Spotted Pony Casino Mysteries

Poker Face
House Edge
Double Down
The Squeeze

The Squeeze

Spotted Pony Casino Mystery
Book 4

Paty Jager

Windtree Press

This is a work of fiction, Names, characters, places, and incidents either are the product of the author's imagination or are used fictitiously, and any resemblance to actual persons living or dead, business establishments, events, or locales, is entirely coincidental.

Contact Information: info@windtreepress.com

Windtree Press
Hillsboro, Oregon
http://windtreepress.com

Cover Art by Covers by Karen

PUBLISHING HISTORY
Published in the United States of America
ISBN 978-1-957638-79-9

About this series

This series is set in and around a fictional casino on The Confederated Tribes of the Umatilla Reservation in NE Oregon. The reservation is real. I have researched, and while I've made up people and where they live, I will try to stay true to the life people live on the reservation.

The casino is modeled a little bit after the real Wildhorse Casino at the reservation. But I changed some things around. The operations of the casino in my series are all my own common sense, not a complete knowledge of how any casino is run.

Chapter One

Dela Alvaro leaned against the corridor wall outside the conference area at the Spotted Pony Casino. As head of security, she was waiting for a casino employee that had been seen sneaking out the fire door by the conference area the last two days.

All employees were to leave through the security area as they clocked out. When Dela checked the woman's time card, someone had been clocking the employee out, three and four hours after she'd been seen leaving the casino by the fire door.

"Athena left the Pony and is headed your way," Marty Casper, head of surveillance's, voice came through her earbud.

"Roger," Dela spoke into the microphone clipped to the shoulder of her polo shirt. Being head of security for this casino on the Umatilla Reservation was the closest she could get to the job she had dreamed of while an M.P. in the Army. After losing her lower leg from an I.E.D. blast, she was shipped home for medical care and physical therapy. If she couldn't be a law enforcement officer, she was going to be the best head of security this casino had ever seen.

Athena rounded the corner typing on her cell phone.

Dela stepped in front of her. "Athena, why are you leaving through the fire door?"

The woman's head snapped up and she stared at Dela.

"Why have you left work the last three days around this time and yet your time card says you worked a full shift?" Dela crossed her arms and studied the woman.

"I've been leaving early because my daughter is sick." The woman's gaze was over Dela's shoulder. She was lying.

"I see. But why would you need to leave early? Shouldn't you be home with her if she's sick?" Dela watched the woman shove her phone into her back pocket.

"She's not that sick."

"But sick enough you can cut out of here and still have someone clocking you out so you get full pay?" Dela wasn't going to let the woman off. This was one of the reasons employees were to clock out in the security office. To keep track that they weren't skipping work and they weren't taking anything home they shouldn't.

"I need the money. In fact, I need more than the casino pays me. That's why I'm leaving early to go to another job." Athena still wasn't looking Dela in the eyes.

"I'm going to walk into the office and clock you out if you walk out that door. And then I'll go talk to HR and see what they want to do about the days you left early and still expected to get paid."

Athena finally looked her square in the face. "Please, I'll tell the place I'm working I can't come in until I finish my shift here. Don't cut my hours short. I need the money." Her gaze darted around the corridor.

"What or who are you afraid of? Why do you need money?" Dela dropped her hands to her sides and stepped toward the woman. "Are you in trouble?"

"I-I can't tell you. I have to go. Please. Wait until tomorrow when I come on shift before you talk to HR. Let me make it okay with the other place to come in later." Athena pleaded in a shrill voice.

"Where are you working?" Dela asked, wondering if it was a bar in town. Athena worked as a barmaid in the Pony Bar and Grill at the casino.

Athena shook her head. "No. I don't want you going in there and causing trouble. I've got enough." She nodded to the fire door. "I gotta go." And ran down the corridor, slammed into the fire door, and left.

The reason the alarm didn't go off, and hadn't the other days, had to do with it having been turned off because employees in the Pony Bar & Grill and Stallion Restaurant used it to go outside and smoke on their breaks. It saved them time from walking to the employee breakroom and out into the outdoor area fenced off for them to smoke on their breaks. Many conference attendees also used the exit to catch a smoke on the patio outside the Stallion set up for outdoor dining.

"That didn't look like it went well," Marty said in her ear.

Dela pressed the button on her mic. "I'm coming in to see if we can find out who has been covering for her. Pull up surveillance video of the last three days an hour before Athena leaves the casino. She has to tell someone she's leaving."

"Roger."

She walked out of the subdued décor and quiet corridor of the conference area and into the bright colors and chaos of machines, voices, and piped flute music. She waved to a security officer and headed to the large mural wall behind the gaming tables that hid the door to the inner workings of the casino.

Tapping her security card on a box on the wall that looked like part of the mural, a door opened and she walked through. Four surveillance employees sat in front of monitors watching the staff and clients at the casino.

"Afternoon, Dela. Things have been quiet," Lionel, one of the oldest surveillance employees and past security officer, said.

"Hi, Lionel. It has been quiet. I'm looking forward to leaving early today and getting a run in before dark." She nodded to the other three employees and walked into Marty's office without knocking.

"Yo, Dela. Did you get the wedding announcement?" Marty's smile spread across his face even larger than usual.

"Yes, but you shouldn't have wasted an announcement on me. After all, I'm the maid of honor." Dela sat in the chair to Marty's right, propping her prosthesis on the box he kept there for her. He was a good friend and a good man. Her best friend was marrying Marty in two months. Molly had always wanted a Fall wedding. They would be married the first week of October. Dela was happy for both of them. Molly had been in a bad first marriage but had come out of it with a wonderful son.

"We wanted you to know you could bring a plus one." Marty grinned. "And we are pretty sure it will be Heath."

"I was thinking about bringing my mom," Dela said, just to see how her friend reacted.

His smile waned. "Your mom? But we sent her an invitation. She can bring a plus one of her own."

Dela laughed at his disappointment. "Bring up the surveillance video, and I'll be bringing Heath. But I don't want either of you two pushing for us to get married. Like tossing me the bouquet or aiming the garter in Heath's direction. My mom doesn't need any more incentive to try and make us a couple before we're ready."

Marty clicked the keys on the keyboard in front of him and three monitors came to life. "The monitor on the right was today."

They watched the video. Athena talked to three people before she went behind the bar, picked up her purse, and walked out.

"Let's see who she talked to the day before." Dela shifted her gaze to the monitor in the middle.

Athena talked to two of the same people before leaving. The bartender and a barmaid. The first day she left early, she talked to the same two people.

Dela pushed her chair back and stood. "It looks like I need to have a talk with Dexter and Natalie."

"Did Athena say why she'd been sneaking out?" Marty asked.

"She's leaving to go to another job. Something about she needed money, but she was also scared." Dela was going to ask Heath what he knew about Athena's husband. She would also ask Rosie, her friend who worked in the deli and knew everything about everyone who worked in the casino and lived on the rez.

"Needed money? Alex, her husband, has a good job doing tech work for Cayuse Industries. I never did know why she was working here as a barmaid." Marty was staring at the monitor as if in thought.

"I didn't know that about her husband. Cayuse Industries is the second place I applied for a job before they hired me here. I figured the casino and Cayuse were the top two employers on the rez where I could get a security job." Dela now wondered if the Kindales were having marital problems for the wife to be working two jobs. She was pretty sure Heath or Rosie would know.

"See you tomorrow. I'm going to visit with the two in the Pony, then Rosie, and head home. Kenny will be here to take over by then."

"Sounds good." Marty pulled a pile of papers toward him as she walked to the door.

Dela scanned the monitors as she wandered through the surveillance room. She spotted Kenny, her second in command, stepping out of the security offices as his voice rang loud and clear in her earbud.

"Dela, I'm here."

She stepped out of the surveillance door and walked toward the large man with a smile on his face. Many had wondered at her picking him as her second, but he had a way of putting people at ease, even if he was six-four and nearly three hundred pounds. And he had an honesty that was rare these days.

"There you are." He smiled. "How was your day?"

Dela smiled back at the man. He was like a big teddy bear. Always welcoming and ready to help where he was needed. "It was a good day, other than discovering Athena Kindale has been leaving early and having someone else clock her out. I'm headed to talk to Dexter and Natalie at the Pony. You're welcome to come along."

"No, I want to check in with everyone on duty."

She nodded. It was their custom to check in with the security guards on the floor when they clocked in. And since only she and Kenny knew the hours they were coming on duty, it kept the rest of them on their toes.

"I'll check in with you before I leave."

Kenny raised a hand as he ambled over toward Bruce.

Dela crossed the gaming floor and entered the Pony Bar and Grill. It was a sports bar. This time of year it was pretty quiet. There weren't as many baseball fans as there were football and basketball fans in the area.

She walked up to the bar and sat down. Her stub was getting better and she could do a full shift without it bothering her, but she took every advantage to sit and take the weight off of it when she could. She'd learned it wasn't a weakness, it was strength to know how to keep her body working at its best. Something it had taken her several years to learn due to her stubbornness.

Dexter Bane, a man in his twenties with long hair, tattoos on his arms and neck, and an easy manner with people, made his way down the bar to her. "Dela, need some coffee or something stronger?" He smiled as he wiped his hands on a white towel hanging from the waistband of his short white apron.

"Nothing to drink. Did you know that Athena has been leaving early the last three days?"

Dexter studied her and said, "It's pretty noticeable

since I only have two barmaids this time of day."

She nodded. "Did you know someone has been clocking her out at her regular time?"

His eyes widened. "No. That I didn't know. She just told me she needed to leave early because her daughter needed picked up from some after-school thing."

The woman had told yet another lie. Dela was beginning to wonder what the woman was mixed up in.

Natalie appeared with a tray, carrying empty glasses. "I need two tap beers, a Pendleton, and two margaritas."

She set the tray of empties on the bar. Dexter picked it up, took it to the sink where the glasses were washed, and started pouring the drinks she'd asked for.

"Natalie, are you the person clocking Athena out at her regular time?" Dela asked, not wanting to take up the time with small talk.

The woman shoved her dark hair back from her face and stared at Dela. "Maybe. She's got problems she's trying to fix. Once she gets things straightened out, she's going to need every dollar she can get."

"But she's stealing from the casino by you clocking her out three to four hours after she leaves. And she's doing it to go to another job."

Natalie's bright red lips parted as she stared at Dela. "Another job? She told me she's been talking to a lawyer about leaving her husband. She wants to make sure he can't take their daughter away."

Dela studied the woman. She honestly thought she was helping Athena with a marital problem. "I'm starting to wonder if she told any of us the truth." Dela slid off the stool. "When she comes to work tomorrow, don't say anything. I'm going to get to the bottom of this.”

"I don't like being played a fool," Natalie said, her eyes glittering with anger.

"She's going to be the fool when I discover the truth."

Chapter Two

Contemplating all the stories Athena had told to cover up for why she was leaving early, made Dela forget where she was headed, until a voice called out, "Dela, why do you look so puzzled?"

She glanced up and smiled. Her friend Rosie was calling to her from the deli.

"Hi, Rosie. Just the person I wanted to see. Do you have a few minutes?" Dela smiled at the woman who was as round as she was tall and as warm and caring as she was smart.

Today she was wearing a purple skirt that flowed around her ankles and a flowered pink and purple blouse. It accentuated her rosy cheeks and lips. Her friend was always in a good mood and had a way of getting people to tell her things they wouldn't tell anyone else. Add to that Rosie's photographic memory and she was better than a computer database for delving into people's histories.

"I'm just getting off work. Do you want to sit here or somewhere else?" Rosie's gaze drifted toward the coffee shop.

"Let's go to the coffee shop, and I'll buy you a piece of huckleberry pie," Dela said, knowing it was the woman's favorite.

"Have I told you lately you are my favorite person?" Rosie's eyes sparkled.

"Besides your family you mean?" Dela said, leading the way to a booth in the corner of the café.

"There are days that I like you better than Willow and Daisy." Rosie slid into the bench seat across the booth from Dela.

"That's because you live with Willow, and Daisy is the complete opposite of you." Dela knew that Rosie only lived with her older sister to help her out with the kids since both her sister and her brother-in-law worked.

"I'm moving out. I'm tired of being bossed around like another one of her kids when I'm the one taking care of them."

Nellie walked over, her order book in one hand and pen in the other. "Can I get you anything?"

"I'll have iced tea and peach pie. Rosie will have huckleberry pie and…"

Rosie grinned and said, "A large cola."

Nellie wrote it down and walked away.

"Why are you buying me pie?" Rosie cocked her head sideways like Mugshot did when he listened intently.

"What can you tell me about Athena Kindale?" Dela asked, playing with the silverware in front of her.

"This must be for work since you don't usually ask me about another employee unless they've done something."

Dela glanced up at her friend's face. "She's been skipping out on work and having someone else clock her out at her regular time. And she gave three different excuses for why she's been leaving early."

Rosie shook her head. "I knew she'd be nothing but trouble for Alex when he married her."

Alex Kindale was a tribal member. His wife was not.

"Why?" Dela asked and leaned back as Nellie delivered their drinks and pie.

Nellie walked away. Rosie picked up her fork, cutting the tip off the slice of pie. "Because she lied to him when they met and she lied to him after they were married."

Dela studied her friend as she slipped the forkful of pie between her lips.

"What kind of lies?" Dela sipped her tea waiting for Rosie to chew and swallow the bite.

"When they met, she said she was studying at the community college to become a nurse. He was there to become a computer technician, what he does for Cayuse. Later he learned she wasn't even going to college, she'd just said that. Even knowing she lied, Athena had him hooked and they were engaged. Then after the wedding, she brings home a little girl, about three years old, and says she was an unwed mother in high school and this is her daughter." Rosie shook her head. "When she applied for a job here as a barmaid, I wondered who was watching the girl and why she needed to work when Alex was making good money at his job." Rosie cut another bite of pie. "I've heard it's so she could flirt with the men." She shoved the bite in her mouth and chewed, staring at Dela.

The Squeeze

"It sounds like she's a chronic liar." Dela went on to tell Rosie the different stories Athena gave her, Dexter, and Natalie.

Rosie picked up her drink. "I bet none of them are the truth and she's up to no good. Whatever she's doing."

♠ ♣ ♥ ♦

Dela and Mugshot, her large, three-legged dog, returned from their jog around the neighborhood as Heath Seaver, her former high school sweetheart and now roommate with benefits, parked his pickup in her driveway. He stepped out wearing his tribal officer uniform.

She had to admit, he was a manly sight in his uniform, buffed up by the body armor under his shirt and standing there with his hands resting on his duty belt as his gaze scanned her up and down.

"Looks like you two had a good workout," he said, grinning at her.

Dela nodded. "It's always a good workout when Mugshot and I can put in several miles. It helps me clear my mind."

"What happened at work that has you needing to clear your mind?" he asked, walking ahead of them to open the gate and enter the backyard.

Jethro, her donkey and Mugshot's friend, stood with his head hanging over the gate looking into the yard.

"Yeah, we're back," Dela said, walking over and opening the gate so the two animals could join them when Heath grilled some burgers and Dela enjoyed her view of the Blue Mountains.

Heath tapped her on the shoulder as she settled into the patio chair. "What's going on at work?"

"Nothing that concerns the tribal police. At least not that I know of. Just an employee slipping out and telling a different story to everyone who confronts her." Dela waved to the back door. "Would you be so kind as to bring me a glass of iced tea before you change?"

Heath smiled. "You know, I'm beginning to think you only let me move in so you could boss me around."

She grinned back. "You know where the door is if you don't like it."

He laughed and entered through the sliding door, leaving it ajar before returning with her tea. "Who is this person?" Heath asked.

"Athena Kindale."

Heath dropped into the chair beside her. "Is her husband Alex?"

This grabbed Dela's attention. "Yeah. Why?" She shifted in the chair to face Heath.

"I read a report that he came in on Sunday dragging his wife and wanting her to press charges against someone who'd assaulted her."

Dela retraced her conversation with Athena. "She didn't look like she had any marks on her. Another of her lies?"

Heath shrugged. "I guess she was working at Harry's in Pendleton and a couple guys got into a fight and she was caught in the middle and took some hits to her body."

"Or that's what she told her husband, and she was beaten up for some other reason." Dela told Heath what Rosie had said about the woman.

He stood. "It sounds like this woman is trouble. I feel for Alex, he's always stayed true to the people and came back to work here when he could have made more money elsewhere."

The Squeeze

Dela nodded, but her mind was sweeping through what could have happened at Harry's and trying to find a way to convince Heath she only wanted to go there to have a drink after dinner, not to snoop.

Sitting in a corner booth at the back of Harry's, Dela sat close to Heath so they could hear each other talk.

"I told you this was a bad night to come here," Heath said.

"When you said there was a biker rally in the tri-cities, I didn't know you meant there would be overflow into Pendleton." Dela didn't like how many people were in the bar. She couldn't watch Athena as easily as she would have on a regular Wednesday evening.

After losing sight of the woman again, Dela scanned the bodies crammed into one of the oldest bars in Pendleton. And the one with the most corrupt history. Less than a year ago, she and Marty had met a drug dealer in this bar to save a woman and her child from retaliation by the dealer.

Tonight, she just wanted to see how the woman who'd told so many lies earlier in the day acted while working here.

"You would have thought he'd stay away on a night like this," Heath said, his breath relieving the heat by blowing across the sweat forming on her neck. She followed his gaze and spotted the drug dealer, Gus Sanders. He had a different bodyguard with him and a young woman. A married man like Gus shouldn't be so handsy with every female he encountered. His wide hands were cupping the young woman's butt as they crossed to what must be Gus's booth as it was the same one he'd sat in the night Dela had handed over his stolen money.

Before Gus and the young woman were seated, Athena arrived at the booth. Bile rose in Dela's throat as the man cupped her butt and squeezed. This was the type of male Dela felt should be castrated. He treated women like they were only put on this earth to allow him to grope and have fantasies.

She did gag as Athena leaned forward brushing her breast against the dealer and whispered into his ear. Whatever she said caught his attention. He stared forward before glaring at her. She smiled, kissed his cheek, and hurried back to the bar with the empty tray she'd held up in the air out of harm's way while talking with Gus.

The drug dealer did a slow scan of the people near him. His gaze landed on her and Heath and his brow furrowed.

"I'd love to know what Athena said to Gus," Dela said in Heath's ear and snuggled closer to make the drug dealer think they were on a date and not there to watch him.

"I like this kind of surveillance," Heath said, kissing her.

Dela enjoyed the kiss but didn't let her mind go anywhere but on what had just happened in front of her eyes. She slowly pulled out of the kiss, peered into Heath's eyes, and asked, "Think there's any chance Gus will tell us what Athena said?"

Heath snorted and picked up his drink. "Nope."

Dela leaned back in the booth and scanned the mass of bodies for Athena. She couldn't see her anywhere. "We might as well leave. I can't see a thing and I think what we did see is a bit telling."

The Squeeze

Heath finished his beer. "I'm ready to get out of this noisy place."

She slid out, waited for Heath, and they walked across the saloon floor to the door. They jostled through men and women dressed in leather, head scarves, and boots.

Heath said excuse me three times to a woman who was blocking the easiest route to the door. She seemed to not hear or not care that she was in the way. He tapped her on the shoulder, and she screamed.

Four men closest to them, turned, making a wall of men around Heath. Dela squeezed his hand to stay by his side when he tried to slip his fingers free. She stepped between two of the men and glared back at them.

"What did you do to my lady?" A tall, beefy, bald-headed man asked.

"I asked her to move politely three times and when she didn't respond I tapped her on the shoulder." Heath had his hands and arms relaxed, but Dela could tell he was evaluating the situation.

This was her fault for dragging him here even after he'd told her what they would encounter.

A smaller man with a scraggly beard and wiry, tattooed arms took a step into the small circle. "Shouldn't you be on the reservation, Kemosabe?"

"Shouldn't you be in prison?" Heath shot back.

The man snarled and lunged.

Dela took a step forward and pushed him sideways into his friend. "We didn't come here for trouble. We're just having a night out. Let us be."

The smaller man straightened and glared at them both. "I heard the womenfolk do everything and the men just sit around. But really? They also fight for you?"

Heath shook his head. "I'm not going to fight you." He put his hand in his pocket and pulled out his tribal badge. "But I will arrest you for attempted assault of an officer if you don't let us go." He stared at the man with calm and authority.

Dela was grinning on the inside, but she kept a stern glare on the small man and a peripheral eye on the other three.

"Common Skeeter, pull your proboscis in and let's get another drink," the largest man of the four said, turning the small man toward the bar.

Heath grabbed her hand and they quickly left the bar. Out in the parking lot, Heath pulled her into a hug, but his tone was anything but loving. "Don't ever jump between me and another man again. You could have been hurt."

She remained in his arms only long enough to be thankful they'd both walked out of the bar unscathed. But his tone made her hackles raise. "You aren't my commanding officer or my boss. I'll do what my training taught me, save whoever is in danger."

"I care for you and don't want you getting hurt trying to save me. Save yourself first." Heath pulled her back into his arms and kissed the top of her head. He knew her well enough to know she was too stubborn to give in already.

He released her and walked to his pickup. "Get in. We both have work tomorrow."

Dela climbed into the passenger side, and he slid behind the wheel. She hadn't really learned anything from this outing, but she was going to ask Athena what she said to Gus when the woman came to work tomorrow.

Chapter Three

Walking into the casino Thursday around noon, Margie, the security guard at the door, practically lunged at her.

"Did you hear what happened?" she asked.

"Here? At the casino?" Dela responded, wondering if she should have come in earlier.

"No. It's Athena. The tribals found her in her car. Dead." Margie's eyes blinked rapidly as if she were holding back tears.

"I'm sorry, was she a friend of yours?" Dela took the woman by the arm, leading her over to a chair and making her sit.

"No. But everyone is wondering since she is a Spotted Pony employee if someone is targeting us." Margie's hands shook as she drew a tissue out of her pocket and blew her nose.

"I don't think Athena's death had anything to do with the casino." Dela had a pretty good idea who could have caused her death since Margie's unease meant it wasn't natural. "How did she die?"

"All I know is someone killed her. No one has said how."

Dela pulled out her phone and scrolled to Heath's number. It rang and went to voicemail. Since he was now the interim detective, until he was officially made detective, he was probably working the case. Since she couldn't butt into that part of the investigation, she'd start asking questions of the casino employees.

"Do you know anything about Athena's family? Her husband and daughter?" Dela asked, pulling a chair up in front of Margie.

The woman shook her head. "No. She only really ever talked about herself. What she planned to do when she wasn't working and rarely had anything to do with Alex or Harper."

"You knew her well enough to know her husband and child's names." Dela pushed to see if the woman knew more than she thought.

"Only because my granddaughter is in the same grade in school as Harper. I went to a school event and my daughter pointed out Alex and Harper. She said Alex does everything with Harper because the mom works all the time." Margie's back stiffened and her eyes glinted with anger. "I told Viola that she didn't work that much. That I knew for a fact she wasn't at work the day of the event. Viola seemed surprised."

Dela nodded. "Most likely Athena had told her a story about having to work to support her family when in fact Alex has a very good job at Cayuse Technologies."

Margie stared at her. "Really? That's where he works? Then why was Athena even working?"

"Exactly." Dela stood. "I need to get to work." She walked over to her desk, put her purse in the cabinet beside the desk she shared with Kenny, picked up her radio, snapped it to her belt, clipped the microphone to her shirt, and shoved an earbud in her ear. She turned on the radio and asked if she was coming in clear.

All her officers on duty responded. She smiled and walked out into the color, noise, and chaos of the gaming floor. Slowly, she made her rounds, talking to each employee and easing into asking how well they knew Athena.

Todd Wilde, a security guard, was evasive when Dela asked if he knew Athena.

"What's her last name?" he asked.

Dela could tell he only asked to stall for time to think about what he wanted to say. "Kindale. Alex Kindale's wife. She's a waitress in the Pony from noon to eight."

The man did a small shake. "No, I can't help you. Why are you asking about her?"

Dela studied the man. Should she be the one to break the news? According to Margie, the staff knew about the death. Then she wondered how they knew. She pretended she had a call on her phone and walked away with her back to the man and called Margie.

"Dela? Why are you calling on the phone?" Margie answered in the security office.

"How did people learn about Athena's death?" she asked. "And are you sure everyone who works here knows about it? So far, the guards I've talked to don't seem to know."

"Rae in housekeeping lives next door. She said she asked the tribal standing guard by the car what was going on. And he said a woman had been killed. She said it was Athena's car and when she tried to get in the house and talk to Alex, another tribal wouldn't let her in."

"And who did you tell about this? And security guards?" Dela was trying to decide how to approach Todd with the news given she could tell he knew the woman and had a reason for saying he didn't.

"I only told you and Nadine."

Dela rolled her eyes. Nadine liked to gossip. She'd have the story all messed up. She was good at her job because she wasn't afraid to approach people and visit with them to find out things, but she liked to reveal everything she heard. Kind of like the telephone game they all played as kids. One person at the front would say something and it would come out completely different by the time it reached the last person.

"Okay. Don't tell anyone else. I'm sure the police will be around to question the people she worked with, and I don't want them getting false information and thinking they heard the correct information."

"Roger."

Dela ended the call and swung around to find Todd gone.

She raised her phone to call Marty when she spotted Heath and Jacob Red Bear, the brother of her best friend in school, walk through the casino entrance. Shoving her phone back into her pocket, she met them as they strode toward the Pony Bar and Grill.

"I heard Athena was killed," she said in a low voice for only the two tribal officers to hear.

"That's where we just came from. Alex is upset, but…"

"Not torn up," Dela added.

"Yeah. However, it isn't very likely he would have

killed her in their driveway."

"Unless he was sitting in the car with her and she said something that angered him and he lashed out," Jacob said.

Dela stopped and swung her body to force both men to also stop. "How did she die?"

Heath peered at her. "This is a tribal investigation. I can't give you all the details."

She smiled and waved a hand at Jacob. "Come on. Jacob isn't going to say you broke any rules. He knows I'm only trying to help solve the murder." She crossed her arms. "Besides, didn't we see a suspect last night?"

Jacob's eyebrows rose. He glanced from Dela to Heath and back to Dela. "Did you two have her under surveillance last night?"

"No. We happened to be having a drink in the bar where she sidelines when not working at the Spotted Pony," Heath said, stepping to the side and evading Dela.

"He's just angry that he almost got in a fight and I had to save him." Dela didn't have time to count before Heath swung back around.

"We shouldn't have been in that bar last night. I told you that. And I wasn't going to get in a fight with an out-of-town biker. You did not save me. You shoved a man and could have put us both in the county jail overnight." He crossed his arms and glared at her.

Jacob whistled softly. "You two sure know how to have fun. Ays? Let's go talk to the bartender." He strode away.

Dela followed, knowing Heath wouldn't remain without someone to glare at.

At the bar, Dexter was restocking. Natalie was wiping down tables and filling salt and pepper shakers.

There were only two patrons sitting at the bar.

Dexter looked up and spotted them in the mirror. He slowly turned toward the bar at their approach. "What brings the Tribal Police to the Pony?"

"Do you notice you are one waitress short?" Dela asked.

Dexter nodded. "It's rare she comes in on time."

"She won't be coming in. Athena Kindale is a homicide victim," Heath said.

Dexter's eyes widened and he took a step back as if Heath had slugged him in the chest. "Victim? Homicide?" The bartender's gaze flashed from face to face as if he expected them to say it was a joke.

"What's going on?" Natalie asked, walking behind the bar and standing next to Dexter.

"Athena Kindale's body was found in her vehicle this morning," Heath said. "We'd like to know if she had any confrontations with anyone while here at work."

Jacob pulled out his notebook, his pen poised over the fresh sheet of paper.

Dela sat on a bar stool. "The only way the police can find who did this is if you tell them everything you know. Including the days she left here early, and you…" Dela nodded to Natalie, "punched her time card when you left."

Dexter let out a whoosh of air. "Athena didn't cause trouble. She smiled and chatted with everyone. Sometimes too much."

"What do you mean by that?" Heath asked.

"She'd spend so much time talking to specific customers, I'd have to work half of her tables and mine," Natalie said in an irritated tone.

Dela latched onto that. "The people she'd spend

lots of time with, were they men or women?"

Natalie looked up as if thinking and then said, "Mostly older, well-dressed men."

"Was she flirting?" Dela asked. She'd seen how the woman had been with Gus Sanders at Harry's the night before. She seemed to be a tease.

"Not really flirting. But she'd smile and talk nice, ask them if they were here alone. That sort of thing." Natalie shrugged. "I just thought she was making small talk to not have to do as much work."

"And yet you let her talk you into clocking her out when she left early," Heath jumped into the conversation.

Natalie folded the towel still in her hands from wiping down the tables and didn't say anything.

"What about you?" Heath turned his attention to Dexter. "Did you see her flirting or conversing more than other waitresses?"

"Only when it wasn't busy. That's the only time I have to watch the waitresses. Usually, I'm busy back here putting out drinks for them to deliver and pouring for people at the bar." Dexter flicked a sideways glance at Natalie.

"Did Athena ever flirt with you?" Dela asked.

He shook his head. "I'm not her type."

Jacob cleared his throat and said, "You have a lot of similarities to her husband, Alex."

Dexter shrugged.

Dela tucked this away. From what Rosie had said and now this observation by Jacob, she was beginning to think that Athena married Alex for a reason other than love.

Chapter Four

Jacob, Heath, and Dela all wandered to the coffee shop after talking to Dexter and Natalie.

"Did you question Rae this morning about possibly seeing anything important?" Dela asked.

Heath studied her. "Who is Rae?"

"The next-door neighbor. She works here in housekeeping. She's the one who told Margie about Athena. She said a tribal officer was standing guard over the car. When she tried to get into the house to see if she could be of help, she was sent away."

She could hear Heath grinding his teeth. "Jacob and I were questioning the husband. No one said anything about a neighbor coming by, and we asked Philips to go talk to the neighbors and see if they heard or saw anything."

Jacob had his phone out as he walked out of the coffee shop. "I'll speak with Philips."

Heath ran a hand across the back of his neck underneath his braid. "I thought working under Detective Jones was incompetent. We have three new officers since I was promoted to interim detective and only one of them has had any classes in criminal justice." A weak smile curved his lips. "But I don't want to complain. Can you have Rae come down here so we can talk to her?"

"If you order us lunch." Dela slid out of the booth and headed to the coffee shop entrance. Once out in the open area, she pulled out her phone and called housekeeping.

"Housekeeping," Mrs. Young answered.

"Hi, Mrs. Young. This is Dela. The tribal police would like to speak with Rae in the coffee shop. Would you please send her down?"

"She's not in any trouble, is she? We can't have people getting in trouble with the police who clean rooms."

Dela smiled. Many of the people in supervisor positions in the casino took their job very seriously. "No, she isn't in trouble. Her neighbor was killed, and they just want to ask her questions about what she might have seen or heard."

"Oh, yes. She did say something about that when she came in this morning. I couldn't believe something like that would happen so close to someone I knew. I passed it off as gossip." The woman cleared her throat and said, "I'll send her right down."

"Thank you." Dela ended the call as Jacob walked toward her. "What did you find out?"

He shook his head. "I wish our budget would allow us to employ better-trained officers. Philips said, he just knew that everyone was to be kept away from a crime scene. Then when he went to the neighbors, no one answered their doors or weren't home." Jacob growled a curse under his breath. "These young people need to know as a tribal officer they have the right to press people for answers and not be afraid of hurting their feelings. What of the feelings of the dead person?" He stared into Dela's eyes.

She knew whom he was talking about. His sister, Dela's best friend, had died at the age of seventeen after being raped and strangled. Only she and Jacob and his family pressed for the tribal police, and later, the state police to do something to find her when she went missing. Everyone matters when they are missing. And everyone alive deserves to have answers about their deceased family and friends. They still didn't know who killed her, but they made sure that no one who is missing or murdered on the reservation is forgotten.

Shortly after returning to the reservation when she received a medical discharge from the army, Dela and Jacob started a monthly self-defense class. She was proud they now had twenty people coming regularly to the free classes.

"Let's get something to eat and talk to the neighbor." Dela led the way back to the booth where Heath sat. He glanced up from his notebook.

Dela slid in next to him and read the questions he had written down. "Good place to start," she said, as the waitress delivered three baskets with burgers and fries.

They had all doctored their burgers with ketchup, mustard, and relish when Rae walked into the coffee shop.

Dela stood. "Over here, Rae."

The woman walked toward them hesitantly as Jacob rose and brought a chair over for her to sit at the end of the table. He slid back into the booth, shoved his basket of food to the far end of the table, and opened his notebook.

The Squeeze

"Rae, this is Detective Heath Seaver, and I think you know Jacob."

The woman nodded, her cheeks darkening.

Dela made a mental note to see if the two were or had been dating. She had hoped her friend would find a wife soon. He was thirty-two and needed a good woman. "They are here to ask you questions about Athena, her family, and anything you might have seen or heard last night or early this morning."

She nodded. "I tried to ask about Alex and Harper this morning but the tribal wouldn't let me in or answer any questions."

"I'm sorry that happened," Heath said. "We have some new officers who don't understand how crucial getting information early in an investigation can be."

Heath had shoved his basket of food away as well when the woman sat down. Dela kept her food in front of her. She wanted the woman to see she wasn't acting as anyone with authority in the murder investigation.

"Do you know if the victim and her husband were having any problems?" Heath led with.

Dela glanced at him wondering how he could start with that when Rae was already nervous about talking with them.

"Problems? You can't possibly think that Alex had anything to do with Athena's death. He took her child in as his own and has done more for her than her own mother." Rae narrowed her eyes at Dela. "I didn't come down here to talk about Alex. I want to tell you what I know about Athena."

Dela glared at Heath to make the woman see she understood and said, "Go ahead. Detective Seaver can wait to ask any questions he might have until after you finish." She bumped Heath's knee to let him know she didn't mean anything by the glare. He pressed back against her leg. He understood.

"Athena has been working more nights lately. She'd go to her job at the casino and then come home at two or three in the morning. Alex has been taking Harper to school and bringing her home, doing work from home. If someone killed Athena, it was for whatever she was doing at night."

Dela asked, "Do you know what she was doing when she left her job at the casino?"

The woman's cheeks darkened, again, and she flit a glance in Jacob's direction. "She was working at Harry's. I was out with some friends one night and we ended up there." Rae leaned across the table. "But she went toward the restrooms with a man. I think she didn't come back for nearly thirty minutes. At least it felt like it was that long before I saw her again."

Heath cleared his throat, pulling the woman's gaze to him. "Do you know who this man was?"

Rae shook her head.

"Can you describe him?" Heath pressed.

"He looked in his thirties. Tall, brown hair, non-Indian and he looked kind of familiar." She shrugged.

Dela had a feeling she knew the man even though it was a vague description. She spoke into her mic. "Todd, would you please come to the Coffee Shop."

"Roger," he replied.

Heath gave her a quizzical look.

"What else can you tell us about Athena?" Dela asked, keeping an eye on the entrance to the café.

"I don't think she liked being married. She said something to me one day that made me think she didn't really even like being a mother." Rae's eyes narrowed. "She never had a good word to say about Alex and never went to any of her daughter's school events. I know because my sister commented that Athena never showed up. My niece is the same age as Harper."

"You wanted to see me," Todd Wilde asked, walking up to the table. His gaze flashed from Heath to Jacob and back to Heath.

Dela smiled. "Rae, is this the man you saw with Athena?"

Todd's tanned face paled.

Rae spun in her chair and looked up at the security guard. "Yes. That's him."

"Todd, you can sit over there until we finish with Rae," Heath said. Then he shifted his gaze to Dela. "How did you know?"

"When I was talking to him this morning and brought up Athena's name, he acted differently. And he had the few characteristics Rae mentioned." She smiled and turned her attention to Rae.

"Did you hear or see anything last night?" Dela knew this was Heath's investigation, but Rae seemed to be responding better to her.

"I went to my sister's for dinner and we watched a movie. I arrived home about ten. I went to bed and didn't hear or see anything until this morning when I left my house to come to work. That's when I saw the tribal vehicles and the officer standing by Athena's car." Rae glanced at Heath.

"You didn't hear Athena come home?" he asked.

"No. The only reason I know she came home late was because a couple of times when she came home my cat Poof woke me up yowling at the window. I'd go to let the cat in and see Athena getting out of the car." She flicked a glance at Jacob, and said, "My bedroom is on the side facing Alex's house."

"Can you think of anyone who would want to kill Athena?" Heath asked.

"Not kill her but she annoyed a lot of people."

"How did she annoy them?" Dela asked, watching Todd squirm in a booth on the other wall.

"She'd make excuses and then people would find out she didn't have car trouble or wasn't sick." Rae sighed. "She told lies as readily as you and I tell the truth."

Dela nodded. "That's what I've discovered as well."

"Thank you for your help," Heath said. "If you think of anything else you can contact me or talk to Dela."

Rae stood, flicked one more glance at Jacob, and walked out of the coffee shop.

Before Heath called Todd over, Dela put a hand on Jacob's arm. "What is with you and Rae?"

He tapped the pen on the notebook. "Nothing."

"Oh no. Those looks she gave you weren't nothing. Did you two go out and something went wrong?" Dela couldn't believe she hadn't heard any gossip about Jacob and Rae.

"We went on a couple of dates. But she made it clear she didn't like me being a tribal officer. I couldn't get her to see that this is my calling." He peered into her eyes. "I really like her, but if she can't believe in me and what I must do…" He did a nonchalant shake of his shoulders. "Then we aren't meant to be together."

Dela could tell he still loved or strongly liked Rae and was hurt she didn't care for him enough to help him follow his dream. But the way she kept looking at him, Rae had strong feelings for Jacob. She'd have to have a talk with the young woman.

The Squeeze

"Todd, you can come over now," Dela said, shoving her friend's love life into a compartment in her brain to dissect later.

The security guard walked over to the chair Rae had vacated and sat.

"Tell us about your relationship with Athena Kindale," Heath said.

The man sighed and his face sagged. "She was a fling. We only hung out for about two months."

"When did you break it off with her?" Heath asked.

Todd ran a hand over his face and mumbled something.

"Could you repeat that without your hand on your mouth?" Heath's eyes narrowed.

"Last week." Todd stared down at his hands.

"Are you sure it was last week and maybe not last night?" Heath asked.

"I wasn't with her last night. I took my wife to Hamley's for dinner. It was our anniversary." The man's cheeks flushed.

"Did your wife know about you and Athena?" Dela asked. Wondering if a jealous wife could have killed her. Then it dawned on her she had no idea how Athena was killed.

"No. Vonnie was clueless. She was always gone to meetings in the evening. I'd go to Harry's, and Athena and I would flirt. Then one night she suggested I go to my car and she'd be out shortly." He shrugged. "After that quicky in the car, she'd drag me out to the alley in back or a backroom at the bar. At first, it was fun and exciting but when I started feeling bad and told her I didn't want to do it anymore, she threatened to tell Vonnie if I didn't pay her to keep quiet."

Dela stared at her security guard. He'd never

shown that he could do something so underhanded as cheat on his wife in a backroom. Knowing this, she wasn't sure she could trust him.

Chapter Five

"The victim was blackmailing you?" Heath said, incredulously.

Todd peered at Dela. "I didn't pay. Last night I told Vonnie all about it. She was hurt, but after our talk she understood, I think. She agreed that I shouldn't pay and if Athena ever came to her, she'd call the police."

"Were you and your wife together all night?" Heath asked.

Todd nodded. "Yes. After dinner we went home and had the best evening we'd had in a long time." His ears reddened.

Dela studied him. "You and I need to have a talk when you get off duty."

He nodded.

"Go back to work." Dela pointed her chin to the café entrance.

The security guard stood. He shuffled his feet before he said, "I promise, I've never done anything like this before and I don't plan to do it again."

"We'll talk about that later." She dismissed him. Dela shifted her attention back to the two officers.

They were both watching her.

"What?" Her gaze flicked from her friend to Heath and back to her friend.

"Why do you need to talk to Todd later?" Heath asked.

"Because I'm not sure I want a man who would cheat on his wife working as a security guard." Her chest tightened with dread. "Do you condone what he did?"

"No."

Heath said it fast enough that she knew he didn't have to think of what to say to make her happy.

"But one indiscretion with a woman doesn't mean he's unfit to continue with the excellent—?" he questioned.

She nodded.

"Work that he's been doing." Heath finished.

Dela crossed her arms. "I guess, but if he was that easily persuaded to break his marriage vows to fool around with Athena, who I don't really think was that pretty or sexy, how do I know he won't be persuaded to help someone who does have both of those qualities?"

"You don't. But I'm pretty sure he learned his lesson," Jacob said. He edged to the end of the booth. "If there aren't any more people to interview, I'll go back to the station and type up what we do have." He stood.

Dela's mind was swirling the fact that Athena had tried to blackmail Todd. "Do you think Todd is the first person she's blackmailed?"

Heath shook his head. "I have a feeling it was something she did as easily as she told lies."

"That's what I was thinking. Remember how she leaned into Gus Sanders at the bar last night, and he didn't look very pleased with what she said to him." Dela's mind conjured up the man's face. "He'd been angry."

"Where was this and when?" Jacob asked, opening his notebook.

Dela and Heath said at the same time, "Last night at Harry's."

Jacob stared at them. "You two went to Harry's on a work night?"

"I'd learned that was where Athena was going when she was cutting out on her work here. I just wanted to see for myself. I'd planned to call her in this morning and discuss the fact she needed to decide which job was her priority or I was going to tell HR." Dela also slid to the end of the bench seat and stood.

"Jacob, let's go have a visit with Sanders," Heath said, standing right behind Dela.

"If you can wait until Kenny comes in, I can go with you." While she'd been intimidated by the drug dealer the first couple of times she'd met him, Dela now knew he was a hot-headed blowhard. He had a bodyguard only because he was scared of everything. Including his wife who might not like him drooling and groping young women.

"This is a tribal police matter, not a casino matter." Heath put a hand on her arm as he walked by.

"She was a casino employee," Dela said, following the two tribal officers.

"But she wasn't killed at the casino. It was at her home on the reservation." Heath turned at the entrance to the casino. "Stay and do your job. I'll let you know what I learn when I get home."

She stopped at the sliding glass doors of the entrance, but her mind followed them out into the parking lot. She still didn't know how the woman died. She pulled out her phone and sent a text to Heath. Please tell me how she died. The method might help them narrow down the suspects. As in male versus female.

"Dela. Dela."

Her name penetrated her thoughts. She turned her head and smiled. "Hi, Arthur." Arthur Simple was one of her favorite casino employees. He was past retirement age but still worked as a valet at the front entrance to make extra money. While he didn't move as fast as he used to, his brain was as quick as a computer motherboard. He had an older male version of Rosie's mind. Between the two of them, they could remember everyone who had ever been in the casino.

She walked over and sat on the slot machine chair he'd pulled up alongside his stool. "What did you want?"

"Heard the bad news about Alex Kindale's wife. Sad, sad thing." The man's droopy eyes watered. He shoved a gray braid away from the breast pocket on his western-style shirt and pulled out a handkerchief. He dabbed at his eyes.

"Did you know Alex and Athena well?" she asked.

"Alex is a nephew. He is a good boy. So smart and talented. But he married that woman. She trapped him. Did you know that?" The sorrow in his eyes was replaced with brightness. He nodded his head.

"Trapped him? How?" Dela would believe Arthur if he said Jethro, her donkey, could talk. He had always told her the truth.

"In college. That's where they met. She told him

how she was putting herself through nursing school and that her mom had kicked her out because she'd been home late one night after studying long hours with her classmates." He shook his head and muttered, "Bullshit. Pure and simple."

"Anyway, Alex fell for her story and asked her to move in with him. Then just as he was seeing through her lies, a big man showed up at their apartment and told Alex he had to marry Athena or he'd make sure she claimed Alex raped her."

Dela's opinion of the woman was going downhill quickly. "How could they prove it?"

"It didn't matter. It scared Alex. He has never done anything that wasn't law-abiding. So they eloped. He seemed happy at first. Then she showed up with her three-year-old daughter, Harper. That little girl is a beauty- inside and out. She's not a thing like her momma. But Alex ended up being the parent to the child. He doesn't know who the father is. Athena would never tell him."

Arthur peered into her eyes. "Please tell me the police don't suspect Alex."

"They only suspect him because most of the time it is the spouse. But from what we've learned about Athena, I'm pretty sure it was someone else. Someone she was blackmailing." Dela watched as that sunk into Arthur's thoughts.

"You know, I've seen her out talking to people in the parking lot a couple of times a month. Usually with the same people." His eyes glistened. "Do you think they were people she was blackmailing?"

"It could be. Did you know any of them?"

"No, but they were all *šuyápu*."

"Whitemen? Not tribal members?" This meant

Athena probably met them at Harry's though she could have met them here at the Pony Bar and Grill. Why did she only pick non-tribal members? Interesting. "Were they all men?" She could have used the same thing on them she did with Todd.

"One was a woman." Arthur closed his eyes. "She drove one of those tiny cars."

Dela thought hard, what did he mean by a tiny car?

"Mini something," Arthur added. "It was blue and had an Oregon license." He recited the letters and numbers.

"Hold on. My memory isn't as good as yours." She pulled out her phone and opened a notes app. "Okay, say it again."

As Arthur recited the license plate, she typed it into her phone. This would help them discover at least one more person Athena could have been blackmailing. "This is great. If you think of or see anyone else, let me know." Dela gave the old man a hug.

His grin stretched across his face. "Any time I can make your day better, it makes my heart happy."

Tears burned the back of her eyeballs. Damn the man for making her feel soft and mushy. Dela was headed to the security office when her phone buzzed.

She was stabbed in the neck. Bled out quickly.

A shiver raced down Dela's spine. She'd witnessed several victims during her tour as an M.P. for the Army in Iraq who had died from shots to the neck.

"Are you okay?" a familiar voice asked.

She shook off the memories and faced her second in command. "Hi, Kenny. Yes, I was just thinking." Dela waved a hand toward the security office. "Come back to the office. There are some things we need to talk about." She continued across the gaming floor.

Kenny fell into step beside her. "Did I do something wrong?"

"No. It's this business about Athena Kindale's murder." She stopped with her hand on the security door handle. "You have heard about it, haven't you?"

"Yes. My wife is a cousin to Alex."

Dela knew the families on the rez were linked not just by blood but by family histories. She didn't know the whole story, but Kenny's wife's ancestors were well-liked and helped many when times were bad, therefore they had become family to groups that weren't blood related.

They walked into the office.

Margie glanced up from a magazine she was reading. "Have you learned anything new?"

Dela was more interested in what others had to say about the victim than what she had learned. "Not a lot. What have you learned?"

"Hardly anyone liked her. She might have married an Indian, but she didn't treat anyone Indigenous well. Not even her husband." Margie scowled. "Everyone knows Alex is a nice man. He had to be to put up with that woman and take care of her illegitimate daughter."

Dela watched Kenny while Margie talked. He was nodding slowly, methodically as the woman spoke. "Is this what you know as well?" she asked.

"Yes. Athena only cared for herself. But no one deserves to die before their time." That was the kind, caring man she knew Kenny to be. He was large, soft-spoken, and took care of everyone. But when he needed to show force and be the boss, he could. It was his even temper and thoughtful approach to life that Dela wanted as her second-in-command of security.

Walking over to the small interview room to the

side of the office, Dela said, "I'll be in here briefing Kenny so I can leave."

Margie nodded, but her face said, she knew they would be talking about more than casino security.

When they were seated, Dela studied the man across the table from her. "I learned today that one of our staff just recently ended a fling with Athena." She waited to see if Kenny knew anything.

"A married man?" Kenny asked.

She nodded. "How did you come up with that?"

"A niece who likes to party mentioned to me that she had seen one of the waitresses at the Pony flirting with married men here and she's witnessed the same thing several times when she was at a bar in Pendleton." Kenny slowly shook his round head. "Athena would pick married men to make sure they did not want more of a relationship."

"No. She picked married men to blackmail them."

Kenny's eyes narrowed. "What is this? And our officer who was with her, did she blackmail him?"

"Yes. Only he refused to pay and told his wife about it."

The man's wide face went from repulsed, to anger, to his usual quiet repose. "What have you decided to do?"

"I'm not sure. I wanted to fire him, but Heath suggested I think about it since he is one of our better employees." Did she tell Kenny about Todd or keep it to herself?

"It's Todd, isn't it?" Kenny said quietly.

She studied him. "Yes. How did you know?"

"He's been acting uptight. Not himself. And he's one of our most reliable people." Kenny shrugged.

"Knowing who it is, do you think he won't do

something that stupid again?"

"He's a quick learner. Let's just see how the investigation goes." Kenny's soulful brown eyes peered into hers. "Everyone has something they regret doing. I have a feeling this will be Todd's."

"I'm going to go with your judgment on this, for now. I'll go talk to him and then I'll be heading out, unless you need me to come back in tonight." Dela stood.

"We should be good. But you know, you are always welcome to lend a hand when you want." Kenny rose to his feet and grinned. "It keeps everyone on their toes."

She smiled and walked to the door. "Have I told you lately how much I enjoy working with you?"

His grin spread across his face. "Yes, but don't stop saying it."

Dela laughed and walked out into the security office. Margie studied her and then Kenny. Their good mood seemed to trigger a change in her as well.

"Are you going home?" Margie asked.

"I have to talk to a couple of people and then, yes, I'm going to go home. Mugshot needs a run and I need to figure out something to make for dessert to take to my mom's on Saturday for a picnic."

Chapter Six

Mugshot woofed at the French door leading out of the dining room to the backyard. Dela's hands were covered in chocolate. Since her baking skills were minimal, she'd decided to dip strawberries in chocolate for her dessert at her mom's party on Saturday. Knowing she'd be at the casino tomorrow night, she wanted to have this done and have one less thing to worry about.

"I'll be there in a minute." There were only three more strawberries to dip in the hardening chocolate. "I have to get these done quickly," she muttered as her phone buzzed and Mugshot woofed again.

Glancing at the phone sitting on the dining room table three feet away, she saw it was Heath.

"Shit." She dropped all three berries in the cooling chocolate, sucked on the chocolate fingers of her right hand, while she swiped the phone, tucked it between her chin and shoulder, and opened the door for

Mugshot.

"Yeah," she answered.

"Did I catch you at a bad time?" Heath asked.

"No. Just chocolate all over my hands, Mugshot wanted in, and…" She glanced at the berries sitting haphazardly in what now appeared to be hardened chocolate. "I can't cook anything!"

"What were you cooking? Dinner?"

She laughed. "No. I was dunking strawberries in chocolate."

"Technically that's not cooking," Heath said, a chuckle in his voice.

"It is to me, and I can't even do that right. Half of the berries look like they were rolled in dirty water and the other half have clumps of chocolate clinging to them, and the last three, are stuck in the bowl of chocolate." She sighed. "Take my mind off my failure, what did you call about?"

"Jacob and I have been playing tag all afternoon with Sanders. It seems he doesn't want to talk to the police. How about I take you to dinner, we swing by a grocery store and buy more strawberries and chocolate, then have a nightcap at Harry's? See if Sanders happens to appear there tonight."

Dela's stomach growled. "I like the way you think. What time do you plan to be here?"

"About two hours. I need to type up what information we do have and see if the medical examiner has had time to do a preliminary check of the body."

"I'll be ready when you get here to change." Dela put the strawberries she'd made in the bowl with the last three and put them in the refrigerator. She didn't want to look at them. Grabbing an apple, she walked down the hall to her bedroom.

Mugshot walk-hopped behind her. As she took off her prosthesis to prepare for a shower, the half German Shepard, half Malamute lay down on his bed with a thump. He only had one leg in the back, making lowering his heavy body a chore.

Dela patted his head. "You and Jethro can have a treat while Heath and I go out for dinner." She would never forget how the donkey and the dog had saved her life just a few months earlier when a money-hungry, vindictive tribal detective had entered this room as she was taking a bath and tried to kill her. If not for the noise her two animals had made, she would have been defenseless sitting in the bathtub. But their rousing brays and barks had given her enough notice to get into the bedroom and grab her weapon.

The memory of that night wasn't something she liked to dwell on, since the man had bled out on her bed. Old bed, she had to remind herself. Heath had bought her a new bed, and her mom had purchased all new linens and comforter. Nothing looked the same as before to keep her from having the scene play over in her mind when she walked into the room. That only happened late at night when she held the photo Detective Jones had tossed on her bed, trying to take her attention off him.

A photo that the detective said was of her father. A man her mother had told her was dead before she was born. Yet, from what she and Heath had been able to determine so far from the mugshot of a man who had her eyes and chin, the photo was taken at a county police station that burned down shortly after she was born. Which meant so did the jail files. They had someone looking into the court documents from when the jail burned down and later. So far that person hadn't come up with anyone that fit the description of the man in the photo.

She wanted to know if the man in the photo was her father and if he was still alive. But the real question was…Why didn't her mom or Grandfather Thunder want her to know him?

These questions, and many others, spun around in her head a good part of every day. She growled her frustration and picked up her crutches to swing into the bathroom and take a shower. Maybe when she came out all these thoughts would be gone.

"Yeah, right," she said, closing the bathroom door.

Heath arrived at seven. He quickly showered and changed and they both slid into her car, with Heath driving.

"Did you learn anything new about the body?" Dela asked, now that they had time to talk.

"Not a whole lot more than we already knew. All the medical examiner had time to do was look at the wound closer and see if there were any defensive wounds on the victim."

"And were there any?"

"He said not that he could see." Heath glanced over at her. "It had to be someone she trusted since they were both sitting in her car."

Dela thought about that. "Not necessarily. Someone could have been hiding in her car either when she came out from work at Harry's, or somehow slipped in her backseat when she stopped somewhere on the way home."

"But why didn't they kill her in Harry's parking lot or where ever they entered the vehicle?" Heath asked.

She tapped her finger against her lips, thinking.

"Well, if it was at Harry's and the person who requested her silence is someone who frequents Harry's, he'd want it to happen elsewhere."

Heath nodded. "That makes sense."

"And if it was someone who wanted her silenced, they could have followed her from Harry's and where ever she might have stopped on the way home and slipped into the back seat. By waiting until she got home, it makes the husband look guilty." She shrugged. "Hopefully after the autopsy we'll have more to go on."

Heath pulled into a parking spot a block from Hamley's Steakhouse. Now that the Confederated Tribes of the Umatilla owned the building and business, it had become more popular with the tribal members.

"You didn't need to spend this much money on dinner," Dela protested.

"We don't go out to a nice meal often enough. We both work and save our money. We can splurge once in a while." He winked.

They entered the building. Dark oak pillars and paneling rose up twenty feet to hold up the copper tiles on the ceiling. A bronze statue of a cowboy dangling a saddle from one hand greeted them alongside the hostess.

She was surprised when the woman smiled at Heath. "Your reservation is ready."

"Reservation? When did you make a reservation?" she asked.

"When I left you at the casino this afternoon." He grasped her hand, leading her behind the hostess. The woman led them to the stairs and took them to the balcony above and seated them at a tall table for two with a view of the interior of the building. Vintage photos hung on the wood walls.

"I'll take your drink orders and your server, Audrey, will be over shortly."

They both ordered iced tea and the hostess walked away.

"I think it's been years since I've been in here." Dela stared down into the middle of the restaurant and farther over at the bank teller wall between the restaurant and the bar. A large stained-glass lamp hung above the area where the hostess stood. Three large cast iron fans over the bar area were spun by a belt that serpentined between them.

"Good evening, I'm Audrey, your waitress, what can I get you for dinner?"

Dela sat up straight and ordered an appetizer for her meal. She figured it would come sooner, since her stomach had been growling all the way into town.

"You can order more than an appetizer," Heath said.

"I know. If I want more, I'll steal it from your plate." She grinned.

"In that case, bring her a side salad with her appetizer, I don't plan on sharing."

The waitress giggled. "Yes, sir. Will that be all?"

"Yes," Heath said, picking up his drink.

"I'll get your order in." Audrey walked away.

Dela glanced down at the bar area. "It looks like the biker crowd has sloshed over into here. I would have thought they'd prefer Harry's and the other run-down bars."

"Not all people who travel across the country on bikes and go to biker events are bikers in the sense you're using it." Heath leaned back in his chair. "When I was in South Dakota, I bought a motorcycle and traveled around on the weekends. Sometimes I'd get into conversations with other bikers in cafes and bars. Most of the people here and probably at Harry's are just people who like to feel the wind in their hair and on their face and eat bugs on a regular basis."

Dela laughed and questioned, "Eat bugs?"

"Yeah, a bit of a hazard when riding a motorcycle if you don't have a face guard. You learn to keep your mouth closed."

Dela studied Heath. "Do you still have your motorcycle?"

"Yeah, it's in the shed at Mom's. I was going to ask if I could bring it over and put it in the feed shed Travis built."

"Only if you take me for a ride. I want to eat some bugs."

He laughed. "You can drop me off there after the picnic at your mom's on Saturday and I'll ride it home."

Warmth swirled in Dela's chest. More and more hearing Heath call her house home was sounding right. She wasn't ready to make a commitment to anyone until she learned who really was her father. Cisco Alvaro, who died before she was born, or the man whom she'd discovered who looked like her. If Grandfather Thunder hadn't warned her that asking her mom would hurt the woman who gave birth to her, she would march up to her mom's house and show her the photo of the man in the driver's license she'd found at Grandfather Thunder's and the mugshot Detective Jones had tossed on her bed. But Dela couldn't hurt her mom. She and Grandfather Thunder had been Dela's boulders of security as she grew up on the reservation surrounded by the Umatilla kids. Most of them were kind. They liked her mom, a school teacher, and they respected Grandfather Thunder and his family, so she was thought of as one of them, most of the time. There were a few times when she'd come home in tears because someone accused her of being one of the people who had caged the Indians.

She and Heath talked about rides they could take on the motorcycle and their food soon arrived. After the meal, Heath offered to make cupcakes in the morning before he went to work. They stopped at the store and he purchased a cake mix, eggs, and canned frosting.

At Harry's, they went around the two blocks closest to the bar twice before they found a place to park.

"The place is packed tonight. I'm not sure how easy it will be to find Sanders if his booth is already occupied," Heath said, holding the door for Dela to enter.

The noise accosted her ears. Between the loud voices and the even louder music, she didn't know how anyone could have a conversation. She twisted her upper body and shouted. "This may not be a good idea."

Chapter Seven

Heath's warm hand on her lower back, propelled Dela deeper into the bar. She had to maneuver around people and tap some on the shoulder to get them to move out of the way. When the last of the cluster of bodies parted, there sat Gus Sanders in his booth. This time with a little older woman than the last, but one dressed just as provocatively as the younger one.

Dela had expected Heath to head to the right and try to snag a corner of a table, but he maneuvered her right up to the booth where Gus sat beaming at the woman across from him.

The man shifted his attention to them and his eyes hardened, as well as his jaw.

Heath stepped around Dela. "Surprised to see you here. From what your secretary told me this afternoon, you are away on a business trip." Heath studied the woman. "This doesn't look like business to me." He said over his shoulder to Dela, "Keep Mr. Sanders company while I snag us a couple of chairs."

Dela stepped forward and held her hand out to the woman, whose questioning eyes and parted lips looked as if she'd walked into the middle of a movie. "Hi, I'm Dela. What's your name?"

The woman held out her hand. "Evelyn Sanders."

Shaking hands with Evelyn, Dela tried to picture her as the woman who had sounded so haughty on the telephone the two times Dela had called Gus's home.

"Pleased to meet you," she said, sitting in the chair that bumped against the back of her knees. Heath had neatly placed her chair so the woman couldn't get out of the booth. She wondered if he knew this was Gus's wife. Though he had to be more than twenty years older than the woman.

Heath placed his chair so that the drug dealer couldn't leave without asking him to move or crawling over him. "Mr. Sanders, as I said, I've been looking for you all day."

"And you are?" Evelyn asked.

"Tribal Detective Heath Seaver, Ma'am." Heath held out his hand.

"Evelyn Sanders. Why are you looking for my father?"

With that one word, father, Dela immediately noted the resemblance between the two. While she was a pretty woman, she had her father's small eyes and large eyebrows. Not to mention his thin small mouth.

"A woman he was having an exchange with in here last night is dead. I wanted to talk to him about that exchange." Heath raised his hand as a barmaid walked by.

When she stopped, he said, "I'll have an iced tea. Dela, what do you want?"

She knew he was driving and this was a night out, but she didn't want to be fuzzy about anything that was said or done tonight. "I'll have the same."

"I'm driving," he said.

"I know." She looked the barmaid in the eyes. "I'll have iced tea."

The barmaid shrugged and walked away.

"Ok, that gave you enough time to decide whether to tell me the truth or make up a story," Heath said.

"How can I do either when I don't know who you are talking about." Gus picked up his drink and stared at his daughter.

"Does your daughter know all about your business dealings?" Heath leaned closer and said with emphasis, "All of them?"

The man shifted his gaze to Heath. The venom shooting out of his beady gray eyes would have cowered many others. In fact, it had made Dela scared of the man the first time she'd met him. But Heath just continued to stare back.

Gus directed his attention to his daughter. His eyes softened. "Evelyn, why don't you and Dela go see if the bartender can change the channel to the Mariner's game?"

The woman narrowed her eyes. "What is it you don't want me to hear about? Surely not your women. I've known about them for years. Mother had no one else to complain to but me."

The man's eyes widened.

Dela held back a snort. Did the man really think the women in his family hadn't a clue about his roaming hands and dick?

Heath paid the barmaid standing beside him for their drinks. He handed one to Dela and took the other one for himself. He swallowed several times, then concentrated on Gus. "When we were in here last night, Athena Kindale, a barmaid, leaned into you and said something that made you angry. What was it? And how well did you know the woman?"

Gus picked up his drink and stared across the table at his daughter. His twitching jaw and perspiration glistening on his temple was a pretty good sign he wasn't ready to talk in front of his daughter, even if she did know he was a lecher.

"Would it interest you to know, you weren't the only person she was blackmailing?" Dela asked. Heath's elbow bumped her arm. She flicked a glance at him. He hadn't wanted to let that out just yet it appeared. However, she continued. "What did she have over you and what were you paying her to keep it a secret?"

The man's gaze bore into Dela. "You said what did she have over me. Why are you using past tense?"

"She was found murdered in her car this morning," Heath said, in a tone that indicated, she had said too much.

Dela leaned back in her chair and sipped her tea watching the daughter. Her beady stare flicked back and forth between Heath and her father.

"Where?" Gus asked.

"In her car," Heath said as if the man weren't quite all there in the mind.

"No. Where was her car?" Gus insisted.

"Why are you worried about that?" Heath asked.

The man ran a hand over his face, peered at his daughter, then said in a low voice. "That car is registered to my construction company. That was her payment for not telling my wife—things."

Dela leaned forward. "Do you want the car back?"

"No!" Gus practically shouted. A few people nearby turned and looked.

"The information she was blackmailing you with, was it something she'd picked up here in the bar or elsewhere?" Heath asked.

"Here. Once she came to work here, my life was hell. She kept track of everyone I talked to and would bring up things she'd noticed or overheard. That woman would threaten me every day with she could tell this to the police, or that to my wife." He glanced at his daughter. "You know I've never been happy with your mom. But I thought she was okay with my wandering."

Evelyn glared at her father and shoved her drink to the center of the table. "I'm going home."

Gus opened his mouth.

"I won't say anything to Mother, but you better either divorce her and let her have some peace or stop hanging out in bars and bedding girls younger than me." She grabbed her purse and pushed to the end of the booth. The anger and misery in her gaze had Dela standing and pulling the chair out of the way.

Evelyn parted the crowd with shoves. She disappeared into the bodies, and Dela sat on the bench she'd vacated.

"Thanks a lot for wrecking my relationship with my daughter," Gus said, glaring at the two of them.

"We didn't do it, you did," Dela said. This man would get no sympathy from her.

"Tell us what Athena was blackmailing you about and if you noticed her talking with other local men who frequent the bar." Heath pulled out a small notebook and pen.

"Don't you cops ever take time off?" Gus asked.

The Squeeze

"Not when there is a homicide to solve." Heath tapped the pen on the pad. "Start talking or I'll haul you into the tribal police station."

The man finished his drink in one swallow and raised the empty glass. When the barmaid came over to get the glass, she brought another drink with her.

"Thanks, Ruby," Gus said, starting to put his hand on the woman's butt. He must have thought about what they'd been talking about and dropped his hand.

The woman looked surprised as she walked away.

"Why was Athena blackmailing you?" Heath asked, again.

"The young women I like to bring in here. One specifically. I like the daughter of one of my wife's best friends. This is the only place we can go in town that her mom and my wife won't hear about us. Athena must have done her research and figured it out. She told me if I gave her a car, she wouldn't tell my wife or the mother." He swallowed half the drink and said, "My wife has turned a blind eye to my women but if she knew about me and Darla, she'd take me to the cleaners, if she didn't shoot me first."

"Athena wasn't blackmailing you about your drug dealing?" Dela asked.

"I passed that on to someone else. I'm getting too old to end up in jail for that." His face paled.

Dela wondered what had made him give up what was more lucrative than his construction company.

"What about other frequent patrons? Did it look like Athena might be blackmailing anyone else in here?" Heath persisted.

Dela knew they needed all the names of the people she'd been pinching for money and it seemed cars. She wondered if the woman had a book or something at her house. If not there, where else might she keep it? A thought came to her. She'd check the woman's locker at work tomorrow.

"She seemed to be chummy with a tall man who came in here once a month, then started coming in a couple times a week. Also, Mack Mahone. But I haven't seen him in here for about a month." The man raised his hands. "Those are the only two I saw her talking with a lot."

"Where can I find Mack Mahone?" Heath asked.

"At Fire Station Two. He's a firefighter paramedic." Gus finished his drink. "I'm going home. You two put a damper on my welcome home party for my daughter." He waved Heath to move and slid to the end of the bench seat.

Heath stood, pulling the chair out of the way.

"The next time you want to talk to me, call and make an appointment." The man walked through the crowd that parted as if the people could feel his anger.

Heath plopped onto the seat across from Dela. "What do you think?"

"A lot," Dela replied. "You messed up his date with his daughter. Did you happen to notice she dresses just like all his girlfriends?"

"Yeah. What about his comments about giving the victim the car and acting as if he didn't have a clue she was dead?"

"The car is easy enough to find out. As for acting surprised… I think he was. But he could have told someone to make her stop harassing him and they went farther than he'd planned." Dela sipped her iced tea.

"True. That could be why he looked so scared."

"But he was more scared when I brought up the drugs. Did you see how his face paled and his eyes dilated? Something about his drug business has him terrified." Dela replayed Gus's actions. He had been scared shitless at the mention of the drugs. Why? Another mystery to solve besides the murder.

"Do you think the person he didn't know is your security guard?" Heath asked.

"Possibly. Are you going to talk to the fireman tomorrow?" Dela asked.

"Yeah. It's getting late. We need to get home so we can both function at work tomorrow." He finished his drink and stood.

Dela slid out of her seat and grasped his hand. She didn't want to get separated in the crush of people still dancing, talking, and drinking as they stood pressed together.

Chapter Eight

Heath was up early to make the cupcakes for the picnic the next day. Dela dipped her finger in the batter. "Yum, this is good. Much better than my ogre-looking strawberries."

Heath laughed and said, "They aren't pretty but I had a couple before bed last night. They taste good."

"Good to know. I'll have some for breakfast." She sat at the table with a cup of coffee. "Are you going to check out the firefighter?"

"That's first on my list after I go to the office and see if any other evidence was found in her car."

Dela nodded. "I'm going to check her locker at work and see if she might have kept a book of the people she was blackmailing."

"Good idea. I'm also going to get a warrant to search the house for anything like that as well. If the husband didn't know about the blackmail, then he wouldn't know there might be evidence of his wife's death in their home. I'm hoping he hasn't touched anything."

"I'm sure he will cooperate. After all, he doesn't want to be mistaken for the killer." Dela was going on her gut reaction to Arthur's fondness for Alex Kindale. If Arthur thought that much of the man, he must be a good person.

Heath sat down at the table with a cup of coffee and a bowl of cereal. The cupcakes were in the oven and making the house smell good. He was dressed in his tribal uniform, all but the bulletproof vest, shirt, shoes, and duty belt. "When I finish eating, I'll put the rest of my uniform on and go. If the cupcakes aren't done, you'll have to pull them out of the oven. Just leave them in the tins, but when they cool cover them with a cloth. I'll frost them tonight while you're at work."

Dela smiled at the man across from her. "You know, you keep cooking and taking care of my animals and I may never let you leave."

He peered into her eyes. "I never want to leave."

The heat in his eyes and the assured tone in his voice, caused a lump to lodge in her throat. Dela held his gaze, unable to speak. She'd asked him to move in as a roommate because they knew each other so well. But it had gone from being just friends to being lovers and growing into feeling like a permanent thing. But she was still too stubborn and frightened to move in that direction.

The oven timer went off. Heath slid his chair back, took his dishes to the sink, and pulled the cupcakes out of the oven. "I see what you did," he said. "You kept me mesmerized so I'd be here to take the cupcakes out."

Dela laughed. It felt better to laugh with him than to think about giving herself over to him completely. She needed to know more about her father before she could give anyone all of her. She had to know if he had really died or if he'd run away when he found out her mom was pregnant with her. If it were the latter, she wasn't sure she could trust any man, even Heath to stick around.

Heath disappeared down the hall to finish getting ready for work. Dela grabbed a protein bar, forgoing the messy chocolate covered strawberries, and called Mugshot. She was ready to start her day with a run.

It was Friday. She'd go to work around three p.m. and stay at the casino until one or two a.m. just to be around when there was a need for more security. After her run, she'd take a shower and meet her friend Molly at Hamley's store. Molly wanted to find a dress for her wedding to Marty. Since it was Molly's second wedding and the first one hadn't gone well, she wasn't wearing a wedding gown. As the maid of honor, Dela needed to show up and help even if she didn't have a very good sense of style.

While helping Molly shop, she could ask her what she knew about the Kindales.

Heath reappeared all dressed. "You still planning on working until two?"

She nodded. "You know how crazy weekends can get this time of year. A lot of tourists passing through think a one-night bender at the Indian-run casino would be a good thing to do." She wasn't a fan of summers only because of the tourists. Yes, they brought in more money, but they also didn't give a rip about the casino or the people who worked there.

He put an arm around her shoulders and pulled her

close, "Just be careful. If you learn anything of interest in the homicide investigation, let me know."

"I will. Same goes for you. Something you learn might help me learn more, too." She wasn't a police officer but she had a good record as an Army military police officer for solving crimes.

"You know I will. Your brain seems to have a knack for figuring things out." He leaned down and kissed her. Then said, "Think about what I said earlier."

It took a second for her to remember what he was talking about. "Yeah that. You know I won't give you any answer until we uncover the truth about my father."

"And I'll be here no matter what that answer is," he said, releasing her.

That was what she loved about him. He wouldn't give up on her. Even if she pushed him away as she had in high school after the death of her best friend, he would be there on the edges waiting to pick her up if she fell.

"You are the one and only person, well you and Molly, who I can count on to have my back."

Heath grinned. "*Táa-minwa.* See you when you get home." He left through the front door as Mugshot barked at the back.

"Always," Dela said the translation of the word Heath had said when they made love as teenagers. Even though they had parted due to her guilt over Robin, she'd always known he would be back in her life by that one word. She walked over and let Mugshot in, unwrapping the protein bar. "Ready to go for a run before it gets too hot?"

Mugshot's eyes brightened and his tongue slid out of his mouth. He loved his runs. Even after they had brought Jethro home. A donkey they had visited on their runs before the owner asked Dela to take the animal. Mugshot having only three legs made him the perfect running partner. He didn't out-pace her.

She threw the wrapper in the garbage and they headed out.

♠ ♣ ♥ ♦

Dela circled the block and found a spot to park in front of the Hamley Store. The building had first belonged to the Hamley Brothers who made saddles and western gear at this spot in 1905. More recently it was purchased by the Confederate Tribes of the Umatilla to preserve the history of the building and the legacy of the Hamleys.

Pushing open the large wood and glass door, Dela stepped into the building with brick walls and tin ceiling up nearly forty feet. Stairs to the right ascended to a loft in the middle of the room. Dela glanced at her watch. She was twenty minutes early. She'd run a couple of errands and was surprised at how quickly she'd finished them.

"Welcome to Hamley's," a clerk said from behind a counter where she was placing jewelry.

"Thank you. I'm waiting for a friend to arrive." Dela rarely bought anything other than sport clothes. She had three dresses besides the polo shirts and slacks she wore for work. Buying clothes wasn't something she enjoyed.

"We have photos of Roundup winners with Hamley saddles and some Native American artwork in the loft if you want to take a look," the clerk offered as if she understood Dela's nervousness at being in the store.

"Thank you." Dela walked over to the stairs and took her time climbing. At the top, she noticed a large print of an Indian Chief she'd seen before. Intrigued she began at the top of the stairs, studying each piece of artwork and photograph she came to.

There was a photo album on a table. She flipped through the photos of saddles and some photos of the cowboys who won the saddles and other Roundup participants. She read the names on each photo.

She flipped a page and there was a photo of the Indian Relay Race winning team for the 1984 Roundup. She scanned the names below the picture to see if she knew anyone. She stopped and read again. Dory Thunder. He stood on the right side of four young men. The other three were smiling and he wore a scowl. She stared. His face looked familiar. Was it because he was related to Grandfather Thunder? She pulled the photo out of the plastic sleeve and snapped a picture of the photo with her camera. Flipping the photo over, she had hoped to learn more. All she found was the photographer's sticker. She took a picture of that with her camera, too.

Dela studied the photo again outside of the shiny plastic sleeve. The face could be a younger version of the man in the mugshot she had and the driver's license she'd found in Grandfather Thunder's kitchen drawer. Her gaze lingered on the name. All the years she'd spent in and out of Grandfather Thunder's house, she'd never heard the name Dory spoken once. It was one she would have remembered. Was he a nephew? Someone not even related? She studied the other names. They were all last names of families at Nixyáawii. This had to be a team from Umatilla.

The clerk sang out, "Welcome to Hamley's."

Dela walked over and looked down at the main floor. Molly had arrived. "I'll be right down," Dela said, putting the photo back in the plastic sleeve and leaving the book open to that page.

Molly was already picking through a rack of dresses when Dela joined her.

"See anything you like?" she asked, her mind still lingering on the photo.

"This one and this one. What do you think?" Molly held up two dresses. One was a sleeveless denim with a tiered skirt and the other was a flowy, flowered dress with wings for sleeves.

"I like the flowered one for a wedding dress. But the other one could be worn for more things afterward." Dela wondered if Heath would think she should wear a fancy wedding dress if they married.

"Always practical." Molly hugged Dela. "I'm going to try them both on and decide which is more comfortable."

They walked over to the dressing room. Dela stood outside the door holding the flowy dress.

"Would you like to try that on?" The clerk asked.

"No, I'm just holding it for my friend while she tries a different one." Dela's gaze drifted to the loft. "Is there a way to learn anything more about a photo I saw up in the album on the table?"

"What was it of?" the clerk asked as Molly stepped out of the room with the denim dress.

"It fits you nice, but I don't see it as a dress to wear while getting married," Dela said. Not that she was an expert on such things.

"I do like it." Molly ran her hands down the front of the garment. "But it is kind of uneventful for the occasion."

"You could wear a pretty shawl or a cute jacket over the top," the clerk said.

The Squeeze

"Try this one." Dela handed her friend the other dress.

When Molly closed the door, Dela asked again, "The photo is of the 1984 Indian Relay Race winners."

"You could probably contact the Roundup Office and see if they keep records from that long ago." The clerk spun around as the dressing room door clicked.

Molly stepped out wearing the flowy dress and Dela smiled.

"That is the dress for your wedding," she said.

"I agree," said the clerk. "You look like a woman ready to take on the world, yet also sexy."

Molly laughed and said, "Wait until I tell Marty I have a sexy wedding dress."

Dela laughed until Molly said, "Let's find a dress for you."

Chapter Nine

Sitting in the Hamley café discussing their dresses and sipping iced teas, Dela told Molly about the photo she'd found earlier that morning and how it seemed familiar.

Molly leaned closer. "Your father? But he is dead."

Dela shrugged. "I'm not so sure." She went on to tell her friend about the driver's license with the scratched-out name she'd found in Grandfather Thunder's kitchen drawer and what Detective Jones had said to her when he threw the mugshot, he said was her father, on the bed before he lunged and she shot him. And now this photo she'd found in an album at Hamley's of a man with the name of Thunder who had a striking resemblance to her.

"But why would your mom and Grandfather Thunder keep that from you?" Molly's gaze searched Dela's.

"I don't know. But you have to swear not to tell

anyone I've found this out. Heath and I have been doing a bit of digging. We know where the mugshot was taken, but the jail and all records burned down after the time he would have been there."

"A dead end," Molly stated.

"Yeah. Until I found this other photo. Now we have a name." She told Molly how Grandfather Thunder had expressed his concern that saying anything to her mom would hurt her.

"That doesn't make sense," Molly said, raising her glass to take a drink.

"Yeah. That's what makes me think the person in the mugshot is my father. He must have done something terrible and she left him, not that he died." She'd mulled this over in her mind many nights since Detective Jones said the mugshot was a photo of her father. She snapped her fingers. "Heath hasn't looked into where Detective Jones had been employed before coming here. He must have run across this Dory Thunder somewhere."

She pulled out her phone and texted Heath. *Can you find out where Det. Jones worked before here?*

She showed Molly the pictures she'd taken of the driver's license and the photo from this morning.

Her friend raised her head and peered into Dela's eyes. "He does have eyes shaped like yours, and your chin and mouth. You definitely have your mom's nose and her blue eyes." Molly put a hand on Dela's. "If you need to talk about any of this, you know where I am. You have always been my sounding board, let me return the favor."

Dela smiled as her phone dinged.

Heath responded. *I'll try.*

She smiled. He didn't even ask why. Maybe he'd

had the same idea.

He added. *The fireman is a possibility. He's got a temper and had a lot to lose. But he has an alibi.*

Ok. She replied.

Dela sipped her tea and then asked, "What can you tell me about Alex and

Athena Kindale?"

"The woman who was killed in her driveway?"

"Yes. That one." Dela sipped her tea and watched her friend arrange her thoughts.

"Alex is a little younger than us. I think he was a year behind my youngest brother. He was smart, but geeky. I don't think he had a girlfriend in school. Then he started going to Blue Mountain and the next thing I know he is married and a child shows up. I would say the woman he married was either very persuasive or he fell hard for her." Molly sipped her drink and continued. "From what my brother and sister say, he attends all the school functions with the little girl and she calls him daddy. A cousin said that he takes sick leave to take care of the child while the mom runs around doing whatever she wants." She took another sip. "I don't know many men who would put up with being the mother and father when the mother was using the home like a rental."

"Has anyone ever seen the two fight? Do you think maybe he liked it the way it was?" Dela asked, having known several people in her life who were content as long as nothing was changed. They preferred to live in dismal housing or have menial jobs with little pay as long as life wasn't disrupted.

Molly shrugged. "Maybe he did prefer the child to the mother. Who knows."

Dela thought about that. It sounded like Alex was a

good parent. The complete opposite of his wife. Maybe they were complete opposites that had been attracted?

"I need to get home and change to go to work. Let me know if you need help with anything else." Dela stood. "And please, don't tell any of what I told you to anybody. Not even Marty. The fewer people who know what Heath and I are doing, the better. I don't want to hurt my mom or Grandfather Thunder."

"I understand." Molly made the motion of zipping her lips.

Dela gave her a hug and left the café. She hurried to her car and headed home.

On the drive home, she'd been tempted to drive to Grandfather Thunder's house and ask him about Dory, but then thought better of it. If he knew she was digging into his family's past, one that it was obvious he didn't want her to know about, he'd clam up and she'd never learn anything from him. Instead, she'd ask some discreet questions of Arthur and Rosie.

♠ ♣ ♥ ♦

As soon as Dela checked in with Kenny and everyone at work, she went to the employee breakroom and searched for Athena's locker. She found it after calling HR for the number and then asked maintenance to come over with a bolt cutter to dispense with the padlock.

Six casino employees were in the breakroom as she pulled out the items in the locker and placed them in a garbage bag. They were mostly personal items. Lipstick, a box of tampons, hair clips, gum, a hard-as-a-rock candy bar, and two small books. One had addresses in it and the other had initials, dates, and items or money listed. She'd found the book listing Athena's blackmail activities.

I found what you need for suspects. She texted Heath.

Be there in 10. He replied.

She tied a knot on the bag and carried it to the security office. Margie stood at the podium reading a magazine.

"Heath will be in to collect this. Call me when he shows up, please." Dela placed the bag in the empty drawer of the desk she shared with Kenny.

"Roger," Margie said.

Kenny's voice came through the earbud. "There are four guys in the Pony celebrating pretty hard."

Dela spoke into the mic, "Can you handle it?"

"Yeah, but they are celebrating the death of a backstabbing whore."

The message clicked in her brain as soon as she heard death and backstabbing. "I'll be right there." She found it interesting that a group of men Athena had been blackmailing would come together here of all places to celebrate their freedom.

She crossed the gaming floor. The machines were dinging, playing music, and congratulating winners. The voices were a dull roar that muffled the flute music. At the Pony, she took a deep breath, placed a smile on her face, and walked over to where Kenny stood back listening to four men, clearly in a good mood as they laughed, raised their glasses in a toast, and threw the drinks down their throats.

"Are they causing trouble?" she asked Kenny.

"No, just get pretty loud now and then." He tugged at his ear peeking out from under a braid.

"Do you know any of them?" Dela thought one of them looked familiar but she wasn't sure where she knew him from.

"I've seen all of them in here a couple nights a week. But I don't know their names."

She glanced at Kenny. "Together?"

He shook his head. "No. This is the first time I know of them being together."

Natalie walked by with a tray of empty glasses. Dela put a hand on her arm, stopping her.

"Do you know any of these men?" Dela tipped her head toward the table of men.

"Every one of them has been in here, first flirting with Athena, then asking for her, talking to her, and leaving with her." She hurried to the bar.

Dela texted Heath. *There are four of Athena's victims in the Pony right now.*

In the parking lot. He responded

One of the men stood as if to leave.

Dela stepped forward. "Sir, I need you to remain here, please."

He peered down at her with bloodshot eyes. "Who are you?"

"I'm head of security for the casino. I'd like you to just sit tight for a few more minutes, please."

"I need to take a piss!" he said so loud it was nearly a shout. Several heads turned and eyes peered at the group.

"Kenny will escort you to the restroom and back," Dela said with a smile.

The man frowned. "I haven't needed an escort to the restroom since first grade."

"There is someone coming who would like to talk to you about Athena Kindale."

The man's eyes widened and he glanced over his shoulder at the other men. "Why?"

"I think you know why," Dela said. "Kenny please

escort this gentleman to the closest restroom."

Heath walked in wearing his tribal police uniform. The man stepped quickly around Dela and Kenny stayed on his heels.

The other three men stared at Heath.

"Do you want to take them into the security office to talk to them?" Dela asked.

"How do you know they are some of Athena's victims?" Heath asked in a low voice.

"Kenny heard them celebrating the death of a backstabbing whore." She raised her eyebrows.

Heath nodded. "Okay, that sounds like pretty good evidence that they knew her."

Dela nodded to Natalie as she went by with a loaded tray. She told him what the barmaid had told her about the men.

"That pretty much clenches it." Heath walked over to the table. "Men, I'd like you to all follow me to the casino's security office. I'd like to talk to you about Athena Kindale."

The men glanced at each other and groaned. "Now?" one of them asked.

"Yes, now. There is an ongoing homicide investigation into her death. You knew her, and I need to question you. It's either here or at the tribal police station." Heath motioned for the men to follow Dela.

She led the way along the outside of the gaming floor to the security office. Dela and Margie were lining up chairs in the main area when Kenny and the fourth man walked into the office.

Heath motioned to that man. "Come on in here with me." He glanced at Dela. "You too. Margie and Kenny can keep an eye on those three."

Dela followed the two men into the small room

they used for talking to people and holding people caught stealing.

The man pulled out the seat closest to the door.

"Over there," Heath said, motioning to the chair across the table from the door.

The man rubbed a hand over his face and sat. "What is this all about?"

"We understand you knew Athena Kindale. And that you know she was murdered the night before last." Heath pulled out his notebook.

"How do you know I know her?" The man's mouth hung open as he stared at Heath.

"Because you and your friends were celebrating it in the Pony," Dela said. He was either really drunk or really stupid.

"Oh, yeah. We bonded over being blackmailed by that bitch."

"What was she blackmailing you for?" Heath asked.

"She came onto me when I came in here without my wife. Next thing you know we were meeting up and having sex. Then boom, she didn't want it anymore and the next time I see her, she shows me a video. Says I need to pay her money or she is going to show it to my wife." The man slammed a fist down on the table. "My wife is the money in our business. If she left me, I would be broke in six months."

"So you paid. How much?" Heath asked.

"First, she asked for five hundred. Then a thousand. I was up to five thousand. I didn't kill her but I'd like to shake the hand of the man who did." The man didn't even blush. Dela knew it was the alcohol making him so loose-tongued. Hopefully, the other three would be just as easy to question.

Heath wrote down the man's name, address, and phone number and told him to send another man in.

At the door the man faced them. "My wife won't find out about this, will she?"

Heath shrugged. "Only as long as we don't need you to testify in court."

The man's shoulders slumped.

"If he's smart, he'll tell his wife and not have to worry about her hearing it from somewhere else," Dela said.

"He won't. He's a man and he'll just hope that she doesn't hear about it."

Dela thought about that as the next man walked in. Did Heath have something in his past he hoped she didn't learn about?

Chapter Ten

The other three men Heath and Dela questioned had similar stories. They all said they didn't kill her but were happy she could no longer blackmail them. When the last one left, Dela was feeling ticked at men in general.

"They were all in the wrong for having sex with Athena, when they were all married. Not one of them felt remorse over doing that to their wives, they only were happy Athena was dead." She peered into Heath's eyes. "If that's what marriage has come to, I'm never getting married. If you can't trust a man who stands before God and his family and swears to love, honor, and cherish his wife, then there is no reason to tie yourself to that person."

"There are many of us who still believe in the sanctity of marriage." He put a hand on her arm.

"Not now. You'll have to tell me about it later. I'm not in the mood to listen to another man right now."

She stood. "I need to walk around. I'll see you at home later."

Dela knew it was wrong to take the other men's attitudes towards marriage out on Heath but their attitude seemed to be normal these days.

She walked out into the office.

Margie was talking on the phone. "No, she's busy." The woman glanced up. "She just came out of a meeting. Hold on." Margie punched a button on the phone. "It's Molly Taylor."

Dela walked over to her desk and answered the phone. "Hi, Molly. What's up?"

"Dela, I didn't want to bother you, but when I was talking to my mother I just kind of slipped the name Dory Thunder into the conversation. She told me that name is to never be said and drop my curiosity about him." Molly's voice was cracking.

"Did she tell you anything about him?" Dela asked. She could tell her friend feared for her.

"Nothing. She just said that there were many people who still remember him. And not favorably. Grandfather Thunder and his brother made it clear no one was to speak of him ever again."

"Which brother?" Dela remembered meeting one when she was small. But all she knew that Grandfather Thunder had left for siblings was a sister. She was older than him.

"He's dead. It was his oldest brother, Samuel. Please, think about this before you go talking to too many people."

"Thank you. I will. I have to get back to work." Dela ended the call, her mind spinning. What could Dory Thunder have done that would make his own father and uncle disown him? And was it before or after he met her mom?

"See you later."

"Huh? Yeah." She was still contemplating what Molly had told her when she glanced up at Heath, changing his direction and walking toward her.

"Now what are you thinking about? Not what went on in there still." He started to put a hand on her arm but dropped it when she glared at him.

She had told him they wouldn't show any signs of being more than friends when at the casino. She didn't need people thinking she was helping the tribal police keep tabs on them. Some of the people who worked here had been in trouble with the law earlier in their lives.

"I'll tell you later." She flicked a glance toward Margie.

"Okay. I'm headed home to frost the cupcakes." He walked out the door into the casino.

"Frosting cupcakes. Is that some new term for waiting up for you?" Margie asked.

Dela glanced at her friend and employee. "No. We are taking cupcakes to my mom's barbecue tomorrow." Which would give her a chance to ask Grandfather Thunder about his brother.

♠ ♣ ♥ ♦

Other than the men getting drunk and celebrating the death of their blackmailer, the casino was quiet. Dela walked into a house that smelled of vanilla and brownies. She hung her purse on the coat rack by the door, locked the door, and found a plate sitting on the table with three brownies on it and a note. *Thought you might like a snack.*

She grinned, poured a glass of milk, and bit into the first brownie as Mugshot walked down the hall and placed his head in her lap.

"Hello to you," she said quietly, stroking his wide head between his ears and eating the brownie. As she started eating the second brownie, feet shuffled down the hall.

Heath, in boxers and bare feet, walked into the kitchen and sat at the table. He picked up the third brownie.

"I thought that was for me," Dela protested.

"No, I figured I'd wake up when you came in and would need it." He smiled as he bit into the treat.

"Thank you for taking care of my dessert for the picnic today and then these waiting for me when I got home." She popped the last bite of the treat in her mouth.

"You're welcome. I thought I'd better prove to you that not all men take their women or wives for granted. Or step out on them." He peered into her eyes.

She could tell he was trying to imprint this scene and his words on her brain. "Molly called at the casino." This was her way of changing a subject she wasn't ready to delve into any deeper.

"Why?" he asked, standing and bringing the rest of the brownies over to the table along with a utensil to get them out of the glass dish.

Dela told Heath about finding the photo at Hamley's. She showed him the picture on her phone. "The name under the man on the end is Dory Thunder. I told Molly about the driver's license, the mugshot, and now this. She asked her mom if she knew Dory."

Heath stopped cutting the brownies and studied her. "What happened?"

"Mrs. Birdwhistle insisted he wasn't to be talked about. That he was Grandfather Thunder's nephew and he was not to be brought up to him or any of the Thunder family." She picked up a brownie, studying it. "Molly's mom said that it would only hurt a lot of people who knew him."

"Who was Dory's father?" Heath asked. He knew the Thunder family well since his mother was a cousin.

"Samuel. I vaguely remember meeting him once when I was small." She'd tried all night while at the casino to bring that meeting up in her mind, but it was fuzzy.

"I remember him at family gatherings. He lost his wife young. They had a son and a daughter. I'll invite mom to the picnic and we can talk to her about if she remembers Samuel's kids. Not Dory in particular. Maybe we can learn more by going around the subject we really want to know." He raised an eyebrow and bit into the brownie in his hand.

She smiled. "I like the way you think." She shoved back from the table, taking her empty glass to the sink. "I need some sleep before we arrive at mom's picnic as a couple and put her in a fluster."

Heath stood, carrying the dish. "I like the sound of that. You calling us a couple."

"Don't let it go to your head. It's how my mom thinks of us now that you are living, as a renter, in my house." She kissed his cheek. "See you in the morning."

A groan escaped Heath. "You are such a tease, call us a couple one minute and send me to my room the next."

She laughed and headed to her bedroom with Mugshot close on her heels.

♠ ♣ ♥ ♦

Dela woke up sweating and feeling as if she'd swallowed a fire bomb.

"Dela, are you okay?" Heath sat on her bed and pulled her into his arms.

She shoved the hair from her face and stared at the man holding her. Her memory flashed over the dream she'd had. It started with her on a regular reconnaissance mission. Then there were explosions and people pointing fingers at her. When she'd made her way past the pointing fingers, she found body parts strewn across her backyard. A leg with a toe tag and her mom's name. A scalp that looked like Grandfather Thunder's hair. And a head with eyes peering up at her, unseeing. It was the man in the mugshot. Her heart felt like her leg had when shrapnel had torn it to pieces.

"Maybe we should heed Mrs. Birdwhistle's warning." Tremors of fear rippled through her body.

"You're shaking." Heath pulled her tighter and ran a hand down her hair. "Why?"

"I just…" She gulped. "A dream. A horrible dream." She eased away from Heath to rub the heel of her hand up and down her breastbone as if to ease the ache she felt in the center of her chest.

"Invite your mom to the picnic, but let's not make finding answers a priority." She'd have to think on this some more. Was it worth ripping her world apart to find a man she had never known?

Chapter Eleven

As Dela had expected, Mom gushed over her and
Heath arriving at the picnic together. Told several
people close to her what a lovely couple they made.

Dela rolled her eyes as she walked by Molly and
Marty, sitting at one of the tables her mother had
arranged on the back patio. They laughed.

In the kitchen, Dela was surprised to see Rosie's
mom, Iris Tapas. "Mrs. Tapas, it's good to see you. It's
been a long time."

"Yes, since your mother and I quit teaching, we
haven't seen as much of each other's children. Rosie
said you are doing a fine job at the casino." The woman
gave her a one-armed hug since the other hand was
plucking fry bread out of a pot of hot oil.

"But it seems you two have remained friends."
Dela felt bad she hadn't even asked her mom what she
did now that she was retired. She figured with her
gardening and keeping an eye on Grandfather Thunder

she didn't do much else.

"Oh, yes. We meet once a week and play cards or do crafts with other teachers who have retired. It is like a sisterhood." The woman smiled. "Like you, Rosie, Molly, and Faith."

Dela nodded but thought it sounded like her mom had more of a sisterhood than she did.

"Dela! I can't believe this is the first time I've seen you since you returned!"

She turned to find another of her mom's teacher friends. "Mrs. Frank. I haven't seen you since I shipped out." The memory of all the people who had turned out as she got on a bus to head to boot camp came flooding back. Nearly the whole community had shown up.

The woman pulled her into a hug. "I'm so glad you came back and are working on the rez. We need young people like you to revitalize the rest of us." Mrs. Frank was a good six foot and two-hundred and fifty pounds. She was all muscle. Always had been. Just the sight of her had kept the kids under control. But she had a huge heart and a ready smile. Dela had learned that the one time the teacher had come over to work with her mom on a presentation to the school board.

"Thank you. And I'm sorry to hear about your husband." Mom had written to her about Mrs. Frank losing her husband in a car accident.

The woman's face fell a little, but she smiled and said, "Thank you. It was such a shock to lose him when we were making plans for our retirement." She glanced at Mrs. Tapas. "But all my friends gathered round and kept my mind occupied."

"Dela, what is taking you so long to drop off your cupcakes?" her mom asked, walking into the kitchen.

"We've been catching up," Mrs. Franks said.

The Squeeze

Mom's face flushed. "Oh, yes. I understand. There is so much love here today, I can feel it." She hugged both her friends and put an arm around her daughter's shoulders. "Come back outside. I have someone I want you to meet."

Dela shot a quick glance at the two women. They smiled and nodded their heads. At least she knew Mom wouldn't be trying to fix her up with anyone since she'd been excited Dela had arrived with Heath.

They stepped out onto the patio as Grandfather Thunder and a Caucasian man, a good head taller than the elderly Indian beside him, walked through the gate that joined Mom and Grandfather Thunder's yards.

Dela studied the man wondering who he was. He had a square jaw, tanned face, silver hair, and was dressed like most ranchers when they came to town. His jeans had a crease down the front of them, he wore a long-sleeved, pale blue with dark blue stripes snap front western shirt, and carried a cream-colored cowboy hat in his hands. Her gaze dropped to his feet and found him wearing shiny expensive leather cowboy boots.

Heath stepped up beside her as her mom held out a hand to the man.

When the newcomer stood beside her mom, their hands clasped, her mom said, "Everyone, I'd like you to meet Lance Truman. He owns a ranch outside of Pendleton. When we get married, I'll be selling this house and moving there."

You could have heard a spider skitter up the wall after Mom finished.

Dela glanced at Heath, then at her mom and Lance holding hands and smiling into each others faces. She'd never known her mom to even look at a man. She thought her father had ruined her for love with another.

Heath gave her a nudge. "Congratulate her," he whispered in her ear.

Stunned, she stepped up to the couple. "Congratulations." She hugged her mom and held out her hand to a man she didn't know.

"I tried to tell your mom we should break this to you alone but she wanted this picnic to tell everyone she cared about the most." Lance returned a firm grip and smiled at her.

"I'm happy for you both. It's just a shock. Mom never, that I know of, went on dates." She studied the man her mom had decided, after decades of being alone, to marry.

"Lance has asked me three times over the years and I always wanted to make sure you were settled and happy before I left the reservation." Mom's gaze landed on Heath before she glanced around at everyone. Her gaze remained on Grandfather Thunder the longest.

It hit her. What was the elder going to do with her mom not living next door?

Dela walked over to the old man, who stood smiling as the others gathered around to congratulate the couple. "Did you know about this?"

He nodded. "Deborah and I have spent many hours with her telling me why she loved him and why she couldn't marry him. Finally, this time she accepted his offer."

Dela glanced at her mom. Her face was glowing. Something Dela didn't remember seeing the whole time she grew up. "I'm happy for her, but you. What will you do?"

He smiled, again, and said, "Hope whoever buys this house takes pity on the old man next door."

She grasped his hand as Heath joined them. "You

can always call Heath or me to come help out.”

"Yes," Heath said, placing a hand on the old man's shoulder. "We are family and we'll help where needed."

The old man studied them with his rheumy eyes. "You two have been the best thing to come out of this family. Keep doing what you are doing and we will be back in favor with the Creator."

Dela stopped her jaw from dropping open. What did he mean? Did it have to do with the man no one would talk about? She started to ask and Heath said, "I think your mom wants you." She glanced at Heath and could tell he knew she was going to bring up the worms she'd told him not to talk about.

With a nod, she walked over to where Mom was talking to all the women present. Marty had pulled Lance to the side. She hoped he was grilling the man. Even though both her mom and Grandfather Thunder said he'd asked her mom several times to marry him, that didn't mean she wasn't going to find out all she could about him. Having this hit her out of the blue, felt wrong.

She listened to the chatter about wedding plans and such until Mrs. Tapas excused herself to get huckleberry sauce. Dela followed her into the kitchen.

"How long have Mom and Lance been dating?" she asked her friend's mother.

Mrs. Tapas was built like Rosie only several inches taller. As a child, she was the teacher with the best hugs. She faced Dela and smiled. "He has been asking your mom since she taught his son. They had meetings at the school over Lincoln's dyslexia. Then when she was no longer Lincoln's teacher, Lance came around asking her out. She never went on a date with him until you joined the Army. She didn't want you to grow up in a blended family." Mrs. Tapas put an arm around her shoulders. "Your mother has always put you before any of her needs. Now it's time to let her be happy. Truly happy." She returned to stirring the bubbling sauce. "Besides, this way you don't have to worry about her when you and Heath start your life together."

"Why does everyone keep shoving Heath and me together?" Dela liked Heath, even loved him, but she wasn't sure it was the kind of love that made a good marriage.

Mrs. Tapas slowly set the spoon down and covered the pot. She turned the stove off and moved, centering her body in front of Dela. "Because everyone knew when you and Heath dated in high school that you were meant to be together. You brought out the best in one another." She glanced out the kitchen window. "Still do." She brought her attention back to Dela. "Don't let pride, stubbornness, or whatever it is that makes you keep him at distance, make you lose him." She put a hand on Dela's arm. "You two make Nixyáawii a better place. Time will show it."

Dela stared into the women's eyes. What did she know? How did she know what the future held for her and Heath?

Laughter in the yard drew her attention out the doorway. Everyone was talking, laughing, and having a good time. She should be out there with them. After all, it was her mom's big announcement, and from what Mrs. Tapas said, it would be Dela's reaction to it that would help her mom be happy.

"Can I come see you tomorrow? I have some questions about the Kindale family."

Mrs. Tapas frowned. "Sad business. Yes, you and

Heath may come talk with me."

"Thank you." Dela rejoined the group outside. Now besides talk of Molly and Marty's upcoming wedding, they were talking about another wedding, on New Year's Eve. Mom and Lance said they had waited a long time for this and didn't want to wait any longer than it would take to make arrangements.

Dela glanced at Heath, he was smiling at her mom and talking with his. She sighed. Did she dare try to bring up the Thunder family today? Because while she felt like family to everyone here, well except the man she still didn't know very well, after her dream and Mrs. Birdwhistle's warning her off asking, she didn't know if she was ready to upset things.

Chapter Twelve

Dela and Heath left the picnic around three to pick up his motorcycle from his mom's and for Dela to take a nap before going in to help out with the Saturday night crowd. There was a local band playing in the Pony. When they had music, the crowds were larger. Meaning more mishaps that would need to be dealt with.

She was dressed for work and standing at the kitchen sink eating a juicy orange when Heath entered the French doors with Mugshot behind him.

"I know you want me to check out Lance, but can't you just be happy your mom is happy?" Heath asked, grabbing the pitcher of iced tea out of the refrigerator.

"If she had told me about him before, I don't think I'd have any problem with this. It just feels off to have her invite people to a picnic and spring on us that she and Lance are getting married New Year's Eve." Dela washed her hands and studied Heath as she dried.

The Squeeze

"It was a surprise. Though Grandfather Thunder and her friends have known about them for quite a while." Heath set his glass down and walked over to her, taking her hands in his. "If Grandfather Thunder likes him, I would say that is a good sign."

She nodded. "I guess. It just—"

"Seems too sudden. I get that. You didn't even know she dated." He peered into her eyes. "You don't always know everything about the people you are closest to."

Dela studied his face. There was something hidden behind the eyes she knew so well. Was it something in his past he wasn't telling her? But then, she had things she hadn't told him either. Things she would go to her grave never telling anyone.

"I realize that and mom's a grown woman who can make up her own mind. I think once I get used to the idea, I'll be happier, less cynical."

Heath laughed and said, "You, Dela Alvaro, will never be less cynical."

She released his hands and headed for the front door. "See you in the morning. And don't take off, we're going to visit with Mrs. Tapas tomorrow. On your motorcycle."

"About?"

"The Kindales and possibly Dory Thunder." She slipped out the door before he could tell her that wasn't a good idea.

♠ ♣ ♥ ♦

Sunday around noon, Dela slowly slid out of bed, took a shower, and smelled breakfast as she padded her stump and strapped on her prosthetic lower right leg. Yeah, there were some pretty good perks to having Heath around.

Walking down the hall to the kitchen, she heard Heath talking to someone but didn't hear any reply. Noting he must be on the phone, she tip-toed into the kitchen to pour a cup of coffee.

He stood outside the open French door on the phone. "Yeah. I can't tell you why, I'd just like to know." He listened. His brow was furrowed and his gaze focused on the patio blocks the two of them had put in place in May. "What is the big secret? I bet I could look up your past history in law enforcement without any problem."

He listened, and said, "Yeah, sure," before ending the call. When he spun around and saw her watching, he smiled but not fully. His eyes didn't sparkle and engage.

"What was that all about?" Dela asked, sipping her coffee as she leaned against the counter.

"It's like Detective Richard Jones never existed before he became a tribal cop." He ran a hand through his shoulder-length hair. "I don't get it. All the places he had listed on his resume never heard of him. Someone had to have talked to a person at each of those places that vouched for him when he applied for the job here."

Dela felt as frustrated as Heath sounded and looked. "That doesn't make sense. He had to have worked at the jail where the mugshot was taken. How else would he have it in his possession?"

At the mention of his name, Mugshot nudged her hand. "Yeah, I know, we keep saying your name and ignoring you." She scratched his head. "Let's worry about that later. I'm hungry." As if to emphasize, her stomach rumbled.

Heath went to work placing a plate stacked with

pancakes and a plate with eggs and ham on the table.

"You're going to make me fat, feeding me like this." Dela forked two pancakes onto her plate.

"I like a good handful of woman when I hold them." Heath grinned at her.

"Is that why you went out with Melvin Smith's sister?" Dela picked up the syrup to keep from looking at his face. She knew he'd lost a bet and had to go out with the girl to save face. But she liked teasing him about it.

"You know I didn't like going out with her. All she talked about all night was how she liked to make things from leather. It was as if she didn't know anything else." He forked two pancakes forcefully.

Dela snickered. "I know. But it's fun to tease you about it."

"I told you, you're nothing but a big tease." He raised his eyebrows and she understood. She had come on to him several times, giving him the idea she was interested in sex then she'd send him to his room and lay awake in hers wondering why she couldn't just live in the moment and forget the consequences. In rehab, some people had said they regretted not doing things before they lost a limb. She lay awake at night regretting so many things that had nothing to do with losing her leg and everything to do with her head and her heart.

"After we eat, we'll head over to Mrs. Tapas unless you want to swing by your mom's first," Heath said as if he understood she wasn't ready to talk about what was really holding her back.

"I don't need to see Mom today. I think I gave her enough congratulations, hugs, and happiness to hold her over."

Heath laughed and tossed a pancake to Mugshot.

Dela cleared the table, Heath put Mugshot out in the field with Jethro, and they headed out the door. Heath handed her a helmet with the largest grin on his face she'd ever seen. "Do you think you're going to scare me on this?"

"No, I'm hoping you love riding it as much as I do. We could take vacations on this and really see the United States." His eyes glowed with excitement.

Heath straddled the Indian Roadmaster and waited as Dela swung her leg with the prosthesis over the seat and settled in behind him, her hands resting on his waist. He started out slow and gradually increased the speed as if he were waiting for her to tell him to slow down.

Dela leaned into Heath, turning her head to stare out to the side. While she was a bit nervous, she trusted Heath with her life. And it was literally in his hands.

It was one-thirty when they parked in front of the Tapas residence. Rosie's yellow Volkswagen sat in the driveway.

"Do you still want to go in?" Heath asked.

"Yeah, I don't want Rosie to think I didn't show up because she was here. I'm sure someone heard or saw us pull up. If not the family, the neighbors next door. Let's stick to information about the Kindales until Rosie leaves," Dela added as they took off their helmets and hung them from the handlebars.

The door opened before they'd taken three steps. Rosie stood on the threshold smiling.

"Hi Rosie, I didn't know you'd be here." Dela gave her friend a hug and entered the house.

Rosie hugged Heath and said, "Go on out to the backyard. It's stuffy in the house today. But then it always is in July."

Dela led the way through the house to the sliding door that stood ajar. Flies were milling around beyond the yellow sticky strips hanging like a curtain from the door opening. She ducked under the strips and onto the wooden deck. Children were playing kickball in the large area behind the house. Mrs. Tapas, two other women, and one man sat in camp chairs on the deck under two large umbrellas.

This wasn't what Dela had wanted when she told Mrs. Tapas she'd be over to visit with her today.

"Heath, grab those two chairs leaning up against the house," Mrs. Tapas said, as Rosie sat in the chair next to her mom.

When Heath brought the two chairs over, he opened one for Dela, placing it next to Mrs. Tapas under the umbrella. Then he opened the other and sat on Dela's other side. His skin already glistened with perspiration from the hot day, and now he sat in the sun.

"You can come over here and sit by me to get out of the sun," Rosie said, smiling and waving to the shade next to her.

Dela smiled at Heath. "Go ahead. There's no sense in you getting sunburned."

He studied her face a moment, she couldn't tell what he was trying to convey, and then carried his chair over beside Rosie.

"Do you know my sister and her husband?" Mrs. Tapas asked.

"No," Dela said.

Introductions were made. The other woman was also a sister to Mrs. Tapas. They had traveled from the Colville Reservation in Washington where they lived, to visit for the day.

"I'm sorry to impose on a family gathering," Dela said, wishing she hadn't asked the woman yesterday about coming by today. She should have called and asked if the woman was busy and then showed up.

"It's fine. My husband has gone with Sherry's husband to get some more drinks. Now is a good time to talk." Mrs. Tapas glanced at Rosie and then back at Dela. "I understand you are interested in the woman who died."

"Yes, Athena Kindale. Did you know her or her husband?" Dela asked.

"Why are you investigating this?" Mrs. Tapas this time studied Heath. "I would think it is a matter for the tribals."

"It is, Mrs. Tapas. Dela has been helping me with the investigation since the victim was an employee of the casino." Heath said, smiling and looking confident.

"I still don't see why Dela should be involved with this. She is security for the casino." Mrs. Tapas now studied her.

Dela glanced at Rosie. "This is for you to hear and not to relay to anyone else."

Her friend nodded.

"Athena was using her job at the casino to blackmail men. That's why I am involved." Dela watched the mother and daughter take the information in.

"I see. Then you must know who wanted her dead," Mrs. Tapas said.

"Unfortunately, she had a lot of victims in her blackmail scheme," Heath said. "We are slowly going through the list but wondered if there was any other reason someone might have wanted her dead."

The Squeeze

"I only know the couple through Alex's mother's cousin. From what I've heard the two did their own things and seemed happy living that way. Alex taking care of the child, and Athena coming and going as she pleased," Mrs. Tapas said.

"Do you know if she had any woman friends she might have confided in?" Dela asked.

Rosie spoke up, "You might talk to Natalie in the Pony. They seemed chummy when they would meet in the deli before work some days."

Dela was surprised. The waitress hadn't acted as if she cared one way or the other about Athena's passing. Could she have also been a blackmail victim? "Really, Natalie? She didn't seem upset about Athena's death."

Rosie shrugged. "They always had their heads together and were laughing."

"Thanks, that's good information," Heath said. He studied Dela.

Was that a 'go ahead and ask look' she wondered.

"I want to make Grandfather Thunder a special gift for his birthday and thought it would be fun to make a family tree for him," Dela said to Rosie. Her friend lit up and practically bounced in her seat. Dela knew Rosie loved doing genealogy for the people of Nixyáawii.

"I thought maybe because you know so many families having grown up here and worked as a teacher, you could help me get started on it." Now she smiled at Mrs. Tapas.

"I'm sure my Rosie can pull up all the information you need. When is Grandfather Thunder's birthday?" Mrs. Tapas asked.

"It's in September. He'll be eighty-five. That's why I thought it would be fun to make a tree and show where he came from and where his family is going."

Dela came up with this on the fly but it was the perfect rumor to get going around and help her get information about his family from people. She was sure she could hire Travis and his artistic friend, Toby, to make a beautiful tree she could put the names and dates on.

"I can start on this tomorrow," Rosie said.

"Do you need me to help?" Dela asked, hoping for an invitation.

"Only if you want to sit and watch me pull up things on a computer. But once I get the names of people in the system, then I'll have to go to the archives and search for the people who passed before it was all put on the computer." Rosie stood. "I'll get us something to drink. Aunties, Uncle would you like something?"

Dela had forgotten about the other three who had sat so quietly listening to everything. She wondered if Mrs. Tapas's sisters had known Dory Thunder.

"This talk about Grandfather Thunder's history reminded me. Dela showed me a picture she took of a photo she found in an album at Hamley's. It was an Indian Relay Race team from nineteen-eighty-four. A name under one of the men was Dory Thunder. I've never heard of him. Is he a relation to Grandfather Thunder?" Heath asked Mrs. Tapas then swung his gaze to the other family members.

Mrs. Tapas glanced at her sister, then back at Heath. "He was a distant relative who swept through this reservation like a bad wind. I can't believe they still have his photo." She turned to Dela. "He won't be added to the Thunder family tree."

Chapter Thirteen

Dela sat in a chair in her backyard, brooding about what they had gleaned from everyone's reaction to Dory Thunder. If he was indeed her father, he wasn't a good person. Did she want to know this about the man who gave her life? Or would it be better to stop pursuing his information?

"What are you thinking about?" Heath asked, carrying their dinner out on a tray. After their trip to visit with Mrs. Tapas, they'd shopped for groceries and Heath had barbequed pork chops. She'd made the salad and pulled rolls out of a bag.

He set a plate in front of Dela with her favorite dressing dripping off the lettuce leaves, a chop, and a roll. Then he placed a similar plate with two chops, salad with the dressing he liked, and two rolls in his spot at the small outdoor table.

Mugshot walked over. Drool hung from the corners of his mouth. He'd been drooling the whole time Heath was cooking the meat.

"Sit. I don't want any drool to end up on my food," she told Mugshot, motioning him to back up and sit farther away from the table.

They didn't have a chance to talk on the drive home wearing helmets and buzzing down the interstate from the grocery store. After the way Mrs. Tapas had shot down any conversation about Dory, she'd been afraid to bring it up while in public buying groceries.

Dela peered across the table at Heath as he cut into his pork chop. "How does it make you feel knowing everyone wants to forget someone from your family?"

He stopped cutting and set the knife down. "I'm not sure. I mean, he is just a family member I picked up through my aunt's marriage, but still, it would be nice to know why he has been erased from the Thunder Family."

Dela stared at the food on her plate, unable to look Heath in the eyes as she said, "Part of me wants to quit looking into him. If he is my father and if he has done some unspeakable thing, I'm not sure I want to know."

A hand grasped hers. She looked up into Heath's face.

"You are Dela Alvaro. Nothing will change that. Even if this Dory is your father and he did something unspeakable, you are not him. You are the goodness that was in him and a lot of your mom. His past will not define who you have made yourself into today."

His words bolstered her. Heath always knew what to say to make her feel better. Except when Robin was found raped and murdered. No one could console her guilt. A flash of it ripped through her as she thought about the call from Robin's mother asking if Dela had seen her daughter. Telling Mrs. Red Bear she'd left

Robin in Pendleton to find a way home that day was never far from Dela's mind.

"Thank you. Let's drop finding my father and focus on finding out who killed Athena." She picked up her utensils and started cutting the meat.

"You said that Natalie had been punching out for Athena when she left work early. Was it because they were friends?" Heath asked.

"Natalie didn't act like they were that friendly, but Rosie knows people and if she says they were friends, then I would think Natalie also knew about the blackmail." Dela lifted the bite of pork chop to her mouth and said, "Tomorrow is my day off. It is also Natalie's. I think I'll go visit her at home."

Heath nodded. "Just let me know what you learn."

"*Táa-minwa.*"

♠ ♣ ♥ ♦

Dela usually took Sunday and Monday off unless a conference was running through Sunday. They were usually the slowest days and nights at the casino. Then Kenny took Tuesday and Wednesday off.

She woke Monday, dressed for a run, and she and Mugshot headed out as soon as Heath left for work. This time of year, when it could be in the 90s or 100 by noon, she liked to get her run in when the temperature was still friendly.

This July had started out mild but had quickly escalated in temperature and hot sun with little moisture. Not that they received a lot of rain in Umatilla County, the summers were usually dry. That's what made it a good area for winter wheat crops. The moisture received in the winter made the grain grow.

She stared at a wheat field as she jogged by. The plants were turning color. She loved the smell of it when the grain was just about ready to harvest. The earthy, grain scent was something that reminded her of hot summers. The next field had cut grass hay. That was another smell she loved. And now she was able to smell the sweet grass and mix of clover every day when she fed Jethro. She wondered how she was such an outdoors type of adult when her childhood was spent mainly at her home or Grandfather Thunder's. Unless she was participating in sports. She did every sport that she could. It kept her busy and she liked competing.

Now they had turned the corner and were headed back to the neighborhood where her house sat off to the side of all the others. It was just the way she liked it. No close neighbors.

Sweat dripped into her eyes as she approached the house. Mugshot caught up to her and woofed, doing his three-legged lope past her. That's when she saw a car parked behind hers.

She stopped, pulled the bottom of her t-shirt up to wipe the sweat from her brow and eyes, and studied the car. It wasn't familiar.

The only way to see who it was would be to go up and ask them. She walked to the car and the door opened. A woman in a fashionable, flowy dress unfolded out of the driver's seat. She had a familiarity to her build and her hair, but Dela couldn't place who she reminded her of.

"Ms. Alvaro?" the woman asked.

"Yes, and you are?"

"Vivian Sanders." The woman smirked and said, "Yes, I am Gus's wife. But if he keeps messing up as he has lately, I won't be for much longer."

Dela liked this woman. "Come in. We'll sit out back and talk." Dela led the woman into her house and through to the backyard.

"Cute place," Vivian said, without any sarcasm.

The compliment meant a lot to Dela since she'd overseen the renovations to the house after she'd purchased it at a reduced cost due to all the things that needed to be repaired. "Thank you. It was a mess when I bought it." Dela motioned for the woman to sit. "I'll grab us something to drink. Do you prefer iced tea or lemonade?"

"Lemonade, please." Vivian's gaze drifted around the yard which still needed a lot of work.

Dela hurried into the kitchen, poured the drinks, and hurried back out. She was curious about this woman's visit.

Settling on a chair across from her visitor, Dela asked, "Why did you come looking for me?"

The woman sipped her drink as she studied Dela. Placing the glass on the table, she said, "My husband seems to think you are a threat to him."

Dela smiled. She liked thinking the man she'd been scared of six months ago, now was scared of her. "In what way?"

"You managed to get him to stop selling illegal drugs and now he seems to think you are a threat to our marriage." Vivian picked up her glass of lemonade. "No offense, but you aren't his type so I know it isn't because he's going to leave me for you."

Dela snorted and put her iced tea on the table. "You're right about that. I don't like lecherous men. Your husband makes me want to gag every time I see him with an arm around someone half his age and his other hand cupping another woman's ass."

Vivian's nostrils flared. "Where do you see this happening?"

"At Harry's Saloon. Vivian, if you don't mind me calling you by your first name…"

"I don't, go ahead."

"Why are you still married to that pig?" Dela sipped her tea and watched the emotions that flit across the powdered face and in the thickly mascaraed eyes. Anger, anguish, determination. It was the latter that interested Dela. This woman had a backbone and seemed to have brains. What was she determined to do? Kill the woman blackmailing her husband to save her marriage? She hardly thought so. Maybe to keep from losing more than she could get in alimony. That seemed more plausible.

"I stayed with him until Evelyn graduated and went away to college because I didn't want to haggle over custody. Even though Gus wouldn't have wanted Evelyn around, he would have dragged both of us through the courts just because." She sipped her drink. "The last two years, because I wanted to learn more about how much money he had and how I could get my hands on it in a divorce proceeding." She held the glass in her hand and smiled at Dela. "I'm ready to make that move now that he isn't encumbered with illegal activities. I knew he was up to something but until that man who cooked meth for him was killed, I didn't really know what he'd been doing to add money to the bank account. He told me it was government contract jobs. But when I looked into that, I couldn't find a record of anything paid to his company."

"He had two men cooking meth that he was distributing. I'm really surprised the Feds didn't go after him. They knew. The tribal police couldn't do anything to Gus because while one of the men cooking for him was a tribal member, there was a corrupt tribal cop who kept all of that hushed up." Dela still fumed when she thought of how many people Detective Jones had coerced and threatened to keep quiet about the meth being cooked on the reservation.

"I see. Well, I'm glad he's through with that now." Vivian sipped more lemonade. "The reason I'm here is my daughter believes you may have something I can use to help wring more alimony out of my husband."

Dela didn't owe Gus Sanders any favors. "He has been sleeping with your best friend's daughter. I believe her name is Darla."

Vivian nearly bolted out of the chair. "That cradle-robbing jackass!" She glared at Dela. "Darla? Really? My best friend's daughter who is a year younger than Evelyn? Oh. My. God." She picked up the lemonade, downed it, and stood. "Thank you so much for this information. I'll make sure he pays for this indiscretion fully." She held out a hand. "You are welcome to come see me any time. I'll be living in the house on the hill when the dust settles from this divorce battle, I can guarantee you that." She smiled. "Darla's grandfather is Judge Peterman."

Dela grinned back at the woman. She didn't have a doubt Vivian would make sure that her lawyer had Judge Peterman oversee the divorce hearing.

Chapter Fourteen

After Vivian left, Dela showered, ate lunch, and then she and Mugshot headed to Pendleton to try and catch Natalie at home on her day off. She'd asked personnel for Natalie's home address that morning.

The waitress lived in a duplex on the south side of the interstate. Dela found the address, drove past, and parked next to a vacant lot. She took Mugshot out on a leash walking around the lot and watching the neighborhood. In the thirty minutes she and Mugshot loitered, no one poked a head out or came by and said anything to them.

She put the dog back in her car and drove to Natalie's address. Dela studied the windows. Nothing moved behind them. There wasn't a vehicle on either side of the duplex. She exited the car and walked up to the number for Natalie's residence.

Knocking on the door didn't get any results in front of her, but the door to the other side of the duplex opened.

The Squeeze

"No one's home," a young female voice called.

Dela faced the young woman who looked to be barely out of high school. As the woman opened the door farther to step out, the sound of a baby crying could be heard.

"Is she at work?" Dela asked.

"No. It's her day off. She's either at the laundromat or visiting her boyfriend." The young woman smiled. "He's cute but a little geeky."

"Does this boyfriend have a name?" Dela asked.

"Drummer boy. That's what Natalie calls him. I think he's in a band or something."

The baby let out a scream that curled Dela's toes from the other threshold. "I'll let you go. Any chance you know which laundromat?"

"Yeah, the one on Emigrant." She started to close her door and asked, "Do you want me to tell her you're looking for her?"

"I'm sure I'll catch up to her at work. Thanks." Dela walked back to her car, slid in, and headed to Liberty Cleaners on Emigrant Avenue.

She parked in the parking lot and walked into the building. The sound of washers and dryers nearly drowned out the radio station playing from speakers in the corners. Dela scanned the room. Natalie wasn't standing anywhere. She walked along the end of the rows of washers to see if she was sitting somewhere looking at her phone or reading. Nothing.

Dela sat down and texted Heath. *Can you tell me what Natalie drives and her license plate?*

Can't find her? He replied.

Her neighbor thought she was at the laundromat but I don't see her. There are several machines going and no one around. I thought if her car is here, I'd wait for her to return.

His next text had the make, model, and plate.

Thank you. She replied. A quick scan of the vehicles and she didn't find the car. *Not here, going home.*

Heath gave her a thumbs-up emoji.

She smiled and walked out to her car. Instead of driving back out to the interstate, she drove toward Main Street. There she took a left and parked next to Hamley's. She had the photo on her phone and had taken a picture of the backside capturing the photographer's name. There wasn't anything more she could learn by looking at the photo of the Indian Relay Race team.

But she could see if the photographer was still around and knew anything more about the team and possibly Dory. She pulled the photo up on her phone and noted the address on the bottom of the sticker. Smiling, she put her phone away and drove to the address listed on the sticker.

There was a large older house that looked as if it could use some repairs. It made her think of the house FBI Special Agent Quinn Pierce was remodeling when she'd met him. She wondered how that was going.

An elderly man stepped out onto the front porch and an equally elderly dog walked stiff-legged out into the yard.

Dela slipped out of the car, while Mugshot whined at the window watching the older dog pee on everything he walked up to.

She was halfway up the walk when Dela asked, "Are you Mr. Dickens who had the photography studio here?"

"Yes, I am. How can I help you?" The man didn't

move off the porch.

Dela continued up the sidewalk and stopped just off the porch. "I was wondering if I could get a copy of a photo you took. It's of the Indian Relay Race team at the Roundup in nineteen-eighty-four."

The man shook his head. "There were a bunch of different teams every year. Do you know which one you are looking for?"

"It would have been the Umatilla team, I'm pretty sure." The fear she wouldn't be able to get another photo eased and she smiled back at the man.

"You're lucky. I was boxing all of those up to give to the Roundup Committee. If they are in this house when I die, my kids will just chuck 'em in the trash."

Dela smiled and followed the man into the house. It was obvious he'd been living alone for a while. The house smelled of liniment, coffee, and stale food. A lot like Grandfather Thunder's house.

He left the door standing open. Dela figured it was so the old dog could come in when he was ready.

Mr. Dickens stopped beside a door that led off the side of the square room that would have been the parlor when the house was built. "This is where I had my photo studio set up. My wife, Eleanor, scheduled people to come in for portraits and the events I did. Like the Roundup. I was their Roundup photographer for over twenty-five years. Up until I couldn't move around very well and they brought in a younger man." He walked into the room and scanned the stack of boxes. "What year did you say?"

"Nineteen-eighty-four." Dela walked into the room and read the labels on the boxes closest to her. "Wow, you have nearly every event that happened in this area when you had a studio."

The man smiled. "I enjoyed capturing moments that would later bring up good memories." He pointed. "There it is. Can you reach it? My arthritis flared up today. My neighbor comes over for an hour on the weekends and helps me box it all up."

Dela reached for the box marked Roundup 1984. She grasped the cardboard carton and spun to set it on an empty table.

Mr. Dickens was pulling on a pair of white gloves. "Have to be careful no oily prints are left on the photos. It could discolor them." He motioned for Dela to take the lid off.

She did as she was told. Stacks of photos in plastic envelopes filled the box.

He handed her a pair of gloves. "What are we looking for?"

"A photo of the relay race winners. I saw the photo in Hamley's and decided I would like a copy of it." She glanced at the man as she pulled on the gloves. "One of the men is a relative and I'd like to give it as a present."

"That's a fine idea." He handed her a stack of plastic-covered photos. "You know what the team looks like, you can find the action shot and I'll look for the winning team photo."

She nodded and took the stack of photos. Her hands shook as she looked through the pile. "Are there more? There aren't any relay race photos in these."

The man handed her more photos. Halfway through the stack, she found not one but three action shots of Dory Thunder as he mounted each of the horses he rode in the relay. His name was written in ink across the bottom. That he was the rider and not just one of the horse holders, made her even more curious about the man.

She stared at the three photos, but they were action shots and his face was small and always faced forward. While it was a good photo, it was hard to see the man's face.

"You found what you were looking for?" Mr. Dickens asked.

"Yes and no." Dela watched the man dig through more photos and finally come up with the photo of the relay team. Dory's expression didn't look as if he'd just become the winner of the Indian Relay Race at the Pendleton Roundup.

"I remember this guy. He was a really good horseman. But he always looked as if he'd just lost his best friend. Even after he made the last race that marked him a winner, he didn't really seem happy." Mr. Dickens took the photos in her hands. "I'll make you copies. You come back by tomorrow afternoon and I'll have them ready."

Dela nodded. "Thank you. I appreciate this."

"No problem. It will give me something to do besides watch television and let Clyde in and out."

Dela figured he meant the old dog. "Can I pay you now?" She pulled her wallet out of her purse.

"Wait until tomorrow. The negative has been sitting so long, I want to see if the photo is worth anything." He pulled out a small tin box and started walking his fingers through cellophane strips with numbers in the corners. "Here it is." He held up a short strip of negatives. "I'll get everything set up tonight and make the photos in the morning."

"If this is too much trouble, I can take it to someone else," Dela offered.

"Those machines they have these days would probably ruin the negative. No, it's fine. Like I said, I need something to do."

"Thank you. I'll be back around three tomorrow." She calculated she could go to work around noon, then take a break at three and run into Pendleton and pick up the photos.

"I'll see you then."

"I can find my way out. Thank you, Mr. Dickens." She smiled at the man and headed to the front door.

It was almost 4 o'clock, she wondered if the East Oregonian newspaper would have a write-up about the Roundup winners in 1984. She headed to the City Library which is part of City Hall.

Her phone dinged as she sat at a light. She glanced at the text.

You aren't home yet.

She'd told Heath she was headed home after the laundromat. Changing the direction of the car, she headed to the interstate. She could always check out the archives when she came for the photos tomorrow afternoon.

Chapter Fifteen

The house smelled of tomatoes, garlic, and basil.
"Are you making spaghetti?" she asked, hanging her
purse on the coat rack.

"No, it's lasagna, the easy way." Heath held up a
jar of spaghetti sauce.

"That works. I'm hungry."

"What took you so long to get home?" Heath
asked, wiping his hands on a towel and walking to the
refrigerator.

"I went to see the photographer who took the
nineteen-eighty-four Roundup photos." She snatched a
piece of French bread from the pan.

Heath held the pitcher of iced tea as he shut the
fridge door. "He was still around?"

"Yes. And I found action shots as well as the one I
found at Hamley's."

He set the pitcher down and faced her. "Can you
see his face any better?"

"No." She sat at the table and scratched Mugshot at the base of his pointed ears. She told Heath about the photographer and how he was making her copies.

"That's lucky. He didn't happen to remember anything about Dory, did he?" Heath asked.

Dela told him how the man had said Dory never looked happy, even after winning.

Heath shook his head. "The more we find out makes me want to learn all we can about him. I feel like he might have had problems no one back then knew about."

Dela nodded. "Even if he isn't my father, I'd like to know why his name isn't to be spoken."

The timer dinged. "Let's eat and I'll tell you what I learned today." Heath opened the oven door. The delicious scents that had made her stomach rumble when she walked into the house, now filled the room.

She poured iced tea into two glasses as Heath put the lasagna, bread, and salad on the table. The way he cooked and took care of her, he was making it hard not to want him around all the time.

Heath settled in the chair across from her and dished up. When their plates were full and Dela had started eating, he began relaying what he'd learned.

"The autopsy and forensics had interesting findings," Heath began.

Dela looked up from buttering her bread and asked, "As in?"

"According to forensics, the blood on a metal fingernail file that was found on the floor of the car was the victim's. The way she bled out it would have been hard for anything in that car to not have blood on it. So not surprising, except the medical examiner says it is the right size to have made the wound."

"She was stabbed by a fingernail file? That kind of leans toward the suspect being female, doesn't it?" Dela wondered if it was Natalie or Vonnie Wilde's fingernail file.

"Considering the roughness of the file, there is no way to get any fingerprints. They are however checking it for epithelial tissue." Heath lifted a forkful of the lasagna toward his mouth. "I plan to have a visit with Alex in the morning. See if he recognizes the file. Want to come along?"

"Don't you need to take Jacob or another tribal officer?" It wasn't that she didn't want to go, but given the position Heath had taken over had a bad cop in it, he would be better off taking someone from the tribal police with him when interviewing so no one could say he was tainted like the last detective.

"Jacob will meet us there. He wanted to talk to Rae one on one to see if he could learn any more about the Kindale's marriage." Heath raised an eyebrow.

"Early as in he might be spending the night? Isn't that against policy to be fraternizing with a witness?" Though she was thrilled that Jacob was dating.

"No. He called and made a breakfast date with her. Something about Rae preferred to get up early rather than go to bed late." Heath buttered a slice of bread. "If for some reason the child is home, you can entertain her while Jacob and I talk to Alex."

Heath's phone rang in the other room. He stood and walked into the room as if the phone didn't really matter.

She heard him carrying on a conversation. From his tone and the questions he asked, it was about the murder investigation.

He returned, set the phone down on the table

beside his plate, and settled his gaze on her. "Looks like we have more to ask Alex about tomorrow."

"Did they find something to incriminate him in the evidence?" Dela asked.

"No. Athena's fingerprints came back. Her name is Marilyn Rathman. She's from the midwest. According to all the medical records they could dig up on her, as Marilyn and Athena, she has never had a child."

Dela sat back in her chair, staring at Heath. "Then where did the child come from? And why did she say it was hers? Where did she get it? Was it stolen? Was she asked to raise it for some reason? This is just—"

"Crazy?" Heath filled in.

"Yeah. You might have to call in the Feds to see if they have anything on Marilyn Rathman." Dela wasn't opposed to working with the FBI but this wasn't really anything they needed to get involved in. Unless Athena happened to be someone on their most wanted list.

"Yeah, I suggested bringing in the Feds to the Chief today when I wasn't finding anything on Athena since before her marriage to Alex." Heath made a face and said in a voice that was a good replica of Chief Steele, "While we have had a good working relationship with them lately, I would prefer you handle this without their help."

Dela laughed even though she knew Heath's hands would be tied trying to find out more about Athena. She sobered. "This adds another angle to who would want her dead."

"Yeah, as if her blackmail wasn't enough, now we have possible child kidnapping." Heath shoved his finished plate to the middle of the table. "I'll update Chief Steele on this new development tonight. And tomorrow I'll ask Alex to give permission for a DNA swab of the child."

"If there is any family that has their DNA in the system." This talk of DNA had Dela wondering if she should take a DNA test and see if it brought up any familial connections. If the man in the mugshot was related to her, his DNA might be in the system and she'd have a name. It might also connect her to her mom's family. She could look up the relatives that had thrown her mom out when she became pregnant and never wanted to see their granddaughter. Then again, maybe she didn't want to meet them. Anger, resentment, and fear all swirled in her chest, making her heart ache.

Tuesday morning, Dela dressed, fed Jethro and Mugshot, leaving the two out in the pasture together, and settled into Heath's pickup. He was taking his own vehicle, though he was dressed in a tribal uniform. He wouldn't be able to dress in street clothes in his detective position until it was made permanent. He was still considered a Tribal Officer and had to do the same duties as well as find out who murdered Athena Kindale.

"Can we stop at the market?" Dela asked.

Heath turned into the parking lot of Mission Market, the grocery store, gas station, and sandwich shop on the rez. "What do you need here?"

"Incentive to become best buds with a child." She exited the vehicle, said hi to the owner of the store as she walked in, and headed to the candy aisle. Not sure what would work for bribery the best, Dela grabbed two flavors of suckers, a package of chocolates, and bubble gum.

"Looks like you have a sweet tooth today," the

owner said, smiling.

Dela grinned back at the man she'd known while growing up. "Looks like it."

"And that's Heath driving you around. Just like when you were in school." The man winked.

She was pretty sure everyone on the reservation knew the two of them were living together even if it wasn't the way they all thought. "I guess some things don't change," she said, when she really wanted to say, it's none of your business. She paid, grabbed her candy, and left.

The pickup springs bounced as she dropped her butt onto the passenger seat.

"Whoa, what made your face all stormy? I thought you were buying candy." Heath shoved his phone into the breast pocket of his shirt.

"The one thing that I dislike about living here is the gossip and innuendo that I get all the time." She buckled her seat belt and peered across the cab at Heath. It wasn't bad being linked to a Tribal Officer moving into a detective position. She just didn't like people talking about her. As a child, she'd felt like people were whispering when she'd enter or leave a room.

"You know it happens anywhere there is a small community. It was like that in South Dakota. Some people would know why I was there to talk to them before I even opened my mouth. Or would tell me gossip about a family that was a rival of my father's family. It happens. You have to smile and ignore it." He put the pickup in reverse and they left the parking lot.

"I'd rather people tell me gossip about Alex and Athena than myself."

Heath laughed and turned into a small housing

complex off County Road 908. He drove to the last house on a small loop.

Dela studied the compact car sitting in the driveway in front of the closed garage door. "You didn't ask Alex to find someplace to stay while the investigation was ongoing?"

"No. It was pretty clear the crime scene was the car. After we scoured the driveway and surrounding area for the murder weapon and any evidence, the car was towed to the State Police Lab in town to be processed for evidence." Heath parked behind the compact. "That's Alex's car. Rae said he hasn't gone to work since Athena's death and he was keeping Harper home from school."

Dela shoved the candy in her purse and followed Heath out of the vehicle. By the time they started walking up the sidewalk to the front porch, Jacob joined them.

This was a housing complex with newer homes. They had been built with money from the casino. Dela always felt good when she saw the benefits the tribal members received from the casino's profits. The Yellowhawk Tribal Health Center, the Government Buildings, Nixyáawii School, and the Tamastslikt Cultural Center, not to mention several businesses that were flourishing. Alex worked at Cayuse Industries. Another business funded by the casino.

The door opened and Dela had her first impression of Alex Kindale. The top of his head came to Heath's shoulder. His body was stout with wide shoulders and short legs. His eyes were red-tinged behind thick glasses. He ran a shaking hand through his close-cropped dark hair. Her first thought was, 'He's not taking this well.'

"Alex, we have some more questions for you." Heath motioned to Dela. "I brought a friend along to play with Harper while Jacob and I talk with you."

She smiled.

The man backed up. "You didn't need to do that. I could just send her over to Rae's until you leave."

Dela liked that idea. Then she'd get to hear the conversation.

"Rae is headed to work," Jacob said.

Heath motioned for Alex to sit. Then Heath took a seat in a chair facing him. Jacob remained standing with his notebook and pen in hand. Dela didn't know what to do, so she sat, wondering if Harper was in her room or outside.

"The first thing I want to ask you is, may we take a DNA swab from Harper?"

Alex's eyes widened. "Why?"

"We have reason to believe she isn't Athena's daughter." Heath kept his tone conversational and soft. He had a much better approach to questioning than his predecessor.

"What do you mean, not her daughter? Why else would she have brought Harper here to live with us?" Alex was clenching and unclenching his fists.

"That's why we want to get a swab from Harper, to see if we missed a medical record somewhere that said she had a child." Heath pulled a swab kit from his pocket.

Alex's lips moved as he shook his head. Finally getting the words to come out, he said, "No. I have the birth certificate. She is Athena's daughter and by her death she is mine. I adopted her when Athena brought her here five years ago. She's my daughter now." His gaze darted around the room as if he were looking for an escape.

"Where is Harper?" Dela asked. "I'll go check on her."

"Her room. Second one on the left," Alex said without hesitation.

Dela stood, caught Heath's gaze, and walked down the hall. The place was clean and tidy. She hadn't expected that. At work, Athena hadn't shown an affinity for the type of labor one would need to keep a clean house. She wondered if Alex cleaned the house as well as taking care of Harper while Athena had run around doing whatever she pleased.

She knocked quietly and entered the room. A child with long brown curly hair cascading down her back, twisted from her spot on the floor where she played with dolls, and peered at Dela.

"Hi, Harper. I'm a friend of your daddy's. He asked me to come in and see how you are doing." Dela maneuvered her prosthesis so she could sit on the floor beside the child. "My name is Dela."

The girl grinned, showing missing teeth and crinkling the sides of her large brown eyes. Her skin was a golden brown. Making Dela think her parents might be African American or East Indian.

"Dela as in Delaware, the state?" Harper asked, her head tipped to one side as if inspecting Dela.

Grinning back at the child, Dela said, "Yes. But I'm not a state, I'm a person."

The child broke into giggles. It was evident either she didn't realize the severity of her missing mother or she hadn't been attached to Athena enough to care.

"You're funny!" the child said, picking up a doll and undressing it.

"Are these all your dolls?" Dela asked, to start up a

conversation.

"Yes. Daddy gets them for me. He says it is good for me to play with them." She smiled and whispered, "I like them because they have pretty clothes. And they don't look like Mommy."

Dela studied the dolls. None of them had pale skin. They all had brown skin tones. "I see. They are all pretty."

"Yes. This one is my favorite." The child smoothed the long black hair. It was a Pocahontas doll. Harper peered up at Dela. "She looks like you."

While Dela was pleased the girl thought she looked like the doll, Dela now wondered at her features that she had thought were Latino could possibly be Indigenous.

Harper thrust a doll into Dela's hands. "Let's dress them for a party."

"Okay." She put her hand in her purse. "Since it's a party, here are some treats."

The child stared at the candy and then up at her. "You are my daddy's friend but you are a stranger. I can't have anything from strangers."

Dela liked that the child had learned a good rule. Many children had been lured to their death by sweets. "Okay, let's play. You don't have to have the candy if you don't want it."

Harper's face lit up. "Okay."

She didn't want to bring up unhappiness but she wondered about her upbringing. As Dela put a fancy dress on the doll she'd been handed, she asked, "Do your mommy and daddy go out to parties?"

Harper shook her head as she put high heels on the Pocahontas doll. "Not Daddy. He stays home and keeps me safe. Mommy likes to dress up and go out. But

Daddy always tells her she shouldn't dress the way she does."

Dela perked up. "How does your mommy dress when she goes out?"

Harper looked at the clothes neatly hung in her doll's wardrobe box. She pulled out a short skirt, short top, and tall boots. "Like this."

Thinking back to the night Athena was working at Harry's, Dela hadn't thought about the way the woman was dressed considering the bar and what she was doing, but it was more something a single woman looking to get laid would wear to a bar, not a married woman with a child.

"Did they argue about it?" Dela asked.

Harper shook her head. "Daddy just says what he thinks and Mommy walks away."

"Where is your mommy?" Dela asked, wondering if Alex had told the child she was dead.

"Daddy said she went away and it's just the two of us." The girl shrugged. "I like this better. Except Daddy cries and won't let me go outside."

A knock at the door startled Dela. She'd been deep in her thoughts over the fact the child didn't care that her mother had left and Alex seemed to be grieving over his wife's death.

The door opened and Alex stuck his head in. He smiled at his daughter. "It looks like you two are having fun."

"Yes. Can Dela come back and play dolls with me again?" Harper asked.

Alex stared at his daughter. "We'll see."

Dela used the end of the bed to help pull herself to her feet. "Harper it was fun playing with you. Are we still strangers?"

"Oh no!" the child said, a smile spread across her face.

Dela faced Alex. "Can I give Harper a treat?"

He nodded.

"Take your pick." Dela held the candy and gum she'd purchased out to the girl.

"I love gum. Thank you!" The child threw her arms around Dela's waist.

"You're welcome." Dela patted the curly hair waiting for the arms to release her. That's when she felt rather than heard the child's deep sigh.

"Can I tell you a secret?" Harper whispered.

Dela leaned down and the child whispered in her ear, "You make me feel safe."

She gave the girl a hug and stood, stepping away. "I'm glad. Your dad can call anytime you need to talk to me." Dela dug in her purse for a piece of paper. She wrote her name and cellphone number on the paper.

"Dela, you ready?" Heath called from the living room.

She peered into Alex's face. "If you or Harper need to talk or she wants to play dolls, give me a call, and if I'm not working, I'll try to come by."

He shoved the paper into his pocket. She had a feeling he didn't want her and Harper to have a connection. Had he pushed her and Athena apart?

Dela hurried out of the room and into the living room. Jacob was gone. Heath stood by the front door. She strode over to where he stood. "Let's go."

He opened the door and they both walked to his pickup. Once they were driving away, he asked, "Did you learn anything?"

She relayed what the child had said. "She's scared of something. She told me I made her feel safe." She stared at Heath's profile. "Do you think Athena was abusing her? Or maybe Alex is?"

"Did she have any bruises or act sore?" Heath asked.

"No. But that's an odd thing for an eight-year-old to tell an adult they'd just met." Dela leaned back in the seat. "What, besides no DNA sample, did Alex have to say."

"That he and Athena got along. He had no idea she was blackmailing anyone. But that made sense given she spent more money than her jobs brought in. He thought she was prostituting because of the way she dressed."

Dela spun her head and stared at Heath. "And he was okay with her prostituting? Harper said her daddy told her mommy she shouldn't go out dressed like that."

"He said, as long as Athena was happy, he didn't care what she did as long as it was off the reservation so no one here knew." Heath pulled into her driveway. "In a way, he was right. She was using her body to get the goods on the men she blackmailed."

"And a woman. Arthur told me that he saw her talking several times to a woman who drove a mini cooper at the casino parking lot." Dela remembered her conversation with the valet. "I forgot to give you the license plate number." She texted it to Heath.

"What are you going to do besides work?" Heath asked as she opened her door and heard both braying and barking.

"I'm going to talk with Natalie about being friends with Athena and see if Marty can pull up parking lot surveillance to see if we can get an idea who the woman she was talking to could be."

Chapter Sixteen

At the casino, Dela encountered a large crowd for a Tuesday. It was Kenny's day off and she'd be staying until they closed down the tables at 2 a.m. Natalie wouldn't come in to work for another two hours.

Dela dealt with paperwork after walking around and checking in with the security staff on duty. By the time she'd finished reading Kenny's reports from the past two days and working on scheduling, it was almost five. Natalie would be in the Pony by now.

She stepped out of the security office and nearly ran into Bernie Moon, one of the board of directors for the casino. "Sorry, Bernie." Dela backed up and studied the man's face. She'd seen him angry and she'd seen him upset, but the paleness of his skin and his red eyes surprised her. "Are you okay?" she asked, leading him by his arm toward the deli since it was the closest place for them to sit down away from the gaming floor.

Once they were seated, she went to the counter and

ordered two iced teas. She asked the girl on duty if it was Rosie's day off.

"Yes. She has been taking three days off and working the four busiest days." The girl glanced at Bernie and lowered her voice. "I think she's taking online college classes."

Dela smiled. "Good for her!" She carried the drinks over to the distraught board member and sat. "What's wrong Bernie?"

The man looked at her. "You don't really care."

"Yes, I do. Even if you haven't believed in me more times than I like to think about, I do care if something is wrong. Does it have to do with the casino?" She sipped her tea and let the man think.

He stirred two packets of sugar into his tea and replaced the plastic lid on the paper cup. After slurping up two large gulps, he licked his lips and said, "My wife came home and said someone has been asking questions about a person who once lived in Nixyáawii. Her nightmares are coming back. I don't get much sleep because of it. I don't know how to make her feel safe. After all, he's dead and can't come back."

Dela studied the man. "What did the person do that gave your wife nightmares?"

"She and several of her friends were coming back from Walla Walla one winter and their car became stuck. This person stopped and offered them a ride. But he didn't take them home. He took them to a shack on Spring Mountain. There were piles of women's clothes in a corner of the structure. They became scared and asked to be taken home. They said he didn't talk once they arrived at the shack. He just sat and stared at them. The four girls huddled together all night listening to the howling wind and what they thought were wolves. It snowed hard that night and when they woke up in the morning, they were snowed in. The man was gone but he'd left what looked like a human arm that had been cooked on the table."

Dela shivered and could see why the woman would be having nightmares. "They must have been found?"

"Yes, but they all have had nightmares since." Bernie finally looked her in the eyes. "That wasn't the first time that man had scared anyone from here. It was as if he enjoyed putting fear into people." Bernie shook his head. "He could also be very charismatic. As many of the girls who were scared of him, there were just as many who fell in love with him."

"What was his name?" Dela asked, wondering why she had never heard about this growing up. But Bernie and his wife and her friends would have been the generation of her mom. They probably told these stories to their friends, not to their children.

"It is never spoken. Thank you for listening. It did help to talk to someone." Bernie stood, holding his drink, and walked out of the deli.

She didn't think her mom would know about this, but she bet Rosie's mom would. Now that Bernie had brought up the story, it intrigued her. Dela picked up her unfinished drink and headed across the gaming floor to the Pony. Hopefully, there wasn't a large crowd in there yet so she could talk to Natalie.

At the door, she stopped and surveyed the room. Only about a dozen people were seated in the room. She spotted Natalie leaning against the bar talking with Dexter.

Dela crossed to the bar and sat on the stool beside the waitress. "Dexter, I need to visit with Natalie for a few minutes."

The Squeeze

The bartender glanced back and forth between them before he said, "Sure," and headed to the other end of the bar.

"Why do you need to talk to me?" Natalie faced Dela.

"I learned that you and Athena were friends. That you would meet in the deli, talk, and laugh. Why didn't you tell me you were friends?" Dela sipped the drink she'd brought in with her.

Natalie looked down at the manicured nails on her right hand. "We were kind of friends, but not real friends like I am with other people."

"What did you talk about when you met up?"

"Where we got our nails done. Our clothes. Nothing much." Natalie still wasn't making eye contact.

"Did she ever talk about her husband or her daughter?"

That got a little flick of a glance up at Dela and back down at her nails. "She really didn't want to be married, but she liked having it as a way to keep men from getting too clingy."

"She told you that?" Dela asked.

"Not like that. But she said being married kept guys from getting serious." Natalie finally raised her gaze and peered into Dela's eyes. "I think she liked the game of seeing who she could get to screw her." She rolled her eyes. "I mean, some of them were well-off married men and others were complete scuzzballs."

"Did you ever tell her husband about her game?" Dela asked.

The woman's eyes widened a bit before she glanced down the bar and back at Dela. "I didn't, but I think Dexter might have said something to Alex one night when he showed up here looking for Athena and she'd slipped out with someone on her break."

"Did Alex seem upset?" Dela asked.

Natalie pressed her lips together and stared at the ceiling. "He looked disappointed more than angry."

Dela thought about what Alex had said about his wife keeping her infidelity off the reservation. Would knowing she was doing it here, at the casino on the reservation, have made him angry enough to kill her?

"Can I get back to work?" Natalie asked.

"Yes." Dela wandered down the bar to where Dexter was chatting with a couple at the bar, playing one of the machines inserted in the bar top. "Can I speak to you?" She nodded her head back the way she'd come.

He said something to the couple, they laughed, and he made his way back to where he'd been when she'd walked in. "What did you need to ask me about?"

Dela studied him. Had he been one of Athena's conquests? "Natalie knew what Athena was doing while working here. Did you?"

"You mean her quickies with anyone who looked like they had money? Yeah. I asked her about it. She said she just wanted to make sure she got good tips." He snorted. "I could tell she was on the hustle, but I never quite figured out how."

"The night her husband came in to talk to her and she was out with a man, how did Alex take it?" Dela kept her gaze on the bartender. She'd dealt with him before and knew his emotions showed no matter how hard he tried to hide them.

"At first, he didn't believe me. But he hung around and saw her and the man she'd left with walk in all smiley. Her shirt was crooked. I had expected Alex to charge across the room and confront her. But he waited until she came over to pick up her tray and all he said was, 'I told you to keep your underwear on when you were on the reservation.' Then he marched out of the Pony and I haven't seen him since."

Dela sat there staring into the mirror behind the bar. She scanned the people visiting and ordering drinks. "That's an odd way to behave having just found your wife messing around with someone else."

"Yeah, I thought so, too." Dexter started filling glasses with beer as Natalie returned with empties.

"Did Athena ever say anything about her husband knowing what she did?" Dela asked Natalie.

"No. She only talked about him in that he was a dandy little housekeeper and babysitter." Natalie loaded her tray back up. "I never understood why they married. She didn't talk like she really liked him and he never treated her in a way a man in love would treat his spouse." She walked away and Dela thought about that. Why had they married?

Because she was stuck at the casino working, she couldn't talk to anyone but the people here. It was Tuesday, she wouldn't be able to visit with Arthur about Alex. All she could do was her usual. Then she remembered wanting the surveillance of the parking lots.

Dela left the Pony, tossed her empty drink cup in a trash can, and headed to the hidden door to the surveillance room. She tapped her security card on the disguised box and the door opeened. Entering a room filled with monitors, she nodded and spoke to each of the four people on duty watching the world as it played out inside the casino and in the parking lot.

"Nice day to be inside where there's air

conditioning," Marie James said. She was the one watching the parking lot footage. There were cameras around the outside of the building as well as on lights in the main parking lot.

"It just keeps getting warmer each day," Dela said, wishing she'd had time for her run early this morning. "Is Marty in?"

"It's Farley today," Russ said, looking away from the screens on the wall in front of him.

"That works. Thanks." Dela continued to the door of the surveillance office and knocked. She wanted to let Marty's assistant know that she was coming in. Not that he would have anything to hide, other than eating over the keyboard, which Marty reprimanded the younger man about often.

"Hey, Dela, figured you were headed in here when you entered our sanctum." Farley was in his twenties and a genius with computers, or so Marty said. But he reminded Dela of the big purple dinosaur loved by many children back when she was young. She hadn't cared for the creature's overexuberance. She understood Farley was just a full-of-energy person, so she tolerated him. And he didn't sing silly songs.

"I would like you to put all the nighttime parking lot videos on a flash drive for me to pick up tomorrow." She continued standing since she didn't plan to stick around.

"By all, you don't mean from several years?" His energy drained a bit at the thought.

She laughed and said, "No, just the last two months should get what I need. I think just the front parking lot is all I need, but if it's easy to do, also the back lot."

"I'll get on it." His cheeks darkened. "You going to save me a dance at Marty's wedding?"

The Squeeze

"As long as you don't hop around."

"Awesome. I'll have that ready for you tomorrow." He started clicking the keyboard.

Dela left the room. She hadn't thought about having to dance with anyone at the wedding. She hadn't danced since losing her leg. Could she dance?

Dela walked out of the surveillance room and into the chaos of the casino. Machines chimed and dinged, voices were muffled, and the flute music in the background didn't lull her as usual. Something wasn't right. Not with the casino but with the information she'd gathered. But which information? About Athena Kindale or Dory Thunder?

Chapter Seventeen

Wednesday morning, Dela told Heath what she'd learned from Natalie. She planned to stop by and talk to Grandfather Thunder about the story Bernie had told her. He was old enough to have heard the story of the stranded girls. As she went to sleep the night before she'd thought how lucky the young women had been that the man hadn't turned out to be someone who raped and murdered Indigenous women. That they were still alive to have nightmares. Robin hadn't been given that chance.

"Alex knew what his wife was doing and caught her messing around on the reservation after he'd told her not to." Heath was buttering his toast. "He doesn't strike me as a jealous man. But he does have strong family relationships and wouldn't want his family to know his wife was selling her body."

"I just don't get it. Is there anyone we can talk to who witnessed their courtship and marriage? They seem like an odd couple, and the way they lived their lives so separately…" Dela had thought about that during the night when her stub had twinged and ached. As was usual, when she became stressed, her phantom pains increased, not helping the situation. She'd almost crossed the hall to Heath's room to have him distract her but didn't want to be the one slipping into his bed and looking needy.

"If you aren't busy this morning, I planned to visit with his family since we can't seem to find any family for Athena, or should I say, Marilyn Rathman. It appears she was in foster homes, never staying in any very long." Heath finished eating his toast. "This identity change and the fact we can't find medical records that she ever gave birth, I was able to convince Chief Steel we could use help from the FBI. Especially if this is a case of kidnapping across state lines. I talked to Pierce last night. He's putting all the info and DNA we have for Athena through their databases. Hopefully, he can come up with some way of finding out who Harper really belongs to."

"That's a good idea. I'm surprised Chief Steele agreed." Dela finished off her cereal and toast.

"He was still dragging his feet until I told him the child could have been kidnapped." Heath rose. "I'll clean up if you want to get in your work uniform. I'll drop you off at the casino after we visit with the Kindales and Pierce."

Dela had dressed in her sweats and t-shirt to go for a run. She'd arrived home so late last night Heath had already been asleep and she'd figured today would be a normal day. It looked like it wouldn't.

She patted Mugshot's head. "Sorry, boy. No run today either." The dog's sad brown eyes tugged at her.

"You can drop me off here when we finish. I'll go to work later."

"Isn't this Kenny's day off?" Heath asked, turning from putting dishes in the dishwasher.

"Yes. They can deal with things until I get there. I'll give Margie a call and have her put someone else on the podium. She can be in charge until I get there." Dela had confidence in the older woman. She had a level head and a good rapport with people. Her temperament was better suited if something came up that required the head of security to intervene.

"Okay. Then if you're ready, let's go. I want to get you back here before noon. Even that's going to be awful hot to be running." Heath walked to the front door, grabbed his hat off the coat rack, and held out her purse.

Dela put Mugshot out the French doors into the backyard and walked to the front door, hooking her purse as she walked out the door Heath held open.

Today they were in his tribal vehicle. A compact SUV. It wasn't made for carrying passengers since he had his computer and a crime scene processing kit in the seat.

"Just a minute. I should have come out here earlier and made room." He put the kit in the back of the vehicle and the computer on the console between the seats.

Dela slid into the seat, buckled up, and smiled. It had been a while since she'd ridden in a law enforcement vehicle.

"Where do the Kindales live?" Dela asked as Heath backed out of the driveway.

"Not far from your mom and Grandfather Thunder."

The Squeeze

Dela bit her bottom lip. Did she tell Heath she planned to see Grandfather Thunder later? And should she tell him about the story? Maybe he'd heard it before. The drive to the Kindales wouldn't be enough time to delve into the story and her thoughts of asking Grandfather Thunder, so she kept it to herself for now.

"Where are you meeting Pierce?" she asked instead.

"He's meeting me at the tribal station. Steele insisted that we not meet out in public. He didn't want word to get out we couldn't handle a murder on the reservation by ourselves."

Dela rolled her eyes. "What does it matter as long as we get the person responsible for taking a life? And reunite Harper with her real parents, if she was kidnapped."

"That's what I tried to say, but he was all about we had lost face with the people of the Umatilla with Detective Jones and needed to prove we were capable of clearing this up." Heath shook his head as he pulled into the driveway of a one-story house that looked as old as the one her mom lived in.

"He's trying to be a politician instead of a cop," Dela said, opening her door when Heath turned off the engine.

"He is. We need a chief of police, not someone trying to make everyone happy." Heath led the way to the front door.

A man about her mom's age answered the door. "Why have you brought this woman with you?" he asked, eyeing Dela in her sweats and t-shirt.

"This is Dela Alvaro. She's head of security at the casino. I brought her along to listen and ask questions. Athena worked for the casino, and Dela has met your granddaughter."

The man waved his hand. "That is not my granddaughter. Alex may have given her our name but she was forced on him. That is not how you make a family. You are offered a child that is not of your blood, not told you will take care of her." The man hadn't allowed them into the house. He stood just inside the screen door.

"Mr. Kindale, we really want to learn more about your son's relationship with his wife. It could help us find out who killed her." Heath nodded to the inside of the house. "We'd like to come in and learn what you know."

"My wife isn't well. She hasn't been since our son brought that woman into our home and said he was marrying her. Now she has brought shame to our family. The stories we are hearing." The man opened the door, but he stepped outside, not allowing them in. "They are saying she was having sex with many men and making them pay. Why would she need to do that? Alex makes good money. Look at the house he has. The car. The money he spends on that child. Why would his wife need to disgrace his name?"

Dela maneuvered the man to a chair on the porch. "Mr. Kindale, sit down. She is a woman who has done many wrong things. We are here to understand how your son, an honorable man, could have married her." She pulled another chair over to sit in front of the man. "Do you know how they met?"

"In Pendleton at the college." The man stared into her eyes. "She was a nursing student. That's what she told Alex. He came home one Thursday night and said he'd met a woman and they were going to get married. That was it. No courtship, no bringing her home for his mother to see if she was suitable." He shook his head. "I thought, they will live well. Alex will make good money with his computer stuff and she would make good money as a nurse. She would be compassionate and kind." His eyes narrowed and his hands shook. "The first time she came to our house, she made fun of us, the family who had gathered to meet her. Alex blamed her bad manners on us. That we shouldn't have overwhelmed her with so much family. That she had none and didn't know how to act around welcoming people." Confusion wrinkled his face and faded his eyes. "How do you not have good manners no matter who you meet?"

"And Harper. When she arrived with the child, what did Alex say or do?" Dela pressed.

The man shrugged. "He was smiling from ear to ear. He was happy about the child. But look at her. That child doesn't look a thing like her mother. And her disposition is too sweet, too caring. I've worried from the beginning that someone would show up and take her away from Alex."

Dela peered up at Heath. How many others didn't believe Harper was Athena's child?

"Did Alex ever mention that he thought the child wasn't hers as well?" Heath asked.

The man's eyes widened. "Is that what killed her? She had taken this child from someone?"

"We don't know that. We are just following all lines of questioning," Heath said.

Dela had noticed the hope that had glimmered in the man's eyes for a second. "Do you think your son killed his wife?"

"No! Alex never had the stomach for hunting and killing. He would starve before he'd kill an animal to eat. I have talked to the Creator that someone would take the child from Alex and he'd come back to us." The man's head drooped, his chin touching his chest.

"Thank you, Mr. Kindale," Heath said and motioned for Dela to stand.

"It was nice meeting you. I hope I can meet your wife the next time I see you." Dela followed Heath back to the vehicle.

Sitting in the passenger seat, she glanced at the man still slumped in his chair and then over to Heath. "How sad that Alex gave up his real family to live a life completely against all he was raised to believe." She was more determined than ever to get to the bottom of the real Athena Kindale.

♠ ♣ ♥ ♦

Heath dropped Dela off after their visit with Mr. Kindale. She and Mugshot went for a run. Dela cut it short because of the heat. Neither she nor the dog could keep up their usual pace. Back home she showered, changed into her work clothes, and put Mugshot out in the pasture with Jethro. Heath could bring him in when he arrived home from work. She wouldn't be home until three in the morning.

Dela passed the casino headed toward Grandfather Thunder's house. The story Bernie had told her the day before continued to play in the back of her mind. Was it a joke someone had deliberately set up for the young women or had there been someone that deranged to put a cooked human arm on the table for them to eat? And where did the arm come from?

She pulled into the gravel and grass driveway. Now that the elder didn't drive and had sold his car, her mom was letting the grass grow up between the rocks. She said it was easier to mow that way. Dela stopped halfway to the house. Who would mow this lawn and tend the flowers once her mom married Lance? She glanced over the bushes separating this property from her mom's and studied the shingle roof of her mom's house.

No, she didn't want to buy that home and live here. She loved her house in Tutuilla. It had been remodeled to her needs and she loved seeing the Blue Mountains out her kitchen window and the glass French doors in the dining room. Not to mention the privacy of being far from her neighbors.

Whoever purchased the place would have to be willing to help with Grandfather Thunder's care. That would make selling her mom's place harder.

"Dela, what brings you for a visit?" Grandfather Thunder asked, standing on the porch holding the screen door open.

"I had a chat with Bernie Moon yesterday and wondered if you could confirm or deny what he said." Dela walked up onto the porch and gave the old man a hug. "You know so much of the history of the people here, that I thought you could clear things up for me."

"What has that old fool Bernie been talking about now?" The man walked slowly into the kitchen and straight to the cupboard where he kept his glasses. "Grab that pitcher of iced tea I made this morning."

Dela did as she was asked, waving the fridge door a bit to help cool off the room. Grandfather Thunder didn't believe in air conditioning. His house had a muggy, hot feel to it. Which accentuated the old house and person smells.

"How about we sit out back, under that cottonwood tree?" Dela suggested. At least there, they would have a breeze.

"If you wish."

Dela filled the two glasses, put the pitcher back, and picked up the glasses, following the old man's slow gait out to the chairs placed under the tree.

Just stepping out of the house felt twenty degrees cooler. She tipped her head, wiping her temple on her shoulder to rid it of the sweat that dripped from her hairline.

When Grandfather Thunder sat in the wooden chair, she handed him his drink and sat in the sagging camp chair. After they had both drained their cups to halfway, Dela began.

"Bernie Moon looked sick when I saw him yesterday." She went on to tell him the story the man had told her. And that it was now plaguing his wife having had the man's name brought up. "Do you know this story? Did it really happen or was it a joke elders played on the young women to keep them from running around?" She'd watched Grandfather Thunder as she'd told the story. She knew by his reactions it wasn't something that had been made up.

The old man put his glass of tea on the ground and folded his hands in his lap. He peered into her eyes. "There was a man at that time who came back from Vietnam and wasn't himself. It was before they realized there was such a thing as PTSD. Elders tried to take away the demons that possessed him but they couldn't. When the demons left him alone, he was a nice guy. Everyone loved him. But when the demons took over, he was like one himself. It has been mentioned many times that the young women were fortunate that night that he was himself and not the demon that had taken him over."

Dela shuddered despite the heat. She knew of

fellow comrades who had taken their own lives and sometimes those of others in their torment from what they saw and did while at war.

"I'm sorry to hear that a fellow soldier came home to such torture. Can you tell me his name so I don't bring up bad memories for someone?" She really wanted to know if this was Dory Thunder, the man she believed could be her father.

Grandfather Thunder shook his head. "No. You would never use this man's name so there is no need to tell you."

"Thank you for sharing this with me. I will give Bernie more sympathy when I see him again. I thought it might just be something he might have made up to cover something else."

The old man's eyes narrowed as he watched her. "You do not trust Bernie?"

Dela thought about that a moment. "He hasn't trusted me. This makes me wary of why he would think I would cause anyone harm or work against the casino. So in a way, his not trusting me has caused me to not trust everything he tells me." She stood. "There are days I wonder if he gives me inaccurate information to cause my termination at the casino."

Grandfather Thunder picked up his glass of tea. "He is not as smart a man as he thinks he is. That is his problem." He sipped his tea, then waved his hand. "Go on. Get to work. Prove how capable you are."

Dela smiled. "I'll drop this off in the kitchen and go. Thank you."

Chapter Eighteen

Stepping into the security office from the employee entrance, Dela met chaos.

"What is going on?" she asked, passing the empty podium and hurrying to the three bodies entangled in the middle of the room.

She grabbed the arm of the person not in a security uniform and wrenched it behind his back. When he tried to round on her, she twisted it higher up his back and buckled his knees.

Margie shoved her loose hair out of her face and grabbed a pair of handcuffs three feet away on the floor. "We've been trying to corral him for the last five minutes." She clicked the handcuffs on the young man who had stopped struggling once he realized Dela knew what she was doing.

Oliver, the oldest member of security, sat on a chair catching his breath.

Dela dragged the young man to his feet. "What is he in here for?"

"He was caught stealing from the gift shop. Jerry brought him in for tribals to pick up." Margie had her hair pulled back into a ponytail but not back in her usual bun. "I'd just finished calling the tribals when he burst out of the holding room." She shot a glare at the young man Dela still held onto. "I stopped him but couldn't get him cuffed. Oliver tried to help me, but you saw how wild this guy is."

Dela sat the young man down in a chair and zip-tied the cuffs to the back of the chair. She turned to Margie. "Go relieve Jerry and have him come in here to write up the report."

The woman nodded and left. Dela walked over to her desk, clipped her radio to her belt, pinned the mic to the shoulder of her shirt, and shoved the earbud into her ear. The radio crackled as she turned it on and spoke into the mic. "Ross, tell me when the tribals arrive to pick up our shoplifter."

"Copy."

She rolled her chair over to sit in front of the young man but far enough back that he couldn't kick her. "Want to tell me your story before the Tribal Police get here?"

He glared at her.

"Okay, I'll take that as a confession." She wanted to get out on the floor and check in with everyone but after seeing how the young man had gotten the better of Margie and Oliver, she felt she was needed here until the Tribal Police took the thief away.

Shoving backward with her feet, she rolled the chair to her desk and started working on reports.

Jerry walked in.

"Fill out the incident report, please," Dela said. "I'd like it finished before they come and pick him up."

She liked to be one step ahead of the Tribal Police when the casino had someone for them to pick up.

Jerry settled his tall, lanky body into the extra desk and pulled a sheet of paper out of a drawer. All her staff knew the forms that needed to be filled out for specific incidents. She had trained them all on how to be vigilant to stop trouble before it started and how to deal with the paperwork involved in an altercation. That way she didn't have to spend most of her shift asking questions and filling out paperwork.

By the time Jerry turned from the desk with the paperwork in his hand, the door opened and the newest member of the Tribal Police walked in.

"Hello, Officer Shaw," Dela greeted the young female officer who had joined the force only a month before. Being new to the force, she was given all the runs to the casino. Dela had been impressed with the young woman's sense of duty and how she handled the people that were handed over to her.

"Dela, I hear you have a shoplifter for me." The woman was close to Dela's build, only ten years younger.

A pang of sorrow wedged in Dela's chest. She rubbed a hand up and down her sternum to get it to leave. "Yes. I didn't check him for I.D. but Jerry caught him trying to take items from the gift shop."

"Expensive items," Jerry added, handing the paper in his hand to Officer Shaw.

She glanced at it and whistled. "Do you have the items he was caught with?"

Jerry walked over to the desk where he'd been writing and picked up an evidence bag. He handed that to her as well.

"Jerry, why don't you help walk this young man

out to the officer's patrol car?"

When Tabitha gave her an inquisitive glance, Dela added, "When I walked in, he was getting the better of two of my smaller guards. He needs to know there are two people who can put him on his knees." She winked at the officer to let her know she wasn't trying to say she couldn't do her job.

When Jerry, Officer Shaw, and the shoplifter left, Dela headed out onto the gaming floor. Not twenty feet out and her phone buzzed. She glanced at the name. Farley.

He'd texted. *I have the video you wanted.*

She smiled, waved a hand, and headed for the surveillance hidden door. Once inside, she said hello to the people sitting in front of the monitors and walked into the office after one knock.

"I wondered when you were coming to work today. It was starting to get late," Farley said, picking up a flash drive. "I have the main parking lot footage for every night the last two months on there." He handed it to her and picked up another one. "And this is the employee and RV parking lot."

"Thank you."

"What are you looking for? I might be able to find it quicker than looking through all of that." He spun his chair around to the table and keyboard.

Dela sat down in the chair and put her prosthesis on the box Marty kept under the table just for her. "I want to see everyone Athena Kindale met in the parking lots. Arthur saw her one night with a woman beside a mini-cooper. And I'm pretty sure she might have met some others in the parking lot for payments."

"I don't know who she is." Farley glanced at her.

"She is the waitress in the Pony who was cutting

out early and was killed last week."

"Oh, the one that thought she was a teenager." Farley started clicking keys on the keyboard.

"Why do you say that?" Dela asked, watching the screen on the monitor in front of her as people and cars entered and left the parking lot in fast-forward.

"Because of the way she dressed and flirted." He stopped the video. There stood Athena and a woman beside a mini-cooper.

"How did you? Never mind. Can you zoom in and get the license plate of that car?"

Farley clicked keys and the plate grew larger.

Dela pulled out her phone and checked to see if it was the same car as the one Arthur saw. "Okay, genius, can you see if she met up with anyone else? I want to specifically see if they hand her anything."

"I've got the rest of my shift to check it out. I'll take stills of the meet-ups I find."

"Perfect. You can just leave them in an envelope on my desk when you leave." Dela stood. "Sorry, you went to all the work of putting these flash drives together. But they might be something the police want when we find the killer."

"I'm using the footage I put together for you to look through, so it really just set me up to help more today." He grinned and began clicking keys.

Dela shook her head smiling and left the surveillance office. Marty was lucky to have such a go-getter working for him.

Walking across the casino floor, she spotted security guard Todd Wilde in an intense discussion with a woman. Dela wasn't sure but she looked a little bit like the woman standing next to the mini-cooper.

Dela walked up to them. "Todd, can I help you?"

The Squeeze

The man and woman both swung around. The woman's face was red with anger, while Todd's face paled as his gaze latched onto Dela.

"No, no, we're fine. This is my wife." Todd waved a hand to the woman. "Vonnie, this is my boss, Dela."

"Mrs. Wilde, pleased to meet you," Dela said, extending her hand.

The other woman acted as if she wasn't sure whether to shake hands or turn and run. She finally grasped Dela's hand and gave her a firm shake. "Pleased to meet you. Todd respects you."

"That's good to know. We don't mind if spouses drop by to leave a message for a staff member, but it looked like you were in a discussion that should be taken care of elsewhere," Dela said as delicately as she knew how.

This time the woman looked embarrassed. Todd's face reddened as well.

"Nice to meet you," Dela said, moving off to talk to Arthur who was at his post inside the main entrance.

The older man nodded his head toward the Wildes. "That's the first time I've seen those two talking when he's on duty. And it looked like an interesting talk." Arthur raised one eyebrow.

"I thought the same thing when I saw it. Does she look like the woman who stood next to the mini-cooper talking to Athena?" Dela asked.

The older man closed his eyes for several seconds. Dela could see his eyes moving underneath the lids. Was he mentally going through the files in his head?

Arthur opened his eyelids and stared at the woman as she strode toward them. "I'm positive it was her. We can watch and see if she gets in a mini-cooper."

Dela stepped in front of the woman. "Mrs. Wilde,

I'd like to visit with you in the coffee shop." She motioned for the woman to walk ahead of her.

When Vonnie Wilde headed toward the coffee shop, Dela glanced over her shoulder at Todd. Worry creased his brow.

When they were seated, Dela ordered coffee for them both and studied the woman. She looked more composed than she had while talking to her husband. Dela waited for the waitress to bring their drinks and then she began.

"Mrs. Wilde—"

"Vonnie, please," she interrupted.

"Vonnie, we have video of you talking to Athena Kindale in the parking lot not long before she was found murdered in her car." Dela sipped her coffee and continued. "Want to tell me what you and the victim were talking about?"

The woman squirmed, adding three packets of sugar to her coffee. She stirred and must have finally found the words to reply. Clearing her throat, she said, "I was telling her to stay away from Todd."

Dela studied her. "But he told me that you didn't know anything about him and Athena until the night she died."

Vonnie shook her head. "I'm not that stupid. I figured it out nearly as soon as it started. His clothes started smelling of someone else's perfume and he had a couple of buttons ripped off his shirt. When I asked him about the buttons, he came up with a lame excuse it was caught in his locker here at work." She sipped the coffee. "The night I confronted her in the parking lot, she laughed and said, he wasn't worth banging anymore if I knew and she couldn't get money out of him to keep quiet." The woman's cheeks reddened. "I couldn't believe she'd made my husband stray only to get money out of him. Believe me, I wanted to kill her, but I only did it in my mind." She glanced toward the casino gaming area. "We're trying to put things back together, but the way Todd's been talking, I think he thinks I killed her."

"Where were you that night?" Dela asked.

"Todd had finally told me what I already knew. But I pretended that I was shocked and horrified. I was secretly happy that by my knowing, she'd pulled her claws out of him. I didn't want him to realize this wasn't new information, so I stormed out of the house and stayed with a friend outside of town."

"You need to give that name to Officer Seaver of the Tribal Police. Do you want to go to the tribal station or I can have him come here and get your statement?" Dela picked up her coffee.

"I just told you. Isn't that enough?" She glanced toward the entrance to the coffee shop.

"No. You are on his list of suspects, as well as Todd. Since you went somewhere, your husband doesn't have an alibi for that night." Dela pulled her phone out of her pocket and texted Heath. *Mrs. Wilde wants to make a statement about her whereabouts the night of Athena's death.*

Heath texted back. *She can come to the station, I'm here.*

She doesn't want to. I'm sitting with her in the coffee shop at the casino.

Be there shortly.

"Officer Seaver is on his way here." Dela sipped her coffee and asked, "Had you ever met Athena before the night you talked to her in the parking lot?"

Vonnie started to shake her head and stopped. "I

think she was at the library on one of my volunteer days. She was trying to look up someone's address on the public computers."

"How do you know it was an address?" Dela asked, wondering why the victim would be using a computer at the library when her husband was a computer technician.

"Because she asked what was the best website to use to get the information for free. I told her unless the person had a landline and she could look in the phonebook or white pages she would have to pay to get the information." Vonnie sipped her coffee. "I'm not sure she found what she was looking for. She left when I was in the back fixing a book."

Heath walked into the coffee shop followed by FBI Special Agent Quinn Pierce. Heath was like a soft flannel shirt, always welcome and comfortable. Quinn always put her on edge, upping her blood pressure and making her feel like she wasn't good enough. But they had made a truce over his letting a rapist go free in Iraq. As an MP she'd caught the rapist and promised the young woman he'd raped that he would be punished. Then Quinn marched in with his special services badge and took him away. Claiming the man would help to save many soldiers' and civilians' lives.

"I didn't expect you to bring back up to collect a statement," Dela said when the two were seated. Heath had slid into the bench seat where Dela sat and Quinn had pulled a chair up to the end of the table.

Heath grinned.

Quinn scowled.

Vonnie's gaze settled on first Heath and then Quinn. "I don't understand?"

"I was with Officer Seaver when Dela texted him.

We hadn't finished our conversation." Quinn held up his hands as if in surrender. "So, here I am along for the ride."

"And you are?" Vonnie asked.

"FBI Special Agent Pierce." He held out his hand and they shook.

"Are you working on this case as well?" Vonnie asked, her gaze sliding to Dela as if to say, 'what have you gotten me into?'

"I am, but not the homicide. I'm helping in another capacity." Quinn turned his attention to Dela. "Good to see you. It's been a while."

Dela gave him a small smile. "We've been busy."

Heath cleared his throat. "Miss Wilde, Dela said you had a statement to give about where you were the night Mrs. Kindale died."

Vonnie told Heath everything she'd said earlier with some coaxing from Dela.

"This doesn't look good for your husband. With you gone, he won't have an alibi," Heath said.

The woman nodded. "If I had known the woman was going to be killed that night, I wouldn't have stormed out of the house. I just wanted him to feel bad for what he'd done."

Dela felt for the woman. "I don't know if this helps, but Athena had targeted over a dozen men that she was blackmailing. We are just narrowing down the list to who finally cracked and decided they weren't paying anymore."

Vonnie peered into her eyes. "That women had slept with other men and blackmailed them? Oooo. You may have more wives to question."

Dela was afraid of that. Especially since the murder weapon was a fingernail file.

"You can go. Thank you for your cooperation," Heath said.

Vonnie didn't wait to be told twice, she slipped out of the bench seat and strode to the entrance.

Dela waited for Quinn to slide onto the vacated bench and for the waitress to deliver coffee before she told them about the victim using a public computer at the library to look up an address.

Chapter Nineteen

Dela stepped out into the parking lot at 2:30 a.m. The rest of the evening and night had unfolded as usual. She stretched her back and breathed in the night air. It was a comfortable 66°. While the July days could be blistering, the nights could be blissful.

She walked to her car, thinking about a glass of milk and cookies when she arrived home.

Lights from a vehicle flashed on. She was the last one from the night shift leaving. All that worked from now until 10 a.m. was a small security, surveillance, and maintenance crew, along with the cleaning crew.

She hurried to her car as the vehicle started moving in her direction. The keys in her hand jingled as she tried to unlock the door. The car stopped beside her. The window slowly lowered.

It was Gus Sanders.

"What do you want?" Dela asked.

"To give you notice. My wife is divorcing me. And

it seems you helped to give her the information that will leave me a pauper." His beady eyes glared at her with hatred. "I'll make your life a living hell for this."

The engine roared to life and the wheels squealed on the asphalt, dispensing nose-stinging rubber smoke that choked her, before the car bolted forward and out of the employee parking.

Dela stared at the taillights. She had to inform someone about this. There was no telling what Gus would decide to do to make her pay. She doubted he would kill her. He wouldn't have any pleasure in that. No, he'd do things that would hurt her family and friends or her job. Things she valued.

Shit! She drove home staring down the side roads and wondering if Gus had really left or was out there watching her.

At home, she hung up her purse and made sure the front door was locked. She stepped out the French doors and called Jethro into the backyard. Dela wanted him close in case Gus retaliated through her animals. With the back door locked, she no longer wanted the cookies and milk. She wanted the blissful oblivion of sleep. If it would come after that encounter.

After finally falling asleep as the sun shone through her blinds, Dela had dreams of trying to get away from someone with only her one leg and crutches. She couldn't see the face completely, one moment she thought it was Gus Sanders, then it looked like Detective Jones, whom she knew was dead because she'd shot him, and then, it was the man in the mugshot.

A wide swath of wetness on her face woke her. She swung her hand at what was tickling her ear.

The Squeeze

A dog yipped.

That woke her completely. "Mugshot? I'm sorry. Come here." She reached out with an arm and the big dog placed his head on her chest, looking at her.

"Did I scare you with my dreams?" she asked, petting his big head. "I'm sorry for that and hitting you. I was still half asleep." Rotating her head, she glanced at the clock on her nightstand. It was almost one in the afternoon.

"Another thing to apologize for. We won't have time to run today." She wiped a hand over her face and moved Mugshot's head off her. "I need a shower and to get ready for work." She sat up and slipped her leg over the bed. The crutches had fallen over and lay on the ground. The easiest way to get them was to lay on her stomach on the bed and try to reach them with an arm. It was that or drop to the floor, scoot to the crutches, then back to the bed and use it to help her stand up.

On her stomach on the bed, she stretched her arm, trying to touch a crutch. Her body started to slide off the bed and she used the arm she was stretching to keep from falling. Mugshot sat beside the bed watching. Now he stood, walked over to the crutches, and picked one up in his mouth.

"Good boy, Mugshot. Bring it here. Come on." Dela smiled and made kissy sounds.

Mugshot carried the crutch over to her.

She grasped the crutch with one hand and patted his head with the other. "Good boy. Can you get the other one?" she asked, pointing to the other crutch on the floor.

Mugshot swung his head in the direction of the crutch on the floor and back to her.

"Go on. Get the other crutch." She reached out

with the crutch in her hand to point and realized she could pull the second one toward the bed. She did and soon was swinging her way into the bathroom to shower. "You'll get a treat for this when I get out," she said.

Mugshot wagged his tail causing a breeze.

Dela showered quickly. When she came out of the bathroom she sniffed. Something was cooking. Heath should be at work. She hadn't told him about locking the doors last night after her encounter with Gus. She hoped it was Heath or her mom. She didn't need to walk into the kitchen and find a stranger making himself a meal thinking no one was home.

She opened the bedroom door and swung down the hall.

Heath stood in the kitchen, flipping grilled cheese sandwiches, in his uniform.

"What are you doing here?" she asked, causing him to jump.

"I know you had a rough time sleeping. I could hear you mumbling and what sounded like fighting someone when I was getting ready for work. Thought I'd stop by and have lunch with you and see what was going on." He glanced at her stub and then back up to her face. "Want to eat now or after you dress?"

"Is it ready?" Her stomach growled as if on cue.

"Yeah, grilled cheese with ham." Heath placed a plate with three sandwiches in the middle of the table. He'd already set it for two.

"Thanks." Dela lowered onto the chair nearest her and took a long drink of the iced tea. She plopped a sandwich on her plate, waiting for Heath to sit across from her.

He settled and studied her. "What's up? You look

like you didn't sleep at all."

"Thanks!" She'd noticed the bags under her eyes matched the dark brown of her hair when she brushed it after her shower. "I had a visit last night from Gus Sanders."

Heath put down the glass he'd just picked up and leaned toward her. "What do you mean by a visit? While you were working?"

She shook her head. "When I was walking out to my car after work."

Heath reached across the table, grasping her hand. "What did he say and do?"

"He threatened me because his wife is divorcing him and taking everything. Said he was going to make my life a living hell." Dela eased out of Heath's grasp and picked up the sandwich. "That's why I didn't sleep well."

"And why you had the guard donkey in the backyard this morning." Heath cut his sandwich in half and started eating.

"Well, it was as much to protect him as him sounding an alarm if anyone tried to get in that way." Dela thanked the dog and donkey every day for alerting her to Detective Jones getting in the house unwanted. "I can't run scared all the time, but he was pretty mad last night when he threatened me."

"You can file a restraining order. You know all of the tribal officers would make sure he was kept off the reservation." Heath picked up his glass and drank.

"Yeah. But that would just make him angrier. I'll just have to be watchful. He threatened my friends and family. How do I keep them all safe?" Dela didn't want anything to happen to the people she cared about because she'd told Vivian Sanders about her husband's affair.

"Be vigilant, and hopefully, he'll calm down when the dust settles after the divorce." Heath picked up the other half of his sandwich.

Dela wasn't that optimistic. She'd taken everything away from Gus by talking to Vivian. At the time, she'd liked the idea of giving the man what he deserved for being a rutting pig, but now… She wondered at the wisdom in that.

"Have you been able to find any more of the people Athena was blackmailing?" Dela asked as she leaned back in her chair, letting the sandwich and a half she'd eaten settle and digest.

"I've talked to a few more. All of them except Todd have alibis. They were all still paying and as far as they knew their wives hadn't found out."

"What about Vonnie Wilde's alibi? Was she with the friend like she said?"

"Yes. Her friend vouched that Mrs. Wilde arrived when she said she did and left the next morning. She also said she couldn't believe Todd would succumb to his desire for another woman. That she'd always thought the Wildes were a loving couple." Heath studied her. "Is this going to be another case where you point out all the errors of males and refuse to even think about marriage?"

She gave him a weak smile. "You have to admit, there are very few faithful couples anymore."

"We could be one of the few." His lips tipped up in the smile that had drawn her to him as a junior in high school. The one that had seduced her into being his girlfriend and her first sexual encounter.

Dela didn't know what to say. She didn't see a reason to be legally bound to a man when they were so fickle. Heath was better than most but in time, he would stray. It seemed they all did. "Now isn't the time to talk about forever. Not with Gus Sanders out to ruin my life, and you, if he believes we are a couple."

"That's not going to make me stop talking to you about it." Heath stood, taking his dishes to the sink.

Dela pushed to her foot and grasped her plate.

Heath plucked it from her fingers along with her glass. "Get dressed. I'll head back to work when you are ready to go to the casino."

"You don't have to babysit me because Gus Sanders is throwing a fit." Dela peered into Heath's eyes.

"I'm not babysitting you. We both go the same direction to work. I'll follow you because I like that sexy bumper on your car."

She humphed and headed down the hall.

"I also like the bumper on the back of you," he said.

She snorted and slammed the bedroom door. His laughter filled the house and made her smile. Damn! He always knew how to make her get over whatever mope she was having.

♠ ♣ ♥ ♦

On the way to the casino, Molly called.

"When can you come over and help me finish the last details for the wedding?" her friend asked.

"I won't really have time until Sunday. Is that too late?" Dela knew as the maid of honor it was her duty to help with this type of thing but she really didn't know why Molly was making such a fuss. She and Marty had decided on a small wedding without a wedding dress or a fancy suit for the groom.

"I guess not. I'm trying to decide if we want to

have someone cater the reception or make it a potluck." Molly sighed. "My mom thinks a potluck and put on the invitation no gifts. But I feel bad asking my guests to bring food even though I don't want presents. Marty and I both have all we need. We're not first-time newlyweds."

"Considering you are having the wedding and reception at the Mission Long House, it wouldn't be any different than any other event there. Ask them in lieu of gifts to bring a potluck dish to be shared at the reception." Dela wasn't sure how she knew that would be the wording but it sounded good.

"See, I knew I picked you for my maid of honor for a reason. You always bring things into perspective. Thanks!"

"Does this mean I don't need to come over on Sunday?"

"Why don't you and Heath come over for a barbecue in the evening? We can go over my list and you can tell me if I'm missing anything."

"How would I know that? I've never been married." Dela pulled into the employee parking at the casino. "I'm at work now. I'll call and let you know if Heath and I can make it. I don't know if he has any plans." Dela had scanned the parking lot as she pulled in. Now she hastily exited her car and headed for the employee entrance.

"Sounds good. Have a good evening." Molly ended the call.

Dela hoped she didn't encounter the angry Gus Sanders when she went home. She entered the building and said hello to Oliver, who was tending the entrance.

"Dela, I'm glad you didn't come in and see the same thing as yesterday. I would have had him any minute, but I was sure glad you arrived and handled that boy." Oliver scratched at the patchy whiskers on his chin.

Dela wasn't sure why he had taken to not shaving his chin. And she didn't want to ask in case he didn't realize he'd forgotten to shave that part of his face. He was in his seventies and working security to help raise his grandchildren. Due to his declining health and napping often, this was the best position to keep him employed. She knew before long, she'd have to let him go, but his youngest grandson still had two more years of high school.

"I'm thankful you and Margie were able to keep him contained. Anything interesting happening today?" She tucked her purse in the usual spot and began putting on the radio, mic, and earbud.

"Seems to be calm. Kenny came in early. He said to take over for someone who wasn't feeling well." The man scratched his patchy whiskers. "I don't remember who he said."

Dela turned on the radio. "Kenny, location."

"Near the Pirate bank."

"Copy." Dela left the security office and headed across the gaming floor to a bank of slot machines that had a cumulative pirate game. She spotted him as soon as she cleared a bank of different slot machines.

"Heard you had a long night last night," Kenny said by way of a greeting.

She studied him, wondering how he would know about Gus Sanders. "The casino was slow. It was an easy night."

Kenny shook his head. "Not that. Farley said some guy nearly sideswiped you in the parking lot."

"No, he threatened me. I'll tell you about it later.

Who are you filling in for?" She had a good idea since she tried to get a look at all the gaming floor security members as she made her way to Kenny.

"Todd called in. Said he wasn't feeling good. I told him I'd fill in since this is a night when we are both here." Kenny shrugged.

Dela studied her second in command. "Did he sound upset or different?"

Kenny pulled his gaze back to her. "You think because of what he told us about him and Athena he's not showing up?"

"No. His wife was in here yesterday and they were having a heated discussion until I walked up. Just wondered if maybe something happened." Dela thought hard about what she was going to say. Kenny was always impartial, but she didn't want him to think the worst of Todd if he wasn't the killer. "So far, of all the people who had a reason to kill Athena, Todd is the only one without an alibi."

"I see. You think he's going to take off?" Kenny asked.

"He actually doesn't seem the type to run, but then I didn't think he would cheat on his wife either." She made up her mind. "I'm going to let Heath know. He might want to send someone around to make sure Todd is really at home sick."

Chapter Twenty

Dela walked toward the Pony and stopped where she had a good view of the area in front of the Pony Bar and Grill and the Stallion Restaurant. Texting Heath, she glanced up after typing each word. She still thought Natalie knew more than she was telling.

Todd Wilde called in sick today. You might want to make sure he is still in the area. Dela sent the text to Heath and walked into the Pony. It wasn't as busy as it would be in another hour.

Natalie was taking an order from a table with two older couples.

Dela walked up to the bar. Someone other than Dexter stood behind the bar. Must have been a new hire. It was a tall, thin woman with long, gray hair, colored purple underneath. She had it pulled up on the sides and held in place with skull-shaped clips. Her right arm had a green vine with purple and red roses climbing along the length and disappearing under her short-sleeved black t-shirt with a skull and crossbones on the front. Her name tag said Norma.

"Hello," Dela said, reaching out a hand. "I'm Dela Alvaro, head of security for the casino."

The woman wiped her hand on a towel and gave her a firm shake. "Norma Toms. New bartender."

"Pleased to meet you." Dela leaned against the bar. "Are you new to the area?"

"Not really. I lived here as a child, went to college, married, raised two kids, and when my husband died, I decided to come home." She shrugged. "He never felt comfortable when we visited."

"Welcome home," Dela said as Natalie walked up with empties on her tray.

The waitress rattled off the drinks she needed and then faced Dela. "Are you in here with more questions?"

"I feel like you haven't told me the whole truth." Dela settled on the bar stool to take the weight off her stub. After her short, and crappy, night of sleep, what was left of her right leg throbbed.

Natalie shrugged. "Can't you talk to me when I'm not working?"

"I tried that. You weren't where your neighbor said you would be." Dela studied the woman. Natalie didn't seem the least surprised that Dela had been trying to find her away from work. The neighbor must have mentioned someone was there looking for her.

The waitress faced the bar and said, "I'm taking a fifteen-minute break. I'll be over there in the corner." She tipped her blonde head toward an empty table in the corner by the small bandstand.

"I can handle things." Norma handed her the tray filled with drinks. "Drop these off on your way by the tables." She smiled, and when Natalie headed off with the tray, Norma winked at Dela.

I'm going to like this new bartender, Dela thought as she walked over to the table Natalie had tipped her head toward.

After her tray was empty, the waitress arrived at the table and slid onto the tall chair. "What do you think I'm holding back?"

"You tell me?" Dela leaned back in her chair, watching and waiting.

"I haven't a clue what you want to know," Natalie finally said.

"How did Athena feel about her marriage?"

Natalie shrugged and studied the fingernail she was picking. "I told you before, she liked being married so the men she targeted wouldn't get clingy."

"Did she like her husband?"

"I don't think she liked any man, actually. To her, they were just a way to get money." This time Natalie looked right at her. "She never had anything good to say about Alex. But what she complained about sounded petty to me." She went back to picking at her nail.

"What about her daughter? Did she ever mention the father?" Dela knew this was a long shot. Especially if the child had been kidnapped.

"She'd mention how much Harper ate and needed new clothes, only complaining." Natalie looked up. This time there was anger in her eyes. "I asked why that bothered her when Alex paid for everything."

Dela tucked that away. This woman seemed to know a lot about the husband. She'd ask Rae if she'd seen Natalie at the Kindale house when Athena was away.

"Did she ever mention being scared of anyone? One of the men she was blackmailing, or someone else?" Dela accepted the glass of water, Norma held out to her.

Natalie, again, looked her in the eyes. "As far as I could tell, she wasn't afraid of anyone. Not even the police. When I told her if she kept using me to fake her hours, I was going to tell HR and the police what she was up to. She laughed and said go ahead."

"That's because she didn't think you would do it." Dela peered at Natalie over the top of the water glass she'd raised to her mouth.

The woman squirmed. "I would if she had killed someone, but the blackmail was as much the men's fault as hers. They shouldn't have cheated on their wives."

Dela had the same feeling, but she wasn't going to let Natalie know that.

"My fifteen minutes are up." Natalie slid off the chair and picked up the tray.

Dela sat sipping her water and running the conversation over in her head. She texted Heath. *Has anyone checked out if Alex had a girlfriend on the side?*

Heath texted back. *We asked him and a few of the neighbors but no one knew anything about it. Why?*

Dela replied. *Natalie is sticking up for Alex in a way that makes me think she knows him very well.*

There was a pause and a reply appeared. *Interesting. I'll have someone dig deeper.*

Dela smiled and texted. *Have Jacob ask Rae.*

You aren't a matchmaker. Heath texted back.

She sent him a smiley face and shoved her phone into a pocket. She had work to do.

The Squeeze

Dela was glad Kenny stayed until it was time for her to leave the casino. He walked her to her car and stood in the parking lot as she drove away.

Before heading home, Dela decided to do a drive-by at Alex Kindale's house. She didn't expect to see anything other than a dark house. It was two-thirty in the morning. To her surprise, Natalie's car was parked in the driveway and the living room light was on. Dela turned off her lights and parked in the street where she could see in the front window. The shadow of a man paced back and forth. A woman sat on a chair, her head bowed. That would most likely be Natalie.

Natalie must have left straight after work to tell Alex the questions Dela had asked. So there was a closer connection than just Natalie being Athena's friend. It appeared Natalie was only friends with the victim to be close to her husband.

Dela moved on by the house, then turned on her lights and headed for home. She caught a movement on the right side of her car. Someone else had been watching the two in the Kindale house. Rae's door opened. Dela caught the silhouette of Jacob Red Bear. Seeing her best friend's kid brother going into a woman's house at, now, nearly 3 a.m., made her happy. She wanted him to find happiness more than she wanted it for herself. The Red Bear family never received answers about Robin's murder. They all still grieved not knowing what had happened, who had picked her up, who took their daughter, granddaughter, sister, niece, and friend's life.

There were so many families across the nation and in Canada who never had closure. They still wondered why or who caused their loved one to be murdered or missing. There wasn't a day went by Dela didn't blame herself for Robin's death. She should have made her friend come home with her. Instead, she'd left her to find a ride. A ride that ended her life.

A tear slid down Dela's cheek as she turned the corner and headed home. She needed to hug Mugshot and wouldn't mind a hug from Heath as well but she wouldn't wake him to soothe her own needs.

The drive home was uneventful. Jethro brayed as she exited the car. It made her smile. Heath had put the animal in the backyard for the night. He knew having the donkey at one of the house entrances would make her feel safer.

She also knew, that while Gus had threatened her, he would wait until she had forgotten or become lax, and then he would strike.

Dela let herself in and locked the front door. She hung up her purse and spotted a plate of cookies on the table. She tiptoed as quietly as she could when one foot remained flat, across the room to open the fridge door. Her hand touched the handle.

"I'll take a glass, too."

Heath's voice caused her to jump but not as much as she would have had she been living alone.

"I wasn't that loud," she said, pouring two glasses of milk and setting them on the table before she settled onto a chair. She placed her prosthesis on the chair across from her. Heath took the chair beside hers.

"I woke up when you should have been home. Saw you weren't and I couldn't go back to sleep." He picked up a cookie and dipped it in his milk.

"Sorry. I swung by Alex Kindale's place. After what Natalie said, I was curious. And her car was sitting in front of the house. She and Alex were having a discussion in the living room." She bit the cookie, chewed, swallowed, and said, "You made cookies tonight." There was no mistaking the soft chocolate chunks in the treat.

"Yeah, I was bored. Quinn is still trying to find out more about Athena. But he did narrow down girls aged three who went missing five years ago. There are still nearly two-hundred unaccounted for." Sadness filled his eyes. "It will take a while for those to be checked to see if they might be Harper. If Alex had agreed to a DNA test, we could have found out what we need to know. Where did this child really come from? Does she have anything to do with our victim's death?"

Dela nodded. "In a way, finding out who the parents really are is something child welfare should step in and do, isn't it? We don't have actual proof Athena isn't the mother. Just because the medical reports you did find didn't note a pregnancy or birth doesn't really mean she didn't have a child eight years ago."

"I'm worried that she may have used other aliases over the years. If that's the case, we may never find all of her medical records." Heath dunked another cookie. "We have her DNA, if Alex would let us take Harper's we'd know for sure without all this paper trail work."

Dela could see the subject of Harper's parentage was bothering Heath. It was kind of like what the two of them had gone through as they became teenagers. Wanting to know more about their biological fathers and being thwarted every time they brought them up. Time to change the subject.

"Was Todd at home?" Dela asked, hoping he was and he was sick. She liked the security guard and didn't want to lose him over Athena.

"He was at home. He wasn't sick. Todd didn't want to face you after yesterday, so he put in for a week off, to lick his pride and get his head back in his job." Heath shoved the cookie in his mouth and chewed.

"Yesterday? I would have thought fessing up to having been a blackmail subject of the victim would have been worse than me seeing him and his wife arguing." Dela finished her milk.

"Apparently, he believes his wife told you something…" Heath left the sentence dangling.

"Nothing I didn't already know, other than he doesn't have an alibi for the time of the murder." She stared across the table at Heath. "Do you think he did it?"

"Forensics hasn't been able to come up with any physical evidence that anyone other than Athena, Alex, and Harper had ever been in the car." Heath studied her. "It appears she wasn't into giving anyone, other than family, a ride."

"So, Alex isn't off your suspect list," Dela stated. She had locked onto all the things people had said about him. She couldn't see him risking going to jail and leaving Harper without family. And his father had said Alex didn't hunt because he couldn't stomach it. The stab in the victim's neck had hit an artery and she'd bled out quickly, according to Heath. If Alex didn't like hunting, how would he know where to stab and how would he deal with the blood?

"Not entirely. The only person who can vouch that he didn't go outside that night is his daughter and she was fast asleep." Heath scrubbed a hand over his face.

"Go back to bed," Dela suggested.

"Only if you come with me. Otherwise, there's no sense in going back to bed when I have to get up in two hours." Heath held out his hand. "Come on. You know you could use a hug."

The Squeeze

Dela picked up their glasses and then grasped Heath's hand, allowing him to lead her down the hall and into his room. She did need a hug and he was the perfect person to make her feel all was right, when it wasn't.

Chapter Twenty-one

When Heath got up to go to work Friday morning, he carried Dela over into her own bed and told her to sleep until work. But she woke up at nine feeling as if she'd forgotten something she said she'd do. Dela sat at the dining room table scrolling through the photos on her phone and came across the Indian Relay Race team photo. She'd told Mr. Dickens she would be there on Tuesday to pick up the photos.

She showered, dressed as quickly as she could while putting on a prosthesis, and loaded Mugshot in the car. She swung by a coffee trailer on a side street in Pendleton and headed to Mr. Dickens's house. Dela hoped the man would be home. She was three days late coming back for the photos.

Standing on his porch, she knocked on the door. Barking echoed from within. Clyde was doing his job of letting his master know there was someone outside.

She waited several minutes before the lock clicked

on the door and it swung open.

"Mr. Dickens, I'm so sorry. Things at work got busy and I forgot until this morning that I was coming back for the photos." She held out the bag with a maple bar that she'd purchased while at the coffee trailer.

The man gripped the bag, looked inside, and grinned. "You didn't have to give me an apology gift, but I'll take it." He stepped backward, "Come in. I have those photos ready for you."

Dela smiled, happy that he hadn't been one of those people who didn't tolerate being stood up.

In the house, he continued through into the kitchen. "Come on. You're going to have to tell me something about you since you kept me waiting for you on Tuesday. You can talk while I have this donut and drink my coffee."

Dela eased down onto a chair and waited while he poured her a cup of coffee and topped his off. He sat down across from her and waved a hand. "Go on. Who are you and why do you want these photos?" He picked up the maple bar and bit into it.

"I'm Dela Alvaro and the man, Dory Thunder, looks like someone who might be from my family. I was interested in getting the photo and asking some family members." She sipped her coffee. He wasn't from the rez and wouldn't tell anyone she knew there what she was doing.

"I see. Can't you just ask them if this person had been in an Indian Relay Race in nineteen-eighty-four?" He took another bite and chewed. His faded brown eyes watched her from behind dirty glasses.

"It's complicated. Very complicated. I don't want to bore you with the details." Dela sipped her coffee.

"I have nothing other than television to occupy my

time these days. While I was developing those photos, I came up with all kinds of scenarios of why you wanted them." He grinned. "I even went to the library and looked up that name in newspaper issues. I couldn't find it anywhere other than mentioned at that Roundup."

That was good information to know. And it made her remember that Rosie was going to look up family history for the project she, Dela, was now making for Grandfather Thunder's birthday.

"See, he seems to be a relative that was here and then gone. If I could have those photos now, I need to visit with someone else before I go to work." Dela rose and placed her empty cup in the sink with half a dozen other dirty cups and dishes.

"Where do you work?" Mr. Dickens asked, wiping his face with a paper napkin.

"I'm head of security at the Spotted Pony Casino." She never got tired of saying 'head of security.'

"Impressive. Then you are a woman who knows how to handle herself. My Eleanor was a tough woman. I never feared for her when she was out late at night going to meetings. She grew up on a ranch with brothers. She knew where a man's vulnerable spots were and she wasn't squeamish to use that knowledge." He stood. "The photos are in my photography studio."

Dela followed Mr. Dickens into the room where they'd found the other photos and negatives. She paid the photographer for the photos and left the house.

In the car, she pulled them out of the envelope and studied them. Maybe with a magnifying glass, she could get a better look at the face.

Her phone rang. Rosie. It was as if she'd heard Dela's thoughts.

The Squeeze

"Hi, Rosie. Are you still at home?" Dela asked.

"Yes. I have a diagram of names along with births, deaths, marriages, and children for you to use on your birthday present for Grandfather Thunder."

"Great, do you want me to come by and get it? I'm in Pendleton right now."

"I can bring it to work unless you prefer to come over." Rosie said something to someone else.

"Yes. I'd like to pick it up now and take it home before I go to work." Dela felt the nervous energy bubbling under her skin. She was so close to finding out more about Dory.

"Okay, but you'll need to get here before two. I'll be leaving for work then."

"I'm headed your way now. Want me to pick up anything for lunch?" Dela knew that would make her friend more excited to see her.

"If you want to pick up a number four from Zhen's Jade Garden I would eat it," Rosie said.

Dela grinned. She was on the edge of town but it was worth making Rosie happy to drive back to Zhen's. "I'll be at your house in forty-five minutes." She turned around, pulled into the first parking lot she came to, and ordered the number four for Rosie and number one for herself. By the time she arrived at the restaurant, the meals were ready. She paid and headed toward the Tapas home.

Since Rosie started taking online college classes, she'd moved back in with her parents to not have her sister's children interrupting her when she needed to do her classes. But Willow, the older sister Rosie had been living with, wasn't happy to lose her live-in babysitter.

Dela hooked the leash to Mugshot and lead him up to the Tapas front door as she carried the takeout food.

Rosie answered the door. "Hey, I'll take the food, you can put Mugshot in the backyard through the side gate."

Dela handed over the food and led her dog over to the side gate. "I'm sure I'll be sitting in back with you. Mrs. Tapas just doesn't like animals other than her grandchildren in the house." She walked through the gate with the dog and unleashed him. She closed the gate and walked to the patio behind the house, figuring that's where they would eat. To her surprise, only Mrs. Tapas was sitting under the umbrella. She had a white piece of leather she was beading.

"Hi, I hope you don't mind if Mugshot hangs out in your yard while I'm visiting with Rosie," Dela said.

"He's fine as long as he doesn't dig or pee on my flowers." The woman gave Mugshot, who stood beside Dela, a stern look.

Dela couldn't guarantee the peeing part, but he didn't dig. "Did you hear that Mugshot?" Dela said to the dog and then walked into the house.

"In here!" Rosie called.

Dela walked down the hall to the bedroom Rosie had as a child. They had played in this room many times as children. Though now it no longer had dolls and horses strewn about the floor. It was a relaxing pale turquoise color with tasteful Native American art and flowers on the walls.

Rosie sat in front of a computer at her desk. "I have this all printed out for you, but," she lowered her voice, "there was one person Mom made me leave off the information. I thought you might want to see it."

Dela leaned over Rosie's shoulder. "Where? Who?"

Rosie pointed to a name. Theodore Thunder.

The Squeeze

It hit Dela. That was why Heath hadn't been able to find out anything about the man in the justice system. They had been looking for Dory, not Theodore. "I'm going to take a picture of that." She pulled out her phone and clicked several times to make sure she would have a clear image. It had his birthdate but there wasn't a date of death. Could he still be alive?

"Thank you for showing me that." Dela shoved her phone back into her pocket as she heard footsteps coming down the hall.

Rosie clicked off the monitor and handed Dela the papers stacked by her keyboard. "Want to eat out in the yard?" she said as Mrs. Tapas stuck her head in.

"It's stuffy in the house. You girls should sit in the shade and visit," the woman said, looking at the empty computer screen.

"That's where we are going," Rosie said, picking up the bag Dela had handed her at the door.

Once they were seated outside, they dug into their food. Rosie asked about Molly and Marty's wedding arrangements and they talked a bit about the surprise of Dela's mom and Lance.

"Don't you think it was odd of Mom to not tell me anything until she announced she was getting married at the picnic?" Dela hadn't spoken to her mom since that day. Not that she was mad or upset. It seemed now that Dela knew about Lance, her mom was preoccupied with her fiancé these days. Before the announcement, Mom would call Dela at least once a day and sometimes three times a day to talk about nonsense stuff.

"She has been dating him since you joined the Army. And she dropped him like a hot potato when you came home injured." Rosie shrugged. "You do come first with her and always will."

"I know that." And deep down she did. But it just felt odd that her mom had never mentioned the man. Not once. "But if she is so in love with him, why didn't she at least talk about him in our conversations?"

"She didn't want you to think you were holding her back," Mrs. Tapas said from behind them. The woman walked up and sat in the chair beside her daughter. "Your mom has always worried more about you than she did herself. Now that you are grown, came home alive from Iraq, and have Heath looking after you, she feels she can begin a new phase of her life." Mrs. Tapas leaned around her daughter and peered into Dela's eyes. "She is finally getting to do things she has always wanted. Lance has the means to make the rest of her days stress-free. Be happy for her."

Dela studied the woman's face. Mrs. Tapas believed this marriage was good for her friend. It was obvious she was closer to her mom than Dela was. "Okay. I'll just embrace that Mom is finally having the wonderful life she deserves." In her head she thought, am I going to ruin it by bringing up a man who could be my father?

Chapter Twenty-two

Dela took Mugshot, the paperwork Rosie gave her, and the photos of the Indian Relay Race team home. After dressing for work, she left the papers and photos sitting on the table and put Mugshot outside with Jethro.

Before backing out of the driveway, she sent the best photo of the information about Theodore to Heath. He could change the name on the searches he'd been doing.

Her phone rang as she drove to the casino. She punched the button on her dash and answered. "Hello?"

"Where did you get this information?" Heath asked.

"Rosie found it while doing the genealogy for Grandfather Thunder's birthday present."

"I'll get busy using this name. Did you learn anything else?" Heath asked.

"I have the photos of the relay team. They're

sitting on the table at home. But nothing new on Athena's death." She hoped this wasn't a homicide that didn't get solved on the reservation. While the victim wasn't a tribal member and wasn't very well liked, it would still be an affront to the people who lived here if her murderer wasn't caught. Too many deaths on reservations were never solved.

"Quinn has been piling up more information about Athena from her real name. And they have been calling all the people with missing girls in our time frame to see if they knew anyone by both of Athena's names. So far, they haven't had anyone recognize a photo or the name."

Heath sounded tired.

"Don't worry. Something will come up and you'll be able to catch whoever killed her." Dela pulled into employee parking behind the casino. "I just arrived at work. Come by about seven and I'll have dinner with you."

"That's something to look forward to. See you then." The call ended.

Dela exited her car and headed to the back of the building and the entrance for employees. Her phone rang. She didn't recognize the number. Leaning against the back of the building, she answered, "Hello?"

"Daddy's mad. It scares me," Harper's young voice whispered into the phone.

"Harper? Are you safe?" Dela asked, pushing away from the wall.

"I'm in my bedroom closet. He's yelling at someone. I'm scared."

"I'll call my friend and I'll be right there. Don't make a sound. I'll be there." As she dialed Heath, she ran back to her car.

"Couldn't wait until—"

"Harper just called. She's scared. She said her dad is yelling at someone. I'm headed over there." She hung up on Heath and dialed Kenny at the casino as she roared out of the parking lot.

"Hey Dela," her second-in-command answered.

"Kenny. I'm going to be even later. I just got a call from Harper, Athena's daughter. She needs me. I'll be in when Heath and I get this taken care of." Dela ended the call. She didn't have time to go into details.

Her foot pressed on the accelerator, racing down the road. She turned to the right at Mission Market barely slowing for the four-way stop and corner. The man might be yelling at someone else right now but he could direct that anger on the little girl.

Pulling up to the Kindale house, she didn't see any extra cars in front. Dela pulled her foot off the accelerator and slammed it onto the brakes, while pulling the vehicle into park.

She could see Alex pacing back and forth in the living room. As she approached the door, she realized he was on his cell phone. Dela wondered if there was a landline and how did the child talk to her in the closet unless the phone was cordless. And how did the child get her number when the father had shoved it in his pocket when Dela handed it to Harper?

With all of these questions bouncing around in her head, she scanned the area for neighbors watching. None. Apparently, this neighborhood didn't watch out for one another. She heard a siren headed this way. She quickly called Heath.

"Turn off the siren. He's on the phone in the living room."

The siren ended, and his car appeared at the turnoff

to the housing complex. Heath parked behind Dela's car.

She hurried over. "I need to get in the house to see Harper. I promised I'd come."

Heath walked up to the door and knocked.

A minute later Alex opened the door. "What do you want now?"

"Dela wants to see Harper," Heath said.

"Why? She's in her room playing." The man continued to stand with the door half open.

"She called and wanted me to come over," Dela said, ducking under the man's arm and heading to the hall.

"Hey! You can't—"

Dela didn't hear any more, she opened the girl's bedroom door. "Harper? It's me, Dela. You can come out." She continued over to the closet. Opening the door, she found the child curled up on the floor of the closet with a blanket over her.

"I'm here. You're going to be okay." Dela put a hand on the girl's shoulder.

"What's going on?" Alex asked in a loud voice.

The child flinched.

Dela didn't want to get the girl in trouble. However, the man needed to know he had frightened the child. "I'm here because Harper called me. She was frightened by your yelling and arguing with someone." Dela sat on the floor by the girl, rubbing her back.

"She what? How?" Alex started across the room. Heath grabbed his arm, keeping him near the door. "You can't hold me. This is my house." The man became agitated.

"Take him to the living room," Dela said, feeling the tremors in the child's body. "He's just making things worse."

When the two men left, Dela spoke quietly to the girl and finally managed to get her to push the blanket off her head and sit up.

"There wasn't anyone here. Your father was talking on his phone." Dela pushed the child's errant curls out of her face.

"He was so angry. I've never heard him yell like that." Harper clutched something in her hands.

"What's that?" Dela asked, pointing to the child's hands.

"Mommy's phone. I found it in Daddy's room when I was looking for the paper with your phone number." She held up the latest brand of cell phone.

Dela's heart thudded in her chest. How had the phone made it from Athena's possession to the bedroom? "How do you know it's your mommy's phone?" Dela asked.

"When she'd take me with her to visit friends, she'd give me the phone to play with." Harper stared down at the phone in her hands. "I didn't miss Mommy until today. She never yelled like Daddy. She just didn't talk to me."

Dela let the child talk. She was learning more about the family dynamics. "How did you get my phone number?"

Harper peered up at her and a smile tipped the corners of the child's mouth. "Daddy washes the clothes on Sunday. It's my chore to bring him the clothes baskets. I found the number in his shirt pocket."

"That was smart of you. Why didn't you just ask him for it?" Dela shifted her position.

The child's bottom lip stuck out a little bit before she said, "He said I wasn't to play or talk to you again.

That you were with the police and they were digging up lies." Harper's dark brows met above the bridge of her nose. "He always told me police are good people."

"Your daddy is upset about your mommy leaving. The police are helping to find out why she left."

"Mommy's dead. She won't come back." Harper peered into Dela's eyes. "Natalie told me that my mommy would never be back, that she was dead. Like the bird we found in the yard. We buried the bird in a hole Natalie dug." The child took a breath and asked, "Is Mommy going to be buried?"

"I'm not sure. It would be up to your daddy." Dela now knew that Natalie had been here and spent time with Athena's daughter and husband. Had she become tired of the other woman's lies and Alex not doing anything to get out of his marriage?

Dela changed the subject. "I know your mommy's phone is the only way you can reach me, but it would be helpful to the police to use it to find out why your mommy died." Dela held out a hand palm up. "Could I give it to the police? I can bring you another cell phone you can use to call me."

The child's eyes lit up. "You'd give me my own phone?"

"Just one that you can call me with. Nothing fancy with games or anything like that."

Harper pouted but placed the phone in Dela's hand.

She texted Heath. I have Athena's phone. You might want to take Alex to the station to question why it was in his bedroom.

Dela looked at her watch. Rae should be home. She could take Harper to her house until Alex returned from being questioned.

Standing, Dela reached out a hand. "Let's go see if

Rae can watch you until I can get you that other phone."

Harper smiled and stood, taking Dela's hand.

Heath walked into the room with Alex. "We're going to the station. Are you going to stay here with Harper?"

"Only if Rae, next door, can't watch her." Dela studied Alex. The color drained from his face. His gaze was on the phone in Dela's hand as she gave it to Heath.

"Thanks." Heath grabbed Alex's arm. "Come on."

When the two had left the house, Dela took Harper next door. Rae's car was in the driveway. She knocked on the door and waited.

The door opened and Rae's gaze landed on Dela and then slid down to Harper. "What's going on?"

"Harper's dad was taken in for questioning. Can you watch her until he gets back? I need to get her a phone and get to work."

"A phone?" Rae's gaze bounced back and forth between Dela and Harper.

"Long story, I'll tell you when I come back. Do you mind watching her?" Dela didn't want to sound like it was being thrust on her even though it was.

"Not a problem, Harper and I like the same cartoons." Rae backed up, opening the door further. Harper stepped forward. "Find which one you want to watch, and I'll be right there."

Harper skipped into the house. Rae stepped out and closed the door. "What's really going on?"

"Harper called me frightened by the way Alex was talking." She went on to tell her about the phone she called on being Athena's.

Rae stared at her. "You mean Alex had Athena's

phone? That means he probably killed her. How else would he get it?"

Dela didn't say one way or the other. "We'll know more after Heath questions him. I have to go get a pay-as-you-go phone for Harper in case she needs to call someone again. I'll drop it by on my way to work."

Chapter Twenty-three

The casino was busy when Dela stepped out of the security office and onto the gaming floor. The noise blasted her first and then the crush of bodies.

She radioed Kenny to meet at the deli. Dela made her way over to stand outside the deli since all the tables and chairs were filled. Rosie was behind the counter taking care of customers. Every fifth person in the casino had on a cowboy hat. The Roundup wasn't until September. Then it dawned on her, Chief Joseph Days in the town of Joseph in Wallowa County was this weekend. Several of her Umatilla security officers had taken the weekend before off to participate in the Tamkaliks powwow in Wallowa.

They had the people traveling to that rodeo in the casino tonight. The perks of being only a mile off the interstate.

Kenny lumbered over to where she stood. "Everything go okay?"

"Yeah. Harper's safe with Rae, and Heath is questioning Alex." Dela hadn't heard anything from Heath since he'd left with Alex. It was getting close to seven. She had a feeling he wouldn't be here for dinner and she didn't have time to sit and eat with him anyway after arriving late.

"What did Alex do?" Kenny studied her with his droopy, soulful eyes.

"That's what Heath is trying to discover. He had Athena's phone." She didn't need to elaborate on what that could mean.

"Oh." He shifted a bit to search the crowd in line at the buffet. "It's a good crowd tonight. So far, no one has gotten out of hand."

"Let's hope it stays that way. You can take a break and I'll check in with everyone." Dela motioned toward the gaming floor. "I'll start with the crew refilling the money machines."

"I'll be in the coffee shop taking a break. Holler if you need me."

She nodded and made her way along the edge of the casino floor before moving through the people to the ATM machines. With this many people playing the games, the machines needed to be restocked more than once a night. Most people didn't come to the casino with cash in hand, they waited until they arrived to get it out of the machines even if there was a fee. And then there were the players who were losing and had to get more money out of the ATM.

She found Shawn and Benji getting ready to make the money transfer from the cart to the machine. Dela nodded to Shawn and then stood guard while they filled the ATM with twenties. When that was finished, they moved on to the change machines. These machines were where a person could put in the printed receipt they'd received from winnings at a slot machine and the change machine would pay out the amount.

This was a job that required three people. Two to fill up the machines quickly and one to keep guard. Because they were down not only Todd, but several who had asked for this weekend off to participate in the events at Chief Joseph Days, she or Kenny would be the third each time the machines were filled during the weekend.

After that task was finished, Dela made her rounds of everyone else. Voices in the gaming area continued to grow in volume. She made her way over in time to see two cowboys chest bump and hoot. The small group around them was laughing. It appeared to just be a boisterous group.

She decided to make a swing through the Pony and ask Natalie a couple of questions. Norma was behind the bar. She was laughing and handing out drinks all while collecting money and putting it in the till.

Dela scanned the busy bar. Every table and stool were taken as well as half a dozen people standing. There were two waitresses on duty. She'd met them before. But no Natalie. She didn't want to bother Norma, she was so busy, but Dela needed to have a word with Natalie.

At the bar, Dela squeezed between two women who were talking to the men on either side of them. "Why isn't Natalie here?" she asked.

"Natalie called in sick, so I called in Jasmine. She was on the list of waitresses to call in if needed," Norma said, not missing a beat as she made a mixed drink.

"When did she call in? Before the time she was to

be here or after she was late?" Dela wondered if the woman had swung by Alex's place on her way to work and seeing the police car called in sick and went home.

"It was about half an hour after she should have been here." Norma nodded toward Jasmine. "She said Natalie passed her going the other way when she came in after my call."

"Thank you." Dela pushed away from the bar and walked over to where Jasmine was pulling empties off a table. "Hi, put those on the counter and follow me. I'd like to ask you a couple of questions where it's quieter."

Jasmine nodded. She finished picking up the glasses and delivered them to the bar.

Dela caught Norma's gaze and motioned she'd only have Jasmine for a few minutes. Then she led the waitress out of the Pony and over to the corridor leading to the events center. The same place where she'd intercepted Athena leaving early over a week ago.

"Is this about Natalie?" Jasmine asked, leaning her back and butt against the wall.

"Yes. Was she leaving the casino parking lot when you saw her?" Dela asked.

"No. I was about a mile from my house when she drove really fast toward me."

"Where do you live?" Dela shifted all her weight onto her full leg.

Jasmine recited the address.

Natalie had to have been leaving the area of Alex's house. Dela wondered if it was before or after Heath had taken Alex away. And if the woman had talked to Rae.

"Thank you. Sorry to say, you need to go back in there," Dela said, waving a hand toward the Pony.

Jasmine pushed away from the wall. "It's okay. I need the extra money. I'm going to take my mom to see her relatives in Arizona in the spring."

"That's nice. Thank you for the information." Dela remained in the corridor where it was quiet and dialed Housekeeping.

"Housekeeping, Sherry. How can I help you?"

"Hi, Sherry. This is Dela Alvaro. Can you get me Rae Cooley's phone number? I have a question for her."

"Sure." The clicking of a keyboard could be heard in the phone. "Here you go." She recited a phone number.

"Thank you." Dela dialed the number.

"Hello?" Rae answered.

"Hi, Rae. Do you still have Harper?"

"Yes. She keeps asking when she can go home." Rae's voice held a tinge of irritation.

"I'm sorry I stuck you with her. But I needed to get to work and I didn't know who else to call." Dela didn't wait for the woman to say anything else. "Did Natalie come around there after I left the first time?"

"Yes. But she just drove through and didn't stop. Harper keeps asking if she can call Natalie and have her come stay with her at the house. I didn't even know that Alex and Natalie knew each other. From what Harper says Natalie has been over a lot. Mostly when I've been at work and Athena wasn't around."

"Good to know. I can call Heath and ask him when he'll be letting Alex go. He's probably still talking to him if the tribals haven't dropped him off by now." Probably waiting to find out what all was on Athena's phone before Heath questioned Alex more.

"I wish I could say call Alex's parents to help

watch her, but when Heath and I were there, they didn't want anything to do with Harper." Dela had thought that was a bit harsh. Just because they didn't care for the mother didn't mean they had to be cruel to the daughter.

"I'll be fine. Jacob is coming over to help when he gets off duty."

Dela didn't miss the excitement in the woman's voice. She grinned. Maybe Jacob and Rae had mended their differences. "I'm glad you won't be dealing with entertaining her by yourself."

"Let me know if Natalie does come by, please," Dela added.

"Okay." Then she whispered, "Do you think I'm safe when Alex comes home and picks up Harper?"

"Tell Jacob your concerns and I'm sure he'll stick around to make sure you're safe."

"Good idea!"

Dela ended the call and returned to her duties.

♠ ♣ ♥ ♦

By the time the gaming tables shut down at 2 a.m. and the Pony Bar & Grill had closed along with the Stallion Restaurant, the crowd had lessened around the slot machines and Dela felt the morning crew that had come on duty could handle things. She walked out to her car at 2:30 with Kenny.

"Thanks again for taking care of things when I couldn't come in on time today." Dela stood at the door of her car. Kenny was standing with his back to the casino, looking at her.

A succession of gunshots sent them both to the ground. It wasn't until she registered hoots of laughter that she realized the sound had been firecrackers going off over by the semi-truck parking area.

Kenny helped her to her feet. "I about shit myself."

Dela laughed. "It's a good thing you weren't in the Army. You'd have been changing your pants twenty times a day."

Kenny laughed. "Either that or they would have put me in diapers."

Dela pictured Kenny as the cartoon character Baby Huey. She laughed so hard tears streamed down her face.

"Hey, glad I could take your mind off things," he said, opening her car door. "Get a good night's sleep. I have a feeling we'll be just as busy tomorrow."

She dropped into the seat and nodded, controlling her laughter. "I agree. I can come in early to make sure there are enough people, help if need be, then go home for a few hours when you come in and then come back to help out at the end of the night."

"Sounds good to me. See you tomorrow night." Kenny walked over to his car.

Dela started her car and headed home. She was physically and mentally exhausted. She planned to sleep until noon and go in at one. Stay until Kenny arrived, then go home for four hours and be back at ten to finish out the night.

Thinking about the next day, she barely registered the road. She was on autopilot. The flash of lights glaring in the passenger side window jerked her out of the stupor. But it was too late to do more than hold on tight to the steering wheel.

Chapter Twenty-four

Why did her body hurt? Did they drive over an
I.E.D.? Dela reached up to take off her helmet, but she
wasn't wearing one. Her head and neck hurt. Slowly,
she opened one eye and then the other. The hay field
and paved road weren't in Iraq. This wasn't a Humvee
that was crumpled around her.

Then the last four years came streaming back to
her. She'd lost a lower leg and was sent to rehab, then
home. She had a job with the casino.

Dela huffed out a breath, to release the helplessness
she felt. White powder swirled on the dashboard and
into the air causing her to cough. Which made her neck
and sides hurt. She clawed at the seatbelt holding her
phone hostage in her pants pocket. With shaky hands,
she released the seatbelt and pulled the phone out.

Heath's number came up first. She dialed that. It
went to voicemail. "Hey, I'm somewhere between
home and the casino. Some asshole T-boned my car.

Please come." She dropped the phone and the world went black.

♠ ♣ ♥ ♦

A familiar voice pulled Dela out of the dark cocoon she remembered when her leg was blown off. There hadn't been a familiar voice or a hand holding hers when she'd awoken in the hospital in Germany. She fought her heavy eyelids, slowly raising them. A blurry face was near hers.

"There you are. I told your mom you'd wake up soon."

Heath. She tried to smile but her lips felt funny. Like they were fatter than she remembered.

"That was some fight you put up with the other car," Heath said.

Car. Gradually the night filtered into her conscience. Kenny walked her to her car. The firecrackers, his joke about a diaper. Driving home and the lights.

She licked her lips. "They were waiting for me."

Heath waved to someone. She tried to move her head but something kept it forward.

"Good to see you're okay," Jacob said, giving her a smile.

"It's hard to kill me. I'm like a cat," she said, to put him and Heath at ease, but she felt Heath's grip on her hand tighten a bit.

"How do you know someone was waiting for you?" Heath asked.

"Was there another car there when you found me?" she countered.

"No."

She tried to nod but again something held her head. Dela reached up and felt a neck brace. She wiggled her toes to make sure she wasn't paralyzed. The toes of her left foot scraped the sheet. "I didn't see the lights until they flicked on and came at me. It was so fast I couldn't react." She tried to push up to sit but her ribs, neck, and head retaliated with sharp shards of pain.

"Stay still. You need to heal and you can't do that if you keep using muscles that need to rest," Heath placed his free hand on her shoulder.

"You need to see where Gus Sanders was at two-forty." She thought about how the firecrackers had scared her and Kenny. She should have been looking for trouble instead of blowing it off.

"I sent a request to the Sheriff's Office to find and question Sanders." Heath sat on the chair that was next to the bed. "Did you see anything that will help us pin this on him?"

Dela started to shake her head and said, "No. But who else would have wanted to hurt me?"

"Alex didn't have very many good things to say about you. How you turned his daughter against him. You keep sticking your nose in his life." Heath studied her. "I let him go home at midnight. He wasn't being cooperative and all we had to hold him was the fact he had his wife's cell phone. It obviously wasn't hidden if Harper found it."

"Didn't you do a search of the house? Why wasn't it found then?" Dela asked.

"The warrant we had was to find the names of the blackmail victims and look for traces of blood. We found neither. There wasn't anything on the warrant about a phone." Heath stared into her eyes. "I don't remember if there was a phone found with the body in the car." He glanced over his shoulder to Jacob. "Go read the evidence report and see what all they found in the car and on the body."

"I will. Do you want me to let Mrs. Bolden know she can come in?" Jacob asked.

"Yes. We've kept her out of here long enough." Heath raised up and kissed Dela's forehead. "I have to say you gave me a scare. That message. I couldn't drive fast enough to find you."

She read the fear and worry in his eyes. "Sorry I couldn't stay awake long enough to see you be my shining knight."

"Dela, oh honey, I have been pacing the hallway waiting to see you." Mom came to the other side of the bed and picked up her hand with the IV.

Dela could make out the dampness around her eyes. "I hope you called Lance to keep you company while you waited."

Her mom smiled weakly. "He picked me up and brought me here."

"Good." Dela was glad her mom had someone to lean on. She wondered if her mom had also leaned on the man when Dela was wounded and going through rehab.

"How did this happen?" Mom asked.

"Some idiot came racing down a side road and rammed into my car on my way home from work," Dela said, holding Heath's gaze. She didn't want him to say anything that would make her mom worry even more.

"Probably some drunk. Really as head of security, I would think you could work better hours, Dela." Mom had the look that meant she was going to talk to someone.

"Mom, I choose my hours. I prefer to be at the casino to help when it's the busiest. And tonight we were several employees short." She tried to sit up again. Pain shot through her.

Heath eased her down. "You can't keep irritating your injuries."

"We are short-handed and now we'll be even more short-handed tomorrow night. Remind me to call Kenny tomorrow and let him know he needs to call in more help." She grasped Heath's hand. He knew how important this job was to her. She wouldn't leave her guards understaffed.

"I'll make sure you call. You need to relax and rest. I'm not going anywhere." Heath smoothed her hair back.

"You have to find a murderer," Dela said.

"You have to find out who did this to my daughter," her mom said.

Heath smiled at both of them. "We will be working on the homicide and the hit and run, I guarantee you both."

♠ ♣ ♥ ♦

Waking up, Dela moaned. Her body ached all over, but especially her neck and back.

"The nurse said I could give you this pain med when you woke up."

She looked to her right and found Heath pouring water into a plastic cup. "What time is it?" She could hear people talking, carts being wheeled, and the sound of cars outside the window.

"It's seven." He placed the pill in her mouth and then a bent straw.

She sucked on the straw and water washed the foul-tasting pill down. She spit out the straw and studied Heath. "Have you been here all night? Don't you need to go to work?"

He grinned. "I said I wasn't leaving you. The doctor said if you didn't show evidence of a concussion, you could go home today. I'll go to work after I take you to your mom's."

She tried to shake her head but the dull thud in her head and the neck brace didn't allow it to happen. "No. You aren't taking me to my mom's. If she wants to take care of me, she has to come to my house. I want to get well with my animals and my things." By things she meant her handicapped bars in her bathroom. She'd lived in her mom's home for almost a year without any of the shiny silver bars she had installed in her home. She liked not having to figure out how to get in her mom's tub shower or getting on and off the toilet when she wasn't wearing the prosthesis.

"Okay, I'll take you home and let your mom know she has to come to our home to pamper you." Heath leaned over and kissed her forehead. "I'm going to the cafeteria to get breakfast. I'll bring it back here, you want anything?"

"Just grab a couple things you know I like."

He nodded and left the room.

Great. Not only was she not going to be able to go to work but she'd have her mom hovering around all day. But she would also have her mom to drive her around.

That started Dela wondering how bad her car had been damaged.

Mom pushed through the door, followed by Lance. Her mom's fiancé had his cowboy hat in his hands. She knew her face must be hideous when Lance quickly looked away. Only people who truly loved her wouldn't turn their heads.

"Dela, where is Heath? He said he would stay with

you." Mom hurried over to the bed and sat in the chair, grasping her hand.

"He—"

"Went for breakfast," Heath cut her off as he carried a tray of food into the room.

"Oh! I figured they would have fed you by now," Mom said, rising and standing by Lance.

"They came by when Dela was still sleeping. I told them to let her sleep." Heath set the tray on the table by the bed and then swung it over the top of Dela.

"Has the doctor been in?" Mom asked.

This answer Dela didn't know. She watched Heath.

"Not since last night. He should be around in another hour. When we spoke, he said as long as Dela doesn't have any symptoms of a concussion or internal bleeding she can go home. But she can't go to work for a week." As he said the last sentence Heath peered into her eyes.

"No one said anything to me last night about internal bleeding." Mom had her mother lion face on. "How could she escape that bomb in Iraq and come home to us only to have a drunk driver possibly take her away."

"Hey! I'm laying here and I'm not going anywhere. I told Heath, I have the nine lives of a cat." Dela glared at her mom for even thinking she would let a thing like a car accident take her life.

"I'm sorry. It's just you've gone through so much already. I just want your life to be easy and smooth." Tears welled in her mom's eyes.

"What would be the fun in that?" Dela asked, joking.

Heath faced her mom. "Why don't you go on to Dela's and feed the animals and get things ready for when I bring her home?"

"Oh, yes. I can do that. I'll make some cookies." She stopped at the door. "You do have ingredients at your house for that, don't you?"

Heath laughed. "Yes. Since I moved in the cupboards are being kept stocked."

"Good. See you at your house," Mom said to Dela. Lance had headed out the door as soon as Heath had mentioned Mom taking care of things.

"Thanks, I think?" Dela said, picking up a piece of cold toast and spreading jam on it.

"Did you want her to keep on chattering here?" Heath asked, sitting on the edge of the bed so he could cut up a piece of sausage.

"No. I'm not sure I want to listen to her chatter all day at my house either." Dela stopped the piece just before her mouth as she remembered the photos. "What about the photos I left on the table of Dory Thunder?"

"I put them in the drawer of your bedside table, where you keep the mugshot, last night." Heath slipped the sausage in his mouth and made a face. "I think this is made out of a plant." He swallowed and picked up his cup of coffee and drank.

Dela chuckled. "What did you expect in a hospital?" Another thought struck. "Did you call Jacob away from Rae's place last night?"

"No. He was there when Alex was released, giving Rae support when Alex arrived to pick up Harper. Then he stayed an hour and went home." Heath scooped up egg onto his fork.

"Jacob had gone home when I was hit. So he wouldn't know if Alex went back out or not." She wondered if the person who hit her was the angry father or the man being divorced.

Chapter Twenty-five

Dela sat in her recliner, listening to her mom bustling about in the kitchen. Heath had brought her home, taken a shower, and dressed in his uniform to go to work. He already had people checking out the vehicles owned by Gus Sanders and Alex Kindale to see if there was any damage to them.

Heath had told her where her car had been towed. Dela called her insurance company and filled them in about being hit and where the car was to investigate her claim. She would be without a car until that was settled. While she'd been thinking she'd like a different vehicle for a while, she'd liked not having a car payment.

It was now three in the afternoon. Rae would be home from work. Dela wanted to know if she learned anything more from Harper and if Rae happened to hear Alex leave after he picked up his daughter.

She dialed her phone as Mom walked into the living room with iced tea and Dela's favorite oatmeal cookie with dried cranberries. Her mom settled onto the couch with her own glass of iced tea as if she planned to turn on the television and watch a show.

Dela didn't know how to delicately tell her mom, this call was private. She just hoped her mom ignored her.

"Hello," an out-of-breath Rae answered.

"Hi Rae, it's Dela. I was wondering if Harper told you anything else last night."

"Are you okay? Jacob told me you were in a car accident last night. Everyone at the casino was talking about it."

"I can't come to work for a few days. Mostly just sore." She was glad she'd called Kenny as soon as she'd been released from the hospital so he would have time to find people to cover for him while he covered for her.

"Was it a drunk?" Rae asked.

"We don't know. Whoever hit me fled the scene. But Heath had officers looking for evidence." She took a drink of her tea and said, "Heath said Jacob was with you when Alex picked up Harper. How did that go?"

"It was after midnight so Harper was asleep. I told him she could stay the night but he insisted she had to be in her own bed when she woke in the morning. So he carried her over to their house. Jacob hung out about an hour afterward and then he went home." Rae seemed distracted. "Tribal cars just pulled up to Alex's house. It looks like Heath and Jacob."

"Does Alex own a car besides the compact I saw in the driveway the other day?" Dela asked.

"I've seen him driving a truck but that was six months ago. I haven't seen it since. I think he sold it. I know Athena didn't like it 'cluttering up the driveway.'" Rae's tone sounded like Athena's.

Dela smiled. There was no love lost between the two women. "What about Natalie? Did you see her over at Alex's yesterday?"

"Yeah, later, about dark. She went in the house and then came back out. I guess she was looking for Alex and Harper since the car was in the driveway."

Now Dela knew for sure the woman had not come to work because of Alex being taken in for questioning. What she didn't understand was why the woman would go into the house if no one was home. Did she think they were hiding from her?

"Did she use a key to go in the house?" Dela asked.

"The door wasn't locked. I went over with Harper to get one of her dolls and we walked right in." Rae didn't act like it being unlocked was unusual.

"Thanks. Let me know if you do see Natalie hanging around Alex's place." Dela couldn't do anything other than tell Heath but at least she could make inquiries by phone.

"I will. Rest up and get well."

"Thanks." Dela ended the call. Her mom made a sound that she knew well. "Yes? What don't you approve of?"

"You're supposed to be resting not trying to solve a murder." Mom picked up the remote to the television.

"I might not be able to go to work but I can help Heath discover either who ran into me or who killed Athena Kindale." She held up her phone. "If you're going to watch TV, I'll go in my room and make a couple more calls."

Mom replaced the remote and stood. "I'll get my crocheting. I don't want you using those crutches any more than you have to with bruised ribs." She walked over to the coat rack where she'd hung her crocheting bag. When she was back sitting on the couch with yarn in her lap, Dela looked up all the body repair shops in the area. She wrote them on the pad she'd ask for when Heath brought her home. She had a lot of phone calls to make. If the person who rammed her was smart, he wouldn't take the vehicle to anyone local, he'd go to the Tri-Cities in Washington or even farther away. Unless…

She texted Quinn. *When you were looking into Gus Sanders, did he own any wrecking yards?*

Her phone rang.

"Hello, Quinn," she answered.

"Are you out of the hospital? I heard you were T-boned. Do you think it was Sanders?"

Dela was always surprised at how easily he understood her. "He's one of the possibilities." She went on to tell him about Gus's threat.

"You took away everything when you talked to his wife." His tone almost sounded like he was impressed.

"Yeah. I didn't think about him retaliating at the time. It just felt good to know I was giving him what he had coming."

Mom had made a noise when she told Quinn about the threat and now she was making a disgusted noise.

"I'll be over shortly with the information," Quinn said.

"No, you don't have to come over." Her first thought went to her mom playing matchmaker and then to the reflection she'd seen in the hospital mirror. The airbag had blackened her eyes, cut and bruised her lips, and caused bruising on her face. She was purple and red with panda eyes.

"Yes, I do. Are you alone? Don't tell me Seaver left you alone?" There was an ongoing gorilla chest thumping over her between Heath and Quinn. She hated it.

"My mom is here with me. Just call me back with the information." She ended the call.

"It will be nice to see Quinn," her mom said.

Dela growled.

♠ ♣ ♥ ♦

Dela was on the phone with Heath when Mom opened the door to Quinn.

"Mrs. Bolden, good to see you," Quinn said, handing her a bouquet of flowers and Dela a box of chocolates.

"Who's there?" Heath asked.

"Quinn showed up. I asked him for some information and it seems he felt he should deliver it in person." Dela opened up the box of candy. She was pleased to see it was a collection of nuts and caramel.

"What did you ask him?"

"If Gus owned any wrecking yards."

"I knew you being laid up would be an advantage. I hadn't thought of that. Call me back with the list when Pierce leaves."

"I will. See you soon." She ended the call before he could remind her he'd called to tell her he'd be late. But her mom didn't know that. Dela could send Mom on her way in an hour, telling her Heath should be home any minute.

Mom walked into the living room with the flowers in a vase. "Aren't these lovely?"

"Yes, thank you for the flowers and the candy," Dela said to Quinn as he sat down on the end of the couch closest to her recliner.

"You're welcome." He grinned at her and let his gaze scan the living room. "I like what you've done with the place."

She snorted. "You've been in here since I finished the remodel."

"It's been a while."

Dela knew exactly when it was. After she'd shot and killed Detective Jones in her bedroom.

"I'm not too crazy about this new makeup look you have going on," he said, drawing her thoughts from that night.

She glared at him. "Leave it to you to find flaws."

"Hey! I'm just saying you need to pay better attention that time of night."

"That's what I told her. She needs to stop coming home after midnight when all the drunks are out," Mom hopped into the conversation.

Dela looked her mom in the eyes. "I won't quit my job at the casino and I won't give any less to the job than I expect from my security team."

Mom sighed and asked, "Quinn would you like something to drink? Water, iced tea, juice, milk?"

"I'll have water, please."

When she left the room, Dela glared at him. "You could have just emailed the information to me."

"I wanted to see for myself that you were okay. Anything else hurt besides your pride and face?"

If it wouldn't hurt to swing her arm, she would have punched him. "I have bruised ribs and whiplash. I'll be back to work in a few days. Where's the information?"

"You and I both know this is probably someone you pissed off."

"I told you about Gus." She stared at him as if he

had short-term memory problems.

"Yeah, but who else have you locked horns with lately?" He pulled a piece of paper out of the inside pocket of his jacket as Mom walked in.

"No one," Dela said, holding her hand out for the paper.

He placed the paper in her hand and took the glass from her mom.

"Since Quinn is here, I think I'll head home. Lance is coming for dinner and I want to have everything ready when he arrives." She drew her gaze from Dela and peered at Quinn. "You can stay until Heath gets here, can't you?"

Quinn met Dela's gaze and then said, "Yeah, I can stick around until he shows up."

"Thank you." She leaned over Dela and kissed the top of her head. "I'll be here in the morning at eight."

"Thanks, Mom. Sorry I'm cutting into your Lance time." Dela saw Quinn's eyebrows raise. She'd have to get him up to speed on her mom's upcoming marriage.

"He understands. He would be at the side of his children if things were reversed. Though he did say his kids have never been in the hospital except to be born." She plucked her purse off the coat rack and said, "Thank you, Quinn. It was nice seeing you," and disappeared out the door.

Dela released all the tension that had been bursting her skin since settling into the recliner and having her mother hover.

"It can't be that bad being waited on by your mom," Quinn said, loosening his tie and leaning back on the couch.

"It wouldn't be so bad if she didn't remind me that I nearly died once before and she didn't like me making a habit of it."

Quinn's laughter filled the house.

Mugshot barked outside and jumped on the French door.

"Could you stop laughing long enough to let Mugshot in, please?" Dela picked up the paper Quinn had handed her while he stood and went into the dining room.

The paper had a Hermiston address for the Neal and Son's Wrecking Yard. She held up her phone to take a photo of the address when Mugshot trotted into the room and nudged her arm. The paper fell down into the side of the recliner and her phone dropped to the floor.

"Yeah, I know, you haven't seen me since I came home." She scratched his ears as Quinn entered the room.

"Can you hand me my crutch? While I'm using the bathroom, could you fish that paper you gave me out of the side of the recliner? Clumsy here knocked it out of my hand." Dela held out a hand, expecting him to hand her a crutch.

"I can just carry you," he said. "Wouldn't that be easier on your ribs and neck?"

Dela shook her head. "No, it wouldn't. Just hand me the crutches." She was glad she had on sweatpants. That way he wouldn't see her stub, just the leg of the pant waving back and forth.

He handed her the crutches and stood back as she used them to stand on her left leg. Then she swung out of the living room and down the hall to the bathroom off her bedroom. Mugshot followed her in. She closed the door and locked it, then did what she needed to do. Enjoying the alone time, she studied her face in the mirror and brushed her hair and teeth. Something she hadn't had a chance to do today.

Mugshot whined at the door and that's when she heard voices. It was too early for Heath.

Chapter Twenty-six

She recognized Jacob's voice as she swung down the hall.

"What kind of information could you be giving her?" Jacob asked, his face practically in Quinn's.

"Hey, he did bring me the information I asked for." Dela stopped in the middle of the living room.

Jacob took a step toward her. "You look like you're made up for a ceremony."

She gave him a weak smile. "Not any ceremony I want to do. What are you doing here?"

"You were pretty out of it last night when I was at the hospital. I heard you went home and just wanted to check on you." Jacob sent a glare toward Quinn, then returned his gaze to her.

"I'm glad you did. Go grab something to drink and come visit with us." Dela swung over to the recliner. "Did you find the piece of paper?" She asked Quinn.

He nodded and pointed to a folded piece of paper

on the table by her chair.

Dela lowered her body into the chair as gracefully as she could on one leg and crutches. Then she opened the paper on her lap and took the picture. She texted it to Heath and replaced the paper on the table.

Quinn sat back down on the couch. Jacob brought a chair in from the dining room and placed it in the middle of the room where he was facing both her and Quinn.

"Have you learned any more about the Kindale murder?" Dela asked.

Jacob flicked a gaze at Quinn. "Not that I can talk about."

"I've been working on it, too, which you should know," Quinn said. "I told Seaver today that as far as we can determine there are two people who might be the parents to the little girl. They are in different towns in the same state and they both recognized the name Marilyn Rathman. She worked for the cleaning company they'd hired."

"Do both these families have money?" Dela asked. Thinking what had gone wrong that she kidnapped the child to collect ransom and ended up keeping her.

"Yes. They said they did receive ransom calls, but when they went to deliver the money, no one showed up." Quinn drank his iced tea.

"Athena must have had a partner and something happened to keep them from collecting the money. But why keep the child?" Dela didn't think it was a ransom gone wrong. Keeping the child and not ditching or killing her meant she wanted the child to hurt someone.

She studied Jacob. "Everything we've found out about Athena, she didn't really care about anyone but herself."

He nodded.

She sat sideways and said to Quinn, "I think you need to get someone investigating Marilyn Rathman. Her ruthlessness makes me think she took the child to hurt someone. I bet she sends this person photos of the child every now and then." She faced Jacob. "Has anyone looked at the information on the phone Harper had?"

"Yeah, it was only local calls to work and people she knew." Jacob shrugged.

"None of the people she was blackmailing?" Dela asked.

"Nope."

"Then she had another phone she took care of business on." Dela tapped a finger on the arm of the chair. "Have you tried looking for phone records for Marilyn Rathman?"

"Or she could have used a burner phone," Quinn stated.

"Yes, there is that." She studied Jacob again. "Did you hear what Alex said about how he came to have her phone?"

"Yeah, he said it was laying on the ground next to where she parked when she left for work. He picked it up and put it in the house." Jacob sipped his drink.

"But Harper found it in her dad's bedroom. To me, that means he was looking to see who his wife called." She sipped her drink and said, "There has to be another phone. The killer must have taken it knowing their number was in the phone."

"You're saying if we find the phone we find the killer?" Jacob asked.

"I think so. But in the meantime, we need to learn more about Athena before she hooked Alex." Dela reclined in the chair. She was feeling tired from all this brain work. "I'm tired. You can both leave if you want. Heath should be here pretty soon." Mugshot had been laying on his bed by her chair. He stood up and walked to the door as if telling the two they needed to leave.

"Go ahead and go," Jacob said. "I'll stay here until Heath gets home."

"I can get the search started on Marilyn Rathman." Quinn rose off the couch, put his glass in the kitchen, and stopped at the front door. "Let me know if you come up with any more good ideas."

"I will," Dela said, closing her eyes. She was in good hands with Jacob and Mugshot.

Her phone ringing woke her. Dela rubbed a hand over her face and winced. She stuck out an arm to grasp the phone when she heard voices talking in the kitchen.

"Hello?" she answered.

"Stay out of other people's business," a raspy, muffled voice said and the line went dead.

"Heath!" she called out.

He and Jacob ran into the room. "What? Are you okay?"

"Write down this number." She held her phone up for him to read the number that had called her.

"Why am I writing this down?" Jacob asked.

"The voice on the other end told me to stay out of people's business. That sounds like a threat to me." She studied Heath's face. His jaw muscle twitched as he peered back at her.

"It does to me, too." Heath pointed to the pad Jacob had jotted the number on. "See if you can find out where the call came from."

"I'll get on it. See you later, Dela. Don't go back to

work too soon." Jacob was out the front door before she could respond.

"I think it was the person who hit me last night." She didn't know why she felt that way but she did. And the only person who would want her out of his business was Gus Sanders.

"Did you find out if Gus borrowed a vehicle from the wrecking yard?" Dela sat up and scooted to the edge of the chair. She grabbed the crutches leaning against the end of the couch and stood.

"I talked to the owner. He said he hasn't seen or heard from Gus in three months. Sanders doesn't own the wrecking yard, he owns the land underneath. He did receive notice from Mrs. Sanders that when the land becomes hers through divorce proceedings that he will have to move." Heath led the way into the kitchen where it appeared that he and Jacob were having a beer and going over the Kindale case.

"How's the case going?" she asked, waving a hand toward the files on the table.

"Slow. Jacob told me about your thoughts on the second phone and digging into Athena's earlier name. Good ideas. Both of them." He held out a chair and she sat. "I'll get something whipped up for dinner."

"Just some soup and a sandwich is good enough." Dela pulled the file over to her and began reading the autopsy report. She scanned the photos of the scene, the body, and the murder weapon. "I don't think this was a planned murder. I would bet she was filing her nails ignoring the person sitting in the car with her and said something that angered the other person. The killer grabbed the file out of Athena's hand and stabbed in rage. That's what it would have taken to plunge that file hard enough to sever an artery." Dela studied the blood in the car. "And that person had to have been covered in blood when they left."

Heath took the file out of her hands and placed a microwaved bowl of soup and a ham sandwich on the table in front of her. "We've come up with the same theory."

"Did you inspect Alex's laundry room for blood? At that time of night, he could have gone in, stripped, and put the clothes in the washer, then showered and Harper would have been sound asleep." Dela picked up her spoon. Harper was a sharp girl. She would have noticed something off. Like when her dad was arguing with someone on the phone and she'd become scared.

"We did have forensics check for blood in the house. There wasn't any." Heath placed a bowl of soup and a sandwich on the table beside her and sat. "There wasn't any trail of blood leading from the car to follow."

"While the murder was committed out of rage, the person then became thoughtful enough to not leave any trace of blood outside the car to show how they got away." She stared into the bowl of soup she was stirring. "Of your suspects, who do you feel could detach after killing someone and logically cover their tracks?" Dela raised her gaze to Heath.

"Alex. While he does seem to have a quick temper, he tends to settle down quickly. I could say the same for Todd."

"What about Gus?" Dela asked.

Heath shook his head. "No. He has proven every time we've pushed him that he doesn't think clearly. I honestly don't think it's Gus. He's pissed at you over his divorce."

Dela had the same feeling. "Do you have any other

suspects, besides Alex and Todd?" She hated to think that Todd was still on the list. He was a good security person.

"If Todd's wife didn't have an alibi, I would have her on the list. She was the only wife who knew what was going on. And it was before Todd told her." Heath picked up his spoon. "Can you think of anyone else who would want Athena dead?"

"All the men she was blackmailing. But if you say they all have alibis then that rules them out. Unless you haven't found everyone." She picked up her sandwich and took a bite.

"We checked off everyone that was in her book. They are all accounted for and extremely happy she is gone." Heath started eating his soup.

Dela chewed the bite in her mouth and ran things over in her mind. A thought came to her and she swallowed, took a drink, and said, "What if the person who Athena took Harper from found her?"

"But wouldn't they also take the child?" Heath asked, wiping his mouth with a napkin.

"Well, wouldn't it seem strange if they came forward now that Athena is dead? And they wouldn't have a chance to take Harper because Alex isn't letting her leave the house except to go to Rae's." Dela liked this idea. It made more sense than anything else. The woman's death was caused by taking a child five years earlier or more. "Does anyone know how long Athena had Harper before she married Alex? We may be looking at the wrong year for her being kidnapped."

"You mean she took the child a year or more before she married Alex?" Heath picked up his phone.

"She could have used another name in between Marilyn Rathman and Athena," Dela said.

"I'll see what Pierce has found." Heath stood and walked into the other room.

Dela knew it wasn't so she didn't hear. He was a pacer when he was on the phone. She caught his side of the conversation. It appeared the FBI had found another alias for Athena.

Her phone rang. It was Jacob.

"Hey, did you find out the number already?" she asked.

"No. It's a burner phone and I've asked the phone company to see if they can figure out where the call originated. I tried Heath's phone but it's busy."

"He's talking to Quinn," she said, picking up her sandwich. "What did you want to tell him?"

"State Police found a pickup registered to Alex abandoned going west off the Interstate. The front end is smashed in. Looks like that's as far as the person got before the radiator ran out of water and the vehicle overheated."

Dela's muscles tightened. How had Alex slipped out of his house and waited for her? She swallowed and said, "I'll let Heath know."

"Ask him if he wants me to pick Alex up for questioning."

"Ok."

Heath walked into the kitchen. He pointed at the phone in her hand. She handed it to him and sat staring at the food that moments before tasted wonderful but now, she wasn't sure if she could eat it. Not having a name to put to the person who had tried to kill her, she'd felt bulletproof. Now, knowing it was Alex, she wondered why. Did he think she had proof he'd killed his wife? She didn't. What would make him think she did?

Chapter Twenty-seven

"I think you'll be safe here alone while I go question Alex," Heath said when he came out of his bedroom strapping on his duty belt. He hadn't changed out of his uniform yet.

Dela nodded. She wasn't worried about being alone, she was just stunned that it had been Alex and not Gus who had slammed into her car. "I'll be fine."

Heath kissed the top of her head and squeezed a shoulder. "Finish your dinner and I'll be home soon."

"I'm not a child," she said.

"Sorry. I didn't mean it to sound like I was treating you as a child. I just worry about you. At least I know you can't drive off to ask questions of anyone." He picked up his half-eaten sandwich and left the house.

She heard his pickup start up. The only thing left here to drive was his motorcycle and she'd never driven one.

Jethro brayed. There was donkey power, but she'd

prefer to stay home and think.

Mugshot wandered over. He set his muzzle on the table. "Get your head down and you can have Heath's dinner." Dela set Heath's bowl of soup on the floor for the dog.

She stared into space, replaying all the information she'd gathered about Alex's movements. She didn't see how he could have driven a pickup that wasn't even at his house when he didn't get home until after midnight.

She looked at her watch. It wasn't too late to call Rae and make sure she gave the same answers about the time last night. After setting all the dishes in the sink and wiping down the table, Dela swung into the living room and lowered into the recliner.

Picking up her phone, she scrolled to find Rae's phone number. Just as she started to push the number to dial, she spied Kenny's name. She should check in with him.

Dialing Kenny instead of Rae, she waited for him to pick up. When it went to voicemail, she started worrying. She quickly found the security office number and dialed that.

"Casino Security, this is Tammy."

Trying to keep her worry from leaking into her words, Dela said, "Tammy, it's Dela. How come Kenny isn't answering his phone?"

"He's not here. He went home for some sleep and said he'd be back at nine. How are you? We all heard about that drunk driver t-boning you."

She wasn't going to say any different. "Who's in charge while Kenny's gone?"

"He put Margie in charge. Changed her hours until you get back."

The radio crackled. Dela listened hard but she

couldn't hear what was happening.

"Roger," she heard Tammy say, and then, "You want me to have Kenny call you when he comes back?"

"Yeah, I'd like to hear how he's shifted people around." Dela really wanted to talk to him some more about Todd and Alex.

"Okay. I hope you heal fast."

"Me, too." Dela ended the call and scrolled back to Rae's number.

She pressed the number and listened to the phone ring.

"Hello?" Rae answered.

"Hi, Rae. Sorry to bug you again but I was wondering if you could tell me when Alex returned last night and if by any chance you heard him leave again." Dela knew she was being a pest but she had to know if it was Alex.

"Jacob just left here asking me the same questions. Why do you need to know if he left again?" Rae asked.

Dela bit her bottom lip. Did she say anything to the woman or let it go "Did he ask you about Alex's pickup?"

"Yes. And I told him the same thing I told you. I haven't seen it for months and figured he sold it because Athena didn't like it."

"Who's watching Harper while Alex is being questioned?" Dela asked.

"How did you know? Oh, because you are living with the head of the investigation." Rae didn't say it snotty, but it had a zing to it.

"Is Harper with you?" Dela asked, ignoring the woman's remark.

"Yes."

"Can you put her on the phone, please?" Dela

could be nice even if others weren't.

"I'm not sure Alex would like that," Rae said.

"I don't give a damn what Alex would like. I want to find out if he was the son-of-a-bitch who tried to kill me last night." Dela hadn't planned on letting that out, but between her aching body and head and Rae's belligerence, she'd had it.

"Really? That's why the police took him away for questioning?" Rae's tone had changed.

"Please, put Harper on. I want to ask her some questions."

"As long as you don't cuss at her," Rae said.

As if she would do that to a child. Sheesh. "Thank you."

"Hello, this is Harper." The shy voice made Dela smile.

"Hello, Harper. This is Dela. Do you remember me?"

"Like the state, Delaware." She giggled.

"Yes, like the state but a person. I have a couple of questions I'd like to ask you about Natalie. Is that okay?" Dela wanted to make sure the child didn't think she was being forced to talk to her.

"Sure. I like Natalie. She gives me hugs and candy. And she and daddy are talking about getting me a puppy."

"That would be nice. Did Natalie come visit before your daddy sold his truck?" Dela didn't want to put words in the child's mouth but it was easier to come to the point than ask roundabout questions.

"He didn't sell it. Natalie is keeping it for him. Mommy didn't like it. Said it made the yard look trashy." There was a pause. "A truck isn't trash. I didn't understand and she wouldn't tell me what she meant."

The Squeeze

Dela didn't remember seeing the pickup at Natalie's duplex. But she hadn't gone behind the building. "When Natalie came over, did she ever go into your mommy and daddy's bedroom?"

"Daddy's not Mommy's."

Another thing she didn't know. Alex and Athena had separate bedrooms. Surely Heath knew that. Why hadn't he told her?

"And did your mommy have a phone other than the one you called me on?" Dela waited as the child breathed into the phone.

"I don't want to get into trouble," she said in a whisper.

"You won't be in trouble for telling me about the phone. Where is it?" Dela asked.

"Mommy didn't want Daddy to know about it. She said it was us girls' secret. She'd use it to take pictures of me. She said it was a surprise for Daddy." Talking about the pictures her voice lightened and Dela could hear happiness.

"Daddy didn't find this phone?" Dela asked.

"N-n-n-no."

"Did you tell someone else about the phone?" Dela had a notion she knew who.

"Natalie was taking my picture one day with her phone and I told her Mommy had a phone she took my picture with. She said I'm sure your parents do take your picture with their phones. And I told her it was a special phone. Did she want to see it?"

"Did you show her where it was?" Dela asked.

"Yes. She looked at the photos and we put it back," Harper said.

"Have you looked for the phone since your mommy died?" Dela asked.

"No."

"Put Rae back on the phone and thank you for answering my questions." Dela would make sure she took Harper a gift as soon as she was well enough to go buy one.

"Okay," the child said.

"I heard most of that conversation," Rae said.

"I'll call Heath or Jacob and have them come get you and Harper to go get that phone. It could have the clue to her murder on it." Dela wasn't going to beat around the bush anymore. If Rae liked Jacob, she needed to know how to deal with police situations.

"We'll be here waiting."

"Thanks." Dela ended the call and tried Heath's phone. It went to voicemail. She left her message and then called Jacob.

He answered on the first ring.

"Jacob. You or Heath need to go to Rae's and collect her and Harper. Harper knows where her mom kept the other phone. Also, Natalie was keeping Alex's pickup and she knew about the phone and where it was hidden." She drew in a breath.

"You've been busy for someone who is laid up," Jacob said.

"Who said I can't do footwork with a phone." She smiled. It felt good to feel like she was accomplishing something. Her phone beeped someone was calling. She glanced at the name. Kenny. "I have to go. Good luck."

"Hi, Kenny. How are things going?"

Kenny explained his reasoning behind why he moved the people around that he did and her phone beeped. It was Heath.

"Sorry, Kenny. It's Heath. He's returning my call,

too. Thanks. I'll talk to you tomorrow."

"Hi, Heath," she said, glad Kenny had made good choices with the people he'd moved up to night shift and the people in charge when he wasn't there.

"How did you find out all of this?" Heath asked.

"I called Rae and talked to Harper. Do you still have Alex in custody?"

"Yes. He's pinched his lips so tight they're turning blue. He didn't tell us that his pickup was at Natalie's. He didn't say anything when we confronted him with the pictures of it with the front smashed in. Either he's trying to not implicate her or he knows more about his wife's death than he has let on."

"I'm betting the clue to all of this is on the phone that Athena kept hidden. Harper said her mom would take pictures of her with that phone and it was their secret. I'm thinking she was sending photos of the girl to someone to make them suffer." Dela had seen that mean streak in Athena more than once.

"Jacob went to see if the phone is at the house. I'll go in and let him know we know that Natalie had his pickup and must have been the one to ram your car."

"Wouldn't she have suffered injuries, too?" Dela asked. "And has anyone gone to her place and brought her in?"

"I sent someone there as soon as I received your message which was two minutes before I called you back."

"If they call in she's not there, have them talk to the young woman on the other side of the duplex. She seems to know a lot about Natalie." Dela wished she could be up and moving around to help.

"You did your part. Relax and let us take care of this." Heath ended the call.

Rather than relax, she wanted to do something. But she still hurt too badly to try to lift weights or put her prosthesis on and go for a walk.

She made popcorn and turned on a movie. She wanted to be awake and aware when Heath either called or came home.

The phone rang thirty minutes later.

"You should have died," said the same muffled, raspy voice as before. The line went dead.

Chapter Twenty-eight

Dela stared at the number. It was the same number as before. Why hadn't the Feds or Heath gotten back to her with who it was?

She dialed Quinn knowing that Heath was busy with Alex and possibly Natalie.

"What are you doing calling me? You're supposed to be resting," Quinn answered the phone.

"That number called again. The one that threatened me? Now it says I should have died. Did you learn anything about it?" Dela asked.

"That person has balls. Why do they keep calling you? It's almost as if they want to be caught. We know it is a burner phone. We'll try to triangulate the call using your phone and the number."

"Have you checked records to see if Gus Sanders owns any burner phones? If it's not him then who and why?" Dela had been scared several times while in Iraq. Always when she didn't know what lay ahead and there was a good chance she would die. It was a different feeling than she'd had when Paul Winters attacked her and when Detective Jones had a gun pointed at her. Both those times she'd known her attackers. This, not knowing who it was who wanted her dead, frightened her more. She was better with action not sitting around waiting and wondering.

"I'm afraid only that person knows why. You do have a way of pissing people off. It could be anything." Pierce spoke to someone near him. "Keep your doors locked. Heath's with you, right?"

"No, he is questioning Alex, and if they find Natalie, her as well. They found Alex's pickup with the front end smashed. He'd been keeping it at Natalie's." Dela glanced at the French doors in the dining room. They weren't locked and Jethro was still out in the pasture. "I'll let you go."

"Don't hang up," Quinn insisted. "Call your friend to stay with you until Heath gets home."

When Dela didn't say anything, he said, "Please, ask someone to sit with you. You're injured and vulnerable. If it's the same person who rammed your car last night, they know that, and may try to finish the job."

"Fine. I'll call Molly. I'm not calling my mom. She might be on a date and I don't want her to think I need her and she shouldn't have her own happiness."

She heard Quinn chuckle.

"Good. As soon as you hang up call Molly." Quinn ended the call.

Dela grabbed her crutches and shoved to her foot. She swung over to the dining room and the doors to the backyard. Peering out the glass door, she studied the yard.

"Mugshot, let's go put Jethro in for the night." She opened the door when the dog joined her.

He went out first, sniffing the air.

Jethro brayed. It sounded as if he was waiting at the gate to be let in. It was still light enough for Dela to navigate across the yard and open the gate to the pasture. Jethro pushed his head against the gate almost knocking her over in his hurry to get in the backyard.

"Do you like spending the night in here that much?" she asked him after she closed the gate and stood scratching the animal around his ears. Jethro raised his nose in the air and curled his lip back.

"I'll take that as a yes. Mow the lawn and we'll see you in the morning." Dela and Mugshot returned to the house. She locked the doors and then scrolled through the phone for Molly's number. She hit the dial icon and waited. Molly didn't answer. She could be out on a date with Marty.

Dela scrolled through her contacts and found Travis, Molly's son.

He picked up as soon as the phone rang. "Dela, are you okay?"

"I'm as good as I can be having been a victim of a hit and run last night. Is your mom out on a date?"

"No. Marty's working. She's at grandma's. She didn't want to go, but grandma insisted. Something about the wedding." The boy's tone sounded a lot like his mom's when she talked about her mother's thoughts on the wedding.

"I see. She's not answering her phone. Not that I'm in trouble or anything but Special Agent Quinn thought it would be a good idea if I had someone stay with me until Heath gets home." She hated asking the young man but she was feeling vulnerable with a neck brace and bruised ribs.

"I can come over. I bet Toby would come with me, too," he added.

"That would be a good idea. I have a project I want the two of you to work on for me. When do you think you'll be here?" she asked, wondering if she'd have enough time to properly think through what she wanted them to make.

"I'll pick him up and we'll be there in twenty minutes." The call ended.

She glanced at the clock. Not a lot of time. Dela found a large notepad and a pencil and began sketching her idea. When she finished that she put on her prosthesis. She wanted to know if anyone had talked to Natalie's neighbor.

♠ ♣ ♥ ♦

Once Travis and Toby arrived and Dela showed them her sketch, it took the two of them about fifteen minutes to converse and Toby to draw what they had in mind. It was much better than she'd come up with.

"That's great," Dela said, amazed by the creativity of both the young men. "How about you drive all three of us to Pendleton, and I'll buy you a case of your favorite non-alcoholic drink." Neither young man was twenty-one yet. Travis would be in six months, she wasn't sure about Toby.

"Aren't you supposed to stay here and rest?" Travis asked.

"I'm bored. And I'd like to know if someone has been home since last night." She smiled and walked over to the coat rack by the front door to get her purse.

Travis dropped onto the couch and picked up the remote. "Nope. I don't want to get yelled at by Mom, Marty, and Heath. Sit down and let's watch a movie."

The Squeeze

"I don't have any popcorn," Dela said, not sure if she was lying or not. "We can get popcorn and the drinks at the same time. Then come back here and watch a movie."

"I can just run up to Arrowhead and get some popcorn and pop," Toby said.

"Good idea." Travis tossed him his keys.

Dela knew when she was beat. But she wasn't defeated. She sat on the couch next to Travis. "I want to know if the person who lives on this side of this duplex can tell you anything about her neighbor the last two days." She had opened her phone map to Natalie's address and brought up a picture of the duplex.

"What is the person's name?" Travis asked.

"I don't know the name of the person you'll talk to, but the one I want to know about is Natalie." Dela studied the young man. "If Natalie is home, don't talk to her. Only talk to the neighbor."

"Got it. I'll go when Toby comes back with my truck. You and him can watch a movie and eat popcorn while I'm gone." Travis turned the TV on.

♠ ♣ ♥ ♦

Toby and Dela were on their second bag of popcorn when Travis returned. He also had a case of root beer with him.

"What do I owe you for the pop?" Dela asked.

"Don't worry about it." He placed the case on the table and pulled out three. He sat on the couch next to Toby. Dela was in her recliner.

Toby turned the television off before taking a can and opening it.

Travis held a can out to Dela. "The girl's name is Leah. She's a single mother who doesn't work."

"Was she willing to talk to you?" Dela asked.

"Yeah, she seems like she's lonely. She said that Natalie hadn't been going to work and when Leah tried to ask her what was going on, Natalie told her to mind her own business."

Dela hoped Natalie didn't decide her neighbor was too nosey and retaliated.

"According to Leah, Natalie drove away late last night in the truck she'd been keeping behind her place for her boyfriend. She said she didn't hear her return during the night and didn't see her at all today." Travis opened his can of pop and chugged.

Dela wondered if Natalie had been hurt in the crash and was lying somewhere injured or dead not far from where the vehicle stopped. "That's good information. Thank you." She rose out of the chair and handed her bowl of popcorn to Travis. "You two continue the movie. I have a phone call to make."

Once she was in her bedroom, Dela called Heath. He answered when she had expected to leave a message.

"Officer Seaver," he said.

"It's Dela."

"I'm on my way home. I can't get Alex to say anything and they can't find Natalie." His frustration vibrated in his voice.

"Travis and Toby are with me."

"What are they doing?" Heath asked.

"Watching a movie."

"No, I mean why are they there?"

She told him about the second phone call and Quinn not knowing who the phone belonged to yet and that he wanted her to have someone with her at all times.

"Good call by Pierce. Did you just call to find out

what Alex said? I'll be home in five minutes."

"Then I'll hang up and tell you in person what Travis found out." She ended the call and walked back into the living room.

Chapter Twenty-nine

When Heath arrived, Toby and Travis grabbed their case of pop and Dela slipped Travis forty dollars. The two left, saying bye to Heath and hurrying to Travis's pickup.

"What was their hurry?" Heath asked, studying the muted movie on the television.

"I expect Travis didn't want you to lecture him." She wandered into the kitchen. "Did you get any dinner?"

"No." Heath went into his room and came back out in a t-shirt, jogging pants, and bare feet.

Dela slapped some turkey between two slices of bread she'd slathered with mayonnaise. On a plate with the sandwich, she put chips and a spoonful of potato salad. Placing the food in front of Heath she turned to the fridge and grabbed a beer.

"Looks good. What did you call me about?" He picked up half the sandwich and bit.

The Squeeze

"Travis talked to Natalie's neighbor."

"How did he know who the neighbor was and why was he talking to her?" Heath put the sandwich down and stared at her.

"I sent him to talk to her. I didn't know her name and didn't have her phone number." She held up her hand when he opened his mouth. "I didn't go. And I was pretty sure Travis would be safe talking to the neighbor. She was the one who gave me all the information when I was looking for Natalie."

He settled back in his chair and picked up the sandwich. "Go on. What did he learn?"

Dela went on to tell him about Natalie driving away in Alex's truck on the night it rammed her. "And according to Leah, the neighbor, Natalie hasn't returned since last night. Did anyone check around the vehicle to make sure she wasn't lying dead or injured nearby?"

"Yes, the State Police combed the area for any survivor. She wasn't there. They also checked the hospital." Heath raised his beer but didn't drink. "Why would Natalie want to kill you? She must have killed Athena and she believes you know that. Why else would she ram Alex's pickup into your car?"

"But I didn't know she killed Athena until today. The only way she would think I'm a threat is if she knew Harper was talking to me." Dela feared for the child. "Is Alex still at the police station?"

"I had to let him go. Without him confessing, we don't have enough evidence to hold him." Heath chugged the beer and picked up the other half of the sandwich.

She could tell he was frustrated that they hadn't found any conclusive evidence.

"Do you think Harper is safe with him?"

"All he talked about was getting home to Harper so she wouldn't be worried. I don't think he'd hurt her."

"That's good to know. But he'd hurt someone who was or would hurt her?" Dela wondered if that was the line of questioning Heath should take with the man.

Heath nodded. "I would guarantee if he saw or thought someone was hurting the child, he wouldn't hesitate to hurt them."

"Harper also talks about Natalie as if the two are close. You don't suppose Natalie and Alex planned to kill Athena to get Harper?" Dela thought about what Natalie had said about Athena's feelings for the child. "Natalie couldn't believe that Athena complained about Harper. I think Harper is the key to all of this." Dela sat for a moment watching Mugshot lick his paw and then Heath eating his potato salad. "What must Harper's real parents be going through if people who aren't even related to her biologically love her so much?"

Dela looked at the clock. "It's midnight. We need to go to bed and see if Quinn has been able to find Harper's parents in the morning."

She rose to clear the table and her phone rang. Travis.

"Travis, are you in trouble?" she asked. Her mind flashed to thoughts of Gus starting his revenge on her.

"No. Toby and I went back to town. We bought groceries for Leah and took them to her."

Travis had always had a good heart. He took after his mother and not his abusive father. "Why are you calling to tell me this now?"

"Because she was telling me more about her neighbor. Natalie told her a month ago that by Christmas she would be married and have a happy family. No more working at the casino. She'd be a stay-at-home mom."

"That means she was thinking about getting rid of Athena," Dela said, watching as Heath put the dishes in the sink.

"Not really. Leah said Natalie said the boyfriend's wife was going to get a lot of money and move away. Then she would be able to marry." Travis sounded confused. "What is all of this about?"

"Best you don't know. Are you still at Leah's?" Dela worried the young mother could be in trouble if she said something to Natalie when she returned.

There was a pause. "Yeah."

"Stay there. On the couch, not in her bed, and bring her to the tribal police station in the morning so she can tell all of this to Heath or Jacob." Dela felt this was good information.

"Okay. What time should we have her at the police station?"

Dela relayed to Heath what Travis said.

Heath stood close to her and said, "Tell him to have her there by nine. And if Natalie comes back, they aren't to approach her. Just call and let you or me know."

"Did you hear that?" Dela asked.

"Yes. I have to call Mom and let her know where I am. She'll be worried." Travis ended the call.

"Travis is a good kid, but he can't befriend every down-on-their-luck person he meets," Heath said, turning out the kitchen light and urging Dela down the hall to the bedrooms.

"You will wake me in the morning and then call after you talk to Leah?" Dela asked, standing at her bedroom door.

"Yes. I need my sleep. I suggest you get some rest,

too." He kissed her and opened her door before pivoting and entering his room.

Dela undressed, took off her prosthesis, and went to bed. But sleep didn't come. She had too many things racing around in her mind to drift off.

She finally turned the light on and made a list of everything she knew and who she'd heard it from. It was after 3 a.m. when she finally turned off the light and slept.

♠ ♣ ♥ ♦

Dela swat at the bug that was tickling her face. Someone chuckled. Her heavy eyelids didn't want to open. She tried to wake and force them up but her muscles all felt heavy and didn't want to work.

"Dela, you wanted me to wake you up." Heath's voice penetrated the sludge in her mind. Loud sniffing echoed in her ear before a wide wet thing covered her cheek.

The sound of paper rustling, had her forcing her eyes open.

"This is why you don't want to wake up," Heath said.

He was a blurry image as she peered up at him.

"Stay asleep. I'll tell your mom you were up late and to let you sleep." Heath leaned down, kissed her forehead, and called Mugshot out of the room.

♠ ♣ ♥ ♦

Dela walked out into the living room at eleven and found her mom sitting on the couch watching a talk show and crocheting. The house smelled of cinnamon, cardamon, and yeast. "Did you make cinnamon buns?" Dela detoured into the kitchen.

"Yes. I needed to keep busy while you slept." Mom entered the kitchen and topped off the cup in her hand with coffee and then filled a clean cup. She set the cups on the table.

Dela put two still warm buns on a plate and sat.

"Were you hurting? Is that why you didn't sleep well?" Mom asked, picking up her cup and sipping.

"No. It was the case Heath is working on. I couldn't sleep because things were bouncing around in my head, so I wrote them down and then it was late. I actually feel like I could take this brace off today." Dela didn't mention she'd taken it off last night and fell asleep easier.

"What are these?" Mom asked, picking up the sketches she and Toby had made.

"It's a tree. A family tree I'm making for Grandfather Thunder to give to him on his eighty-fifth birthday." Dela smiled at her mom. She was proud of the idea and the way she and Travis would build the wall decoration.

"Why do you think Silas would want a family tree?"

Her tone had Dela looking up from the sketch and into her mom's face. Mom didn't think the idea was a good one.

"Don't you think it would make him smile to see all of his family from as far back as Rosie can find to now on his wall for him to look at every day?" Dela wondered if her mom knew about Dory, Theodore Thunder. And if she did, was he Dela's father? But she didn't want to come out and ask. Not when it was clear her mother didn't like the idea of her poking around in the Thunder family tree.

"If he wants to see his family he can go to the cemetery or to the homes of the ones who are alive." Mom shuffled the pages together and stacked them away from her. "You know how he likes to talk. A tree hanging on the wall with names won't make him as happy as you taking him to visit relatives."

"I don't have time to drive him all around. I just thought this would be a nice present. Travis and Toby are going to carve the tree and I'll have metal plates engraved with names and dates. It will be beautiful." She didn't want her mom to put a stop to this project. Now that she had it set in her mind, Mom wasn't going to end it before she even got started.

"You know, he has some people in his family he wishes to not be associated with. If you put those names on the inscription, he won't like it." Mom's eyes were downcast, not letting Dela see what she was really thinking or feeling.

"You would know those people. Maybe I could put them out to the side as if they don't matter but are still there?" Dela wasn't going to give in until Mom said what she really wanted to say.

Her phone rang. Dela rose and walked into her bedroom to answer it. "Hello?"

"Dela, it's me, Travis. Leah's talked to Heath and I'm taking her and the baby home. Do you need me to come stay with you?"

"No. My mom is here. But I would love it if your mom would come visit. Could you call her and mention it? Talking to her about the wedding would be a nice distraction."

"Sure thing. Talk to you later."

Dela wondered if she would be intruding if she called Heath. Wondering if he was any closer to finding out anything, she decided to at least leave a message and let him know she was awake and curious.

"You're up," Heath answered her call.

"Yes. Was Leah helpful to your investigation?"

"Very. She gave us lots of good information to use when we find and question Natalie."

"She's still missing?" Dela wondered where the woman could be. "Are you checking with relatives and friends?"

"Yes. Jacob has been calling everyone we can find who is related to her, and Quinn got her phone records and is calling the people on her contacts. She called Alex every day and sometimes more than once."

"We know they were having a relationship from what Harper has told me." Dela heard her mom moving around in the hallway. "Do you know if Quinn learned any more about my caller?"

"No more than he told you last night. The calls are coming from a burner phone and he is trying to get a record of the calls the phone has made." Heath said something to someone else. "I have to go. If your mom needs to leave you call someone to come stay with you."

"I know. I hope you find Natalie today."

"Me, too. I'll let you know when I think I'll be home."

"Okay." Dela ended the call as her mom opened the door and walked in.

"Has Heath learned anything more about your hit and run?" Mom asked.

"They found the pickup that they think hit me. I'm sure by the end of the day forensics will know more." Dela shoved her phone in her sweatshirt pocket and moved to the door, making her mom step into the hall.

"If they found the vehicle that hit you, they know who did it?" She insisted as they walked back to the living room.

"It's not that easy. The vehicle belonged to someone who has an alibi." Dela didn't want to talk about this with her mom. If she slipped about the second threat her mom would never go home.

"But they can get fingerprints."

"Only if the person driving the vehicle wasn't wearing gloves," Dela said, sitting in her recliner.

"Why would a drunk be wearing gloves?" Mom stood in front of her chair, peering down at Dela. She felt like a teenager again being interrogated about coming home late.

"I don't know. It's just something that would keep them from getting fingerprints." Dela grabbed the remote. "Want to watch a movie?"

"Don't change the subject. What do you know about the person who hit your car? Did you make another enemy?"

Dela groaned inwardly. Mom didn't need to know all of Dela's enemies. She'd never get any sleep. "No. I'm just giving you the facts about why it takes a while to find out who was driving the pickup."

There was a knock on the door. Mom moved to the door and opened it.

"Flowers for Dela Alvaro," a voice said.

"Thank you. I'll take them," Mom said and the door closed. "What a lovely potted plant. You don't see chrysanthemums much this time of year." She set the flowers on the table beside Dela's chair and plucked the small envelope stuck in a plastic pitchfork out. "Who do you think these are from? They don't speak of love or friendship," Mom said, handing Dela the card.

"I won't know until I read the card." She opened the flap on the tiny envelope and pulled the card out. SORRY TO HEAR YOU DIDN'T DIE was typed on the card.

"That is an awful joke!" Mom tried to grab the card out of Dela's grasp.

"No! I need to give this to Heath or Quinn. It might be a clue to who sent the flowers." Dela put the card back in the envelope and stuck it back on the plastic pitchfork. "Move these to the dining room table, please. I'm going to text Heath and Quinn. Someone needs to go talk to the florist where they came from."

"Oh! I just remembered. Chrysanthemum is one of the flowers that represent death or goodbye." Mom stared at her with wide eyes. "How awful for someone to do that."

Dela wrote up a text and sent it to both Heath and Quinn in the same conversation. She didn't want to deal with answering them both in separate texts.

Her phone rang. Heath.

"How did the flowers get delivered?" he asked.

"Mom answered the door. Do you want to talk to her?" Dela motioned for her mom to walk over to her.

"Yes."

"Here Mom. Heath wants to know who delivered the flowers." She handed her phone to Mom.

"Hello, Heath." Her mom nodded. "Yes. I answered the door. It was an older man. There was a dark brown small van parked in the driveway behind my car. No. No writing on the van. The florist? Just a minute." Mom crossed the living room to the dining room and read off the florist's name on the envelope. "Yes, that's all I know. Why would anyone do such a mean thing?"

She listened, her gaze on Dela. "I understand. Thank you for being frank with me. My daughter wouldn't answer my questions. Yes. I'll be here when you get home. Thank you." Mom held the phone toward Dela. "It's making a beeping noise."

Dela grabbed the phone and answered a call from Quinn. She answered all of his questions which were the same as Heath's, as she'd listened intently as her mom had given Heath the answers.

Chapter Thirty

"Can you tell me if you have any clue where Natalie is?" Dela asked Quinn when he finished telling her to be careful and don't go anywhere alone.

"I did get a hold of a man who was one of the phone numbers that Athena had called six times in the last month before her death. It sounds like he may be Harper's father. He is a public figure. I have an agent interviewing him today. I should know more by tonight. I'll send someone to check out this florist."

Dela ended the call and stared into her mom's concerned face. "It's okay, both Quinn and Heath are looking into who purchased the flowers."

"Who is this Natalie you asked about?" Mom walked into the kitchen and came back with two glasses of iced tea.

"You heard about Athena Kindale being murdered, didn't you?" Dela asked. There was no sense in not telling her mom what they knew. She told her mom all they knew about the victim and that they suspected Natalie of possibly being the murderer.

"If Heath knows all of this, why can't he arrest her?" Mom asked.

"Because no one has seen her since before she rammed Alex's truck into my car." Dela wondered if Natalie ever told Dexter anything about her friends or family or a place she liked to go. "I need to call Kenny." Dela picked up her phone and scrolled for his name and number. Tapping on the name, she dialed her second in command.

"Hey, how are you feeling?" he answered.

"Not bad. I hope to be back to work in a couple of days."

Her mom cleared her throat but Dela ignored her.

"I'm presuming Natalie hasn't been to work since the police and FBI can't find her," Dela started.

"Yeah, personnel had to hire on two new full-time waitresses for the Pony," Kenny said.

"If Dexter is bartending, would you go in and ask him if Natalie ever talked about visiting any friends or family on a trip and if she ever talked about a place she liked to go?"

"Is she a suspect in Athena's murder?" Kenny asked.

"Possibly, but we also believe she was driving the vehicle that T-boned me." Dela tried hard to keep the anger out of her voice. She didn't need Kenny to feed off of her frustration and resentment.

"Yeah, I can do that. Call you back when I get done."

"Thanks, Kenny." She ended the call and received the 'Mother' look. "What?"

"You heard what the doctor said. You aren't to go

back to work for a week." Mom crossed her arms and tapped one foot.

"Tomorrow is Monday and it will be a new week." Dela knew she was being flip and counterproductive to getting back in her mom's good graces.

"You know—"

Someone knocked on the door. Dela thanked whoever it was, hoping it was Molly and not another bouquet of flowers.

Mom answered the door.

"Mrs. Bolden, I forgot you would be here watching Dela. I have some wedding things I wanted Dela's help with." Molly's voice made Dela grin. Finally, someone who wouldn't glare at her.

"Come in Molly. You must have so much to do with the wedding only a couple of months away."

Molly walked in, spotted Dela in the recliner, and took the seat on the couch closest to her chair. "Hi. Do you mind helping me?"

"I have nothing else to do since I don't have a car and no one will let me do anything other than sit here." Dela threw a glance at her mom and then smiled at Molly.

"Would you like something cold to drink?" Mom asked.

"Iced tea would be great," Molly answered and opened up the box she was carrying.

As soon as Mom was in the kitchen, Dela leaned closer and whispered. "Thank you for coming. She's making me say and do things I don't want to do, but I turn into my teenage self when I'm around her too long."

Molly laughed. "I understood the code when Travis relayed the message. I went through some of that last night at my mom's. She has some really tacky ideas for the reception decorations. And she seems set on that is what we will have, forgetting it is mine and Marty's wedding, not hers."

"What's this about the wedding?" Mom asked, carrying in Molly's iced tea and a plate with cinnamon buns.

"Yum! I love your cinnamon buns! Thanks." Molly picked up the sweet roll and took a bite. She chewed, swallowed, and smiled. "I can never make them taste as good as yours."

"It's my special ingredient," Mom said, pulling a kitchen chair in to sit facing the two younger women.

"She hasn't even told me the ingredient," Dela said.

"That's because you would never make cinnamon buns. When you marry Heath, I will tell him." Mom smiled and sipped from her tea.

Molly laughed.

Dela felt as if that was a challenge. Her mom knew she never backed down from a challenge but marrying someone just to get a special recipe... Dela didn't think she could do that.

"What is in the box that you need my help with?" Dela asked.

"We need to bead these bands. They will go around the glasses holding a candle in the centerpiece for the tables." Molly produced pieces of soft leather and small seed beads. Dela only knew this because she had watched some of her friends and their mothers and grandmothers beading when she was younger.

"You want me to hold a needle and bead on your reception decorations?" Dela peered into her friend's eyes. "Wouldn't you be better off asking your older relatives to do this?"

Molly shook her head. "Marty and Farley, his best man, made the leather from a deer hide my father gave them to tan. Now they need to be beaded and I want my maid of honor, or best woman, to help me do the beading." She handed Dela a piece of leather and a little bag with black, yellow, red, and blue beads. "I have an easy pattern, you'll be fine."

Molly took a piece of leather and a bag out of the box and handed the box to Mom. "Mrs. Bolden, would you be so kind as to count how many of each color I have and then dump one bag of each color altogether into one bag? That's how many it takes to bead each one of these."

"Why can't I do that," Dela asked, staring at the tiny little beads and wondering how many she was going to lose in the chair.

Molly smiled patiently. Like she did when a dog wasn't being cooperative during an exam. "You'll be fine. Here is your needle. I've already threaded this one for you. Watch what I do."

Her friend deftly pulled the string through the leather at one edge, slid five black beads on the needle, and then pulled the needle down through the leather to the back. "That's all you have to do all the way across the starting end of the leather. When you get one row done then you use the red beads and go all the way across. When that row is done, you start a row with the yellow beads and then the blue. When you have those four colors then you start over with the black."

Dela had always been all thumbs with any kind of needle work, but she started stressing less as she made it halfway across the first row.

"That's good. Try to make them bump up against

the last row so it's a snug fit and you don't see the leather between the beads," Molly congratulated her.

Dela was putting beads on her needle when her phone rang. She was going to ignore it until she saw it was Kenny. Setting the beading down, she picked up the phone.

"Kenny, what did you learn?"

"Natalie didn't usually talk much about her life. She just listened to Athena complain, according to Dexter. He did remember her going somewhere on her vacation and coming back in a happy mood. But couldn't tell me more than that."

"I was hoping he'd know something." Dela felt like they were never going to find the woman.

"So, I went over to the deli and talked to Rosie," Kenny said, breaking into Dela's thoughts.

"Oh, that was a good idea. Did she know anything?"

"She heard Natalie telling Athena about her vacation and Athena glared at her and said that was where Alex had just gone with Harper."

"Kenny, you may have just helped the police locate Natalie. I'll call and tell Heath to ask Alex where he and Harper went on their vacation. Thank you!" Dela ended the call and felt happier than she had since she'd learned about Athena's death.

"Good news?" Mom asked.

"It's the best lead we've had so far." She set the beading on the table and shoved to her feet. "I'm going to call Heath. I'll be right back."

She crossed to the French doors and opened them, stepping out into the hot sun and smell of donkey manure and grass. Mugshot followed her out the door and sniffed the pile of donkey apples and then peed on them.

Dela found Heath in her contacts and hit the dial icon.

"Hey, how are things going there?" he answered.

"Much better." She told Heath about asking Kenny to question Dexter and ultimately, he found out the best information from Rosie. "You should contact Alex and ask him where he and Harper vacationed. That may be where Natalie is hiding out since it was a special place for the three of them."

"Good job to all three of you. If he knows that's where Natalie is hiding, he may not tell me." Heath burst her happy bubble.

"True, but if he didn't have anything to do with Athena's death, you'd think he'd want to be cleared of it," she countered.

"True. I've been thinking about this. Do you think Natalie could have been angry enough or jealous enough of Athena to kill her in such a personal way?" Heath was stomping on her bubble again.

"Or Natalie is hiding because she knows that Alex killed Athena and doesn't want to testify against him." She liked that theory.

"But why ram his truck into your car if she was trying to keep from having to say anything against him? It just made him look even more guilty?"

"I don't know. But if she's the one who has been threatening me, I want her stopped. Did you find out anything at the florist shop?" Dela needed to know who was threatening her.

"No one purchased chrysanthemums from that florist in months. She said anyone could wander around and pick up one of the cards and envelopes. They have them in easy reach on the front counter."

"Then where were the flowers purchased?" Dela asked, feeling like her control was unraveling. "If they purchased the flowers elsewhere and picked up a card from that florist, this was more than a mean gesture, it was premeditated. That doesn't sound like something Natalie would do."

"I agree with you. All the more reason you need to stay at home until we get this murder solved and your threats. Can you take a vacation?" Heath's tone didn't sound like a question, more like he was telling her to take a vacation.

Her back bristled. She didn't like taking orders from anyone other than an Army superior. Because they didn't get in your personal life. They only gave orders that dealt with your job.

"No vacation. I'm going back to work next week and whoever is doing this, most likely Gus Sanders, you're going to catch him and get my life back to normal." She stated it with indignation.

"Dela, we'll talk about this when I get home." He ended the call.

"Errrr." She growled between clenched teeth. She wasn't going to hide in her house until the person burned it down around her or until Heath or Quinn figured out who was threatening her. She wasn't a coward and wasn't going to hide.

Mugshot walked over and whined, looking up at her. Dela petted his head and soon her anger disappeared. Once she told Heath her concerns, he'd quit harping on her staying home.

"Are you going to stand out there all day? We have beading to do," Molly said from the door.

"I'm coming." Dela walked back into the house and plopped into the chair.

The Squeeze

After another hour of beading, they took a break. Dela wasn't going to admit it, but she liked the repetition and mindlessness the beading gave her.

Now that they weren't concentrating on the beading, Mom told Molly about the threats.

"Did Heath have any news about where the flowers came from?" Mom asked.

"No. The person who sent them is smarter than we thought." Dela didn't want to talk about the threats or anything else that pushed her buttons. "What kind of wedding preparations will we be doing for your wedding with Lance?"

Her mother glowed as she talked about the event. Dela tried to listen as she nodded her head, but she was thinking about Natalie and how she fit into all of this.

Chapter Thirty-one

Molly was leaving when there was a knock on the door.

Dela was standing by the door and opened it. Rae and Harper stood on the porch.

"Come in. What are you two doing over here?" Dela knew Heath was coming home in thirty minutes and hoped they'd stick around.

"Harper wanted to talk to you. I told her you had been in a car accident and she insisted she had to see you." Rae had a hand on the girl's shoulder.

Harper threw her arms around Dela's waist.

"Whoa, I'm fine, see. I can take this neck brace off tomorrow." She stared at her mom, daring her to say anything different. Mom nodded as if she understood this child needed to hear Dela would be okay.

"This is my friend, Molly. She's getting married in a couple of months and as her maid of honor, I was helping her with decorations." Dela drew Harper over to the couch as she talked. "And that is my mom." Dela pointed.

"Pleased to meet you, Harper. Would you like something to drink? We have iced tea, juice, and water?" Mom asked.

"Juice, please," the child replied.

"And you?" Mom asked Rae.

"Water is fine. Thank you."

Mom went into the kitchen.

"I need to go. It was nice meeting both of you," Molly said, opening the front door and leaving.

Left alone in the living room, Dela glanced from Rae, who stood, to Harper sitting on the couch beside her. "Sit down Rae. What is it you wanted to tell me, Harper?"

The child shoved her curly locks out of her face and looked up at Dela with the saddest eyes she'd ever peered into. Tears glistened in Harper's brown gaze.

"It can't be that bad," Dela said, putting an arm around the girl.

"I said too much," Harper started and hiccupped.

"About what?" Dela asked as her mom started into the room. She turned around and returned to the kitchen out of sight of the child.

"You. Mommy always ignored me, and Natalie always talked to me, like I was a grownup. I liked that. She'd tell me things like one day she'd be my mommy. When I told her you saved me from daddy's shouting and I liked you, she shook me and said I was to only tell her things, no one else. Her fingers hurt my arms. Daddy saw the blue spots on my arms and asked what happened. He asked if Rae did it, and I told him no, she would never hurt me. That it was Natalie." She hiccupped and wiped at a tear rolling down her face.

"Did he believe you?" Dela asked.

She shook her head. "He called Rae and then he called Natalie. He said things. Mean things to her. How she was going to ruin everything if she didn't control herself."

"Do you remember when this was?" Dela asked.

Rae cleared her throat. "Alex called me and accused me of hurting Harper right after he picked her up from my house the night he was questioned until midnight."

Dela stared at Rae. The night Alex's truck rammed her car.

"Have you or your daddy seen Natalie since he called and talked to her?"

Harper shook her head. "When I heard Rae and the policeman talking about you were hurt, I thought it was because of me." She threw her arms around Dela again and started crying.

Dela smoothed the child's hair. "No. It wasn't your fault. Sometimes adults get over-emotional about things and say or do things they later regret. I'm sure your mommy and daddy had fights but they made up later." She had her doubts considering the marriage was basically for looks.

Dela's phone rang. It was Quinn.

"Mom, bring those drinks in now. I have to take this call. I'll be right back." She released Harper's arms and Rae took Dela's place on the couch, comforting the child.

"Quinn, what have you found out?" Dela asked, walking down the hall to her bedroom.

"I'm ninety-nine percent sure I have the child's real parents with me right now. But there isn't anyone at the Kindale house. Any ideas where to look?"

The Squeeze

"You're not just walking them in and saying, here are your real parents, are you?" She knew the emotional roller coaster the child was on and didn't see that helping matters.

"No. They just want to see if she is the girl that Athena has been sending them photos of." Quinn said.

"How about, I'll take a photo of her, send it to you, you can show them and then put them up in a hotel until tomorrow. Heath should have Natalie arrested soon and you'll need to break the news to Alex." She wasn't going to put Harper through any more trauma tonight.

"How can you send me a photo?" There were two seconds of silence. "She's at your house. Why is she there?"

"Do not, I repeat, do not bring those people over here. Harper is upset. She thinks she is the reason I'm hurt. I'm trying to calm her down. Mom's here and Rae. We don't need to make this any more of a circus than it already is." Dela pleaded with a higher being to make Quinn's thick head understand the child was fragile right now.

"Okay. Send me a photo, I'll tuck them in, and then I want you and Heath to fill me in."

"You'll have to come here. I'm not allowed to go out and play right now." She ended the conversation and walked back into the living room. To her dismay, they were looking at the beading she'd done that day.

"Hey, I'm a beginner," Dela said, walking over and taking the leather and beads out of her mom's hands.

"Actually, for a beginner, you are doing a nice job," Rae said.

Dela stared at the other woman. Her expression wasn't mocking and didn't hold pity. She was smiling and nodding.

"Really?" Not that she was going to become a beadworker or anything like that. Though she did find it relaxing.

"What did Quinn want?" Mom asked, spoiling her good mood.

"He's coming over to talk to Heath and me later." Dela held up her phone. "Harper, could you hold up my beadwork? I'd like to send a photo to my friend. She'll be surprised to see me beading."

Harper held up the leather and beads.

"Can you smile? I know it's been a bad day, but it can only get better, right?"

The child smiled, and Dela snapped two shots. "Perfect. My friend Rosie will like this." She sent one of the photos to Quinn and tucked her phone in her pocket. "Did you finish your juice?"

Harper shook her head.

"Then let's go to the kitchen and see what kind of snacks I have in my cupboards, I missed lunch today."

"That's because she didn't wake up until nearly lunchtime and ate breakfast instead." Mom chimed in.

Harper laughed, then said quietly, "When I don't feel well, Daddy lets me sleep in as long as I want."

"Rest is good for a body," Mom said, placing a bag of chips on the table as Dela placed the bread and peanut butter on there as well.

"How about we make our own sandwiches," Dela said, grabbing knives and plates and passing them out.

Rae sat next to Harper and helped her spread peanut butter on a slice of bread.

Dela did the same and was taking a bite when the door opened. Knowing it was Heath, she remained seated.

But it was Jacob who walked into the kitchen.

Rae's eyes lit up at the sight of him.

"We're having peanut butter sandwiches, pull up a chair," Dela said.

He shook his head. "I can't. Heath asked me to pick you up."

"She didn't do anything!" Harper shouted and jumped up from the chair.

"I know she didn't," Jacob said. "You know how smart Dela is?"

Harper nodded.

"We have her help us with things. That's why I'm taking her to the police station. My boss needs to get her opinion on something." Jacob smiled. "She's not under arrest. She's helping us."

Dela stood. "Well, I guess I'll be taking my sandwich for the road." She gently sat Harper back in the chair. "Finish your snack. Mom will stay here until you are ready to go." She glanced at her mom. She nodded. "Let Harper meet Mugshot before she goes."

"Who is that?" Harper asked.

"My dog. And if someone opens the top of the back gate, you can pet Jethro's fuzzy ears." Dela glanced at Rae.

The woman smiled.

"Okay, let's go." Once she and Jacob were in the police car, she asked, "Why does Heath need me?"

"He thinks you can convince Alex to give up where Natalie is." Jacob didn't sound as if he had the same feelings.

Neither did she. "Alex doesn't like me."

Jacob shrugged as he pulled into the public safety parking lot.

They both entered the station from the back entrance and Heath met them.

"I don't think this will work," she said.

"Come in here." He led her into a small office and closed the door. "Hear me out. He isn't giving up Natalie's whereabouts. I'm sure he knows about her ramming your car. But I'm not sure he believes she killed Athena. I thought you could use some of what you heard from Harper to sway him to give Natalie up."

If she hadn't heard from Harper a short time ago about Natalie hurting her, she wouldn't have anything. That, given they believed Alex was devoted to Harper, should help them to get him to give Natalie up.

"Okay, I'll give it a try."

Heath led her down to a small room with only a table, three chairs, and a camera on a tripod.

Alex sat in the single chair on the far side of the table. He scowled when she walked into the room.

She sat and watched Alex while Heath sat and shuffled papers in a folder.

"Why did you bring her in here?" Alex asked.

"Because she has been an adult your daughter has felt comfortable confiding in," Heath said.

"She's just making stuff up," Alex said.

"Who, your daughter or Dela?" Heath asked.

"Her. Harper loves me and wouldn't want to lose me like she did her mother." Alex's gaze didn't hold either of theirs. If he wanted them to believe that he needed to make eye contact.

"Alex, I know you love Harper and she loves you. She talks about you all the time," Dela started. She wanted him to feel she was on his side. And she was, knowing he was going to lose that little girl to her real parents. Ones he didn't know anything about.

"The best way to help her and yourself is to tell us where Natalie is. We know she is the one who rammed your truck into my car. I don't know if she wanted me dead because Harper did talk to me, or she was just trying to scare me. She was the one seen driving your truck, not you. If you want to go home to Harper you need to tell us where Natalie is." Dela continued to watch him. He was torn. He may not have ever loved Athena, but he did love Natalie. It was in his indecision and hands that were still on the top of the table.

"I know you would never hurt your daughter. But Natalie did, didn't she? She left bruises on Harper's arms, she grabbed her so hard. I know you three want to be a family, but would you feel comfortable leaving Natalie alone with Harper knowing she bruised your daughter?" She had to appeal to his love for Harper over Natalie.

"Natalie will never love Harper as much as you do. You have patience with her and she loves all the things you've done for and with her. You are her hero. Continue to be that hero and help us find Natalie. I'm sure you'd like to hear her side of things, as do we."

"She wasn't driving my truck when it hit you," he finally said. "But when she heard about you being hit and it turned out to be my truck she panicked."

"Where is she so we can get her statement?" Heath asked.

Alex studied Heath. "She didn't do it. I asked her to sell the truck so we had money to go on a trip. I wanted to take Harper away from all this mess that Athena's death has become."

Heath nodded. "I understand. We just need to find out who she sold the truck to."

"She hasn't done anything wrong." Alex insisted.

"Then she has no reason to be afraid. Where is she?" Heath asked.

Alex ran his hands over his head and finally said, "She's staying at the lodge at Wallowa Lake. We had a fun long weekend there earlier this summer."

"Thank you. I'm going to have you stay here until we contact her." Heath rose, picking up his file.

Dela remained sitting. This man loved Harper. How was he going to feel when her real parents swooped in and took her away?

"Dela?" Heath said, standing by the door.

She wanted to say something but it wasn't her place. She stood and exited the room, following Heath to the office. He picked up his phone and asked for Jacob Red Bear.

Jacob arrived at the door. "Did you get anything?" His gaze landed on her.

"Natalie is staying at the Wallowa Lake Lodge. Go up there, contact the Sheriff's Office, and then bring her back here." Heath sat down behind his desk. "And call me when you get onto the reservation bringing her back. I'll make sure I'm here when you return."

"Copy." Jacob disappeared.

"Are you going to hold Alex until you talk to Natalie?" Dela asked.

"Yes, I don't want him contacting her and I would like to hear her side of things." Heath stood. "I'll take you home. We can have dinner while I wait for Jacob's call."

"Quinn is showing up at some point. He found Harper's parents. In fact, he was running around with them in his vehicle looking for her today." She couldn't hide her disapproval of what the Special Agent was doing. He wasn't thinking of Harper like she was.

Chapter Thirty-two

Dela texted Quinn to let him know she and Heath would be at home for a few hours if he wanted to come enlighten them.

By the time the special agent arrived, Heath had barbecued chicken and Dela had made a salad. Luckily, there was enough for three.

Once their plates were filled and they sat outside around the patio table, Quinn filled them in. "We started contacting all the numbers on the burner phone that weren't local. Surprisingly there were two that belonged to people who had a child abducted. The first one had their child returned after they paid the ransom. I asked if they had been in contact with Marilyn Rathman after the abduction. They had called her to let her know the child had been returned. She had been in their employ at the time of the abduction, having been let go harshly for not being at work that day. They felt bad afterward and called to apologize and let her know the child was home."

Dela snorted, "She knew that because she kidnapped the kid."

"I had the same thought but didn't say anything to the parents," Quinn said. "Now the second kidnapping, there was a ransom demand. But no one ever showed up for the money. The Hunts have felt that their daughter was killed and the people ran rather than get the money."

Dela shook her head. "Did you run Athena's other name past them?"

Quinn nodded. "That's when the husband made an excuse for the wife to leave the room."

"He got caught in Athena's blackmail scheme?" Heath asked.

"No, it seems he had actually been ready to leave his wife for Marilyn when his wife became pregnant. Then during his wife's pregnancy, he realized how manipulative and lying Marilyn was and didn't want her ruining his move up the political ladder. Mr. Hunt said he had wondered if Marilyn took the child out of revenge, but he could never find her."

"Because she'd changed her name and probably was using a fake social security number and the whole thing." Dela sipped her iced tea. The woman had been one of the best cons she'd come up against.

"She took Harper when she was a year old, not three years old," Quinn added.

"Which means Harper isn't going to have any recollection of her real parents." Dela felt sad for the child. She was going to have a tough time being taken from the only father she knew and being told these people are your parents. "Are they willing to take it slow? Not just rip her away from everything and everyone she knows?"

"Yes, as much as they want her back, they do understand she has thought Athena and Alex are her parents." Quinn sat down the chicken leg he'd just picked up. He peered into Dela's eyes. "I do have more feelings than you give me credit for. I wasn't going to barge in here this afternoon shouting, I found your parents, to Harper."

She wiggled in her chair. That was what she thought he was going to do. "Good to know."

"Should I mention you've found her real parents to Alex?" Heath asked, drawing Quinn's gaze from Dela.

"It might be a good idea. Let the knowledge sink in before we show up. Maybe he can say something to Harper." Quinn bit into his chicken.

"Do you think what Alex said is true, that Natalie sold the pickup to someone?" Dela asked. That had been playing over and over in the back of her mind.

"What is this about the pickup being sold?" Quinn asked.

Heath told what they'd learned from Alex about where Natalie was and that she had sold the pickup on his instructions.

Dela set her glass of iced tea down so hard Mugshot jumped to his feet and barked. "Sorry, boy. Remember he said it was so they would have money to go on a trip." She peered at Heath, then Quinn, and back to Heath. "I know he said to take Harper away from all of the mess around Athena's death, but what if Mr. Hunt called the burner phone while Natalie had it and she answered? She would have found out that Harper wasn't Athena's." She faced Quinn. "Didn't you say that number had been called half a dozen times in the last month? Mr. Hunt had to know Athena had his daughter. He must have either been negotiating or calling to have someone find her so he could, possibly kill her?"

Quinn's face reddened and he threw the chicken bone on his plate and stood. "I'm going to have a talk with Mr. Hunt in front of his wife."

"Be careful, politicians can be accomplished liars," Heath said.

Quinn glared at him and stomped into the house and out the front door.

"I thought he'd never leave," Heath said.

Dela laughed and said, "He did give you more ammunition when you talk to Natalie and Alex."

"When we talk to them. I'm not leaving you alone here if it's true Natalie sold that pickup to someone and you seemed to have hit Alex's soft spot, his daughter."

♠ ♣ ♥ ♦

At 9 o'clock Heath's phone rang. "It's Jacob."
Dela muted the TV.

"Okay, we'll meet you there." He ended the call and stood. "Time to go interview Natalie and Alex."

Dela turned off the television and stood. "I'm surprised we haven't heard anything from Quinn after he talked to Mr. Hunt."

"He may be holding him for some reason." Heath put Mugshot out in the backyard with Jethro and locked the door. "Let's go."

Dela headed to the front door, grabbing her purse as she opened the door. The sun was going down to the west. The yellow and orange glow of the sky was reflected in Heath's pickup window. She stopped to enjoy the colors when she spotted someone running away.

"There! Someone is running." Dela pointed in the

direction the person had run.

Heath yelled, "Get inside and lock the door," as he sprinted after the person.

Dela locked the door, but she went to his pickup, climbed in the driver's side, and backed out of the driveway, heading in the direction she saw Heath chasing someone.

The person Heath pursued was struggling to stay upright, from what Dela could see in the waning light. By the time she parked on the side of the road, Heath had the person in a restraining hold and was putting handcuffs on him.

Dela opened the door.

"Stay in there. You'll drive. I'll sit in the back with him." Heath lowered the tailgate and shoved the person in the bed of his pickup.

That's when Dela saw who it was, Gus Sanders. She smiled as she drove to the Tribal Police Station. With this, she could get a restraining order against him.

At the station, Heath handed Gus over to Jacob to hold until they finished with Natalie.

Natalie's eyes widened when Dela walked in ahead of Heath. "You're not a cop."

"No, but I seem to have been dragged into this homicide," Dela said, sitting.

"Did Officer Red Bear tell you why we brought you back here?" Heath asked.

"Something about Alex's truck. I sold it like he asked."

"When? What time?" Heath asked.

"On Friday night, about ten. I told the guy he shouldn't be driving it before he gets the title changed and insurance put on it." Natalie's gaze was fixed on Heath.

"What was the man's name?" Heath asked.

"He didn't tell me. He paid cash, the amount we wanted, no haggling, and I handed him the keys and the title. Alex had signed it a couple of weeks ago when he told me to sell the truck. I had several people come, drive it, and try to pay half of what we wanted. This was the first guy to pay us the full amount so I took the cash and then went to the Wallowa Lake Lodge. Alex told me, he and Harper would meet me there."

Heath glanced at Dela.

She nodded. She had a pretty good idea who the man was who purchased the truck with cash and didn't haggle.

"I'll be right back. You and Dela can catch up." Heath left the room, leaving the door open.

Natalie frowned. "What is he doing?"

"Just watch the door." Dela didn't want to say, you might see the man who bought the truck.

"How is Harper?" Natalie asked.

"Confused. She told me about you hurting her." Dela glared at the woman. "Everyone has more than one friend. You didn't have to make her feel like she had to choose between you and anyone else."

"I…it's been stressful the last month. Athena found out about me and Alex. She was a bitch about it. I didn't think she cared enough about her husband or her daughter to mind me stepping in." Her gaze flicked to the door. "That's him! That's the man I sold the truck to."

Dela turned in time to see the surprised expression on Gus's face before he saw her and glared. There was justice. She faced Natalie. "Did you know he used that truck to ram into my car and try to kill me?"

Natalie's eyes widened. "I heard you'd been in a

car accident, but I didn't know it was Alex's truck. I'm so sorry. Why would he do that?"

Heath returned. "I heard her out in the hallway. I have Jacob arresting him for attempted murder." He peered into Dela's eyes. "Jacob found a burner phone on him with only calls made to your phone."

Gus had sent the threats. She was safe unless he got out on bail, but she didn't think he had enough money to get out. And she knew his wife and daughter wouldn't bail him out.

"Back to you and Alex," Heath said, sitting down. "Did you slip into Athena's car when she pulled up to her house on the night she died? Maybe just to have a talk with her and when she angered you, you took a fingernail file and stabbed her in the neck?"

Natalie's face paled. "No! That's how? That's awful. No, I didn't do it. Granted there were times when Alex would tell me about something she did that I thought our lives would be much better if something happened to her, but I would never…"

"What about Alex?" Heath said quietly.

The woman went stone still. Only her eyes moved as her gaze flicked back and forth between them.

"He loves Harper and he would do anything to keep her," Dela said. "We know Harper told you about Athena's other phone."

"You didn't have it with you when Jacob picked you up. What did you do with it?" Heath asked.

Natalie's head vibrated. "No, I only found it when Harper told me about it. I showed it to Alex. I- didn't Athena have it on her when she died?"

"No. We didn't find any phone on Athena." Heath opened the file he'd brought in with him after parading Gus by the door.

"Harper told me she found her mom's phone in Alex's bedroom. After Athena was dead. How did he get that phone?" Dela asked.

Raising her hands to her ears, she shook her head. "I don't know. Did you ask Alex?"

"He said he found it on the ground beside where the car was parked after she left that night." Heath leaned over the file. "Does that seem plausible to you? Wouldn't she have called back to the house on another phone to see if she'd left it?"

"Not if she had the other one," Natalie said, with more attitude than she'd shown since they walked in the room. Dela studied her. Was she coming to the same conclusion they had? Alex must have killed his wife. But there was the matter of no sign of blood anywhere in his house.

"When did you figure out Alex had killed Athena?" Heath asked.

"I hadn't. He would never kill anyone. He isn't mean." Natalie stared at Heath.

"But he loves single-mindedly, doesn't he?" Dela said.

Natalie nodded.

"He loves Harper. He would do anything to keep her. Did he tell you she wasn't Athena's daughter? That Athena had been talking to the real parents, asking for money to return her?" Dela saw the flicker of her eyes. He had said something to Natalie.

"Athena didn't like Harper. She was just a pawn for her to make money. We love Harper. We would never do anything to harm her," Natalie said, pointing and glaring.

"But you did. You put bruises on her arm when she mentioned talking to me. Were you worried she would say something to give you and Alex away?" Dela wasn't going to let this woman pretend she loved the little girl. She wanted the man and would put up with the girl to get him.

"What I'm hearing is you didn't kill Athena but you know that Alex did to keep Harper." Heath was watching her intently. Dela did the same.

"I want a lawyer," Natalie said.

Heath stood and walked to the door. He disappeared for a few minutes and then returned. Tabitha walked in and escorted Natalie out.

Jacob arrived with Alex. The man's shoulders slumped, his eyes were downcast, and his face sagged. The man was seated in the chair across from them and Jacob left, closing the door behind him.

"As you saw when you were brought into this room, we have Natalie. She told us about you wanting her to sell the truck so you two and Harper could have traveling money. From conversations with her and Mr. Hunt…" Heath paused.

Alex's head came up and his eyes widened.

"It seems you knew he was Harper's biological father and that Athena, also known as Marilyn Rathman, kidnapped her from the Hunts when Harper was one year old. From Athena's phone records and cooperation from Mr. Hunt, we've learned she was negotiating the return of Harper." Heath pulled a paper out of the file.

"She had no right to take my daughter away from me! To sell her!" Alex said, slamming a hand on the table.

Dela jumped even though she'd seen him raise his hand. Up until now, she wouldn't have thought the man would have the anger and courage it would take to kill someone. But apparently, his love for Harper was stronger than anyone knew.

"Was it planned?" Dela said softly. "Did you plan to kill Athena?"

Alex peered into her eyes. "No. I knew what time she usually came home. I'd found the phone, saw the text messages between Athena and this number. It looked like she was selling our daughter. I couldn't believe it. What mother would do that?" His eyes glistened with unshed tears. "I just wanted to ask her about the texts. She told me he had been her lover and when he chose his pregnant wife over her, she stole the baby. Harper, she'd stolen her. And now she wanted to get as far from this nasty reservation as she could get and wanted money. She was ransoming Harper back to her parents. When I said how could she. We loved her. She laughed at me and called me a soft-hearted sap." His eyes grew hard and his hands fisted. "She sat there laughing, filing her nails as if we weren't talking about a beautiful little girl. I grabbed the file to make her stop. She laughed harder and said, what are you going to do about it? I lost it and jabbed the pointed end into her neck." He ran his hands over his short-cropped hair. "The blood. It was everywhere. I dropped the file, opened the door, and took my shoes off before I stepped out of the car. I ran to the neighbors next door. I knew they were on vacation. I stripped and used their garden hose to wash off. Then I buried my shoes and clothes in the far corner of their yard, in a dirt spot."

"Even though you claim you want the best for Harper, you killed your wife and put the child in the middle of a murder investigation," Heath said.

Alex drooped his head and shoulders, staring at the table.

The Squeeze

"Alex Kindale, you are under arrest for the murder of Athena Kindale." He went on to read him his rights and Dela stood up and walked out of the room.

Athena had pushed all the right buttons to cause her death. She should have known her husband had grown attached to the little girl. Dela pulled out her phone. She texted Quinn. *I want to be there when you introduce Harper to the Hunts. She'll need a friend. Alex just confessed to killing Athena.*

Chapter Thirty-three

Dela stood on one side of Harper and Rae on the other when Jacob let Quinn and the Hunts into Rae's house. She immediately knew the woman was Harper's mother. Mrs. Hunt had the same bone structure and nose. Where her mother's skin was ebony, Harper's was lighter due to her father being Caucasian and he had Harper's ears and mouth.

Dela and Rae had told Harper what was happening. That Athena wasn't her mother and Alex wasn't going to be able to take care of her anymore, because her real mother and father had finally found her. They didn't say Athena kidnapped her or that Alex had killed the only person she thought was her mom. The Hunts could do that when she was older.

"Harper, you have grown into a beautiful little girl," Mrs. Hunt said. Dela could tell the woman wanted to pull the child into her arms, but restrained herself.

Dela leaned down to Harper. "Why don't you and

Mrs. Hunt go to your house and pack up some clothes and the toys you'd like to take with you?"

Harper looked at her with wide scared eyes.

"I'll go with you, if you'd like," Rae said.

Harper looked up at her and nodded. "I'd like that."

Rae smiled. "Come on. She held out her hand and led Harper, followed by Mrs. Hunt, out of the house.

Dela faced Mr. Hunt who was looking pleased. "I don't like men who cheat on their wives."

His face grew dark and he started to open his mouth.

"Dela, we aren't here to judge anyone's life choices," Quinn said.

"You know I don't give a rat's ass what this man thinks of me, but," she stared straight at Mr. Hunt, "I gave Harper my phone number and told her if you don't treat her right or she feels unwanted, she's going to call me. Because we have a whole community, here, who loves her and will support her."

"I can assure you that she will have the best care and my wife will be the doting mother she wanted to be when our daughter was stolen."

"Because of your actions. Does she know that?" Dela asked.

His face reddened and he looked at the ground.

"I thought not. Remember that I do know and I know how to find your wife should I hear anything." Dela walked to the door. "I'll say goodbye to Harper."

"She can't threaten me like that," she heard Hunt saying as she closed the door and walked over to the Kindale house.

Her heart ached for Harper. So much change in a short time. But if she looked closely, she would see herself in Mrs. Hunt and understand why she was living with them. And she had no doubt the woman would love her with her whole heart.

She found them in Harper's room, filling two suitcases. One with clothes and one with toys Harper picked out. "Write to me," Dela said to Harper. "And have a good life." She said this to the mother. Mrs. Hunt nodded and smiled.

Harper wrapped her small arms around Dela. "Thank you for being my friend."

"I'll always be your friend. Just call if you need me." She released the arms. "I have to go. Someone is waiting for me. Good luck," she said shaking Mrs. Hunt's hand.

"Thank you," the woman said, tears of happiness glistening in her eyes.

Dela walked out to where Heath sat in his pickup. She slid in and sighed deeply. "She's going home even if she doesn't know it."

Heath pulled her into his arms and kissed her. When he released her, he said, "Where to?"

"The cemetery. I want to see if we can find Theodore Thunder's gravestone."

Thank you for reading book four in the Spotted Pony Casino Mystery series. If you enjoyed the book, please leave a review where you purchased *The Squeeze*. Reviews are the best way to let an author know you enjoyed the story.

As I continue the series there will be surprises about Dela's heritage and more murders that she, Heath, and their friends will solve.

If you enjoyed this mystery series you might like my Shandra Higheagle Mysteries and my Gabriel Hawke Novels listed on the following pages.

Paty

Shandra Higheagle Mystery Series

Double Duplicity

Tarnished Remains

Deadly Aim

Murderous Secrets

Killer Descent

Reservation Revenge

Yuletide Slaying

Fatal Fall

Haunting Corpse

Artful Murder

Dangerous Dance

Homicide Hideaway

Toxic Trigger-point

Abstract Casualty

Capricious Demise

Vanishing Dream

Gabriel Hawke Mystery Series

Murder of Ravens

Mouse Trail Ends

Rattlesnake Brother

Chattering Blue Jay

Fox Goes Hunting

Turkey's Fiery Demise

Stolen Butterfly (continued)

Churlish Badger

Owl's Silent Strike

Bear Stalker

About the Author

Paty Jager grew up in Wallowa County in NE Oregon and has always been amazed by its beauty, history, and ruralness. She has always had an interest in the Indigenous people and their culture and enjoys learning more every time she writes a book.

Paty is an award-winning author of 51 novels of murder mystery and western romance. All her work has Western or Native American elements in them along with hints of humor and engaging characters. She and her husband raise alfalfa hay in rural eastern Oregon. Riding horses and battling rattlesnakes, she not only writes the western lifestyle, she lives it.

By following her at one of these places you will always know when the next book is releasing and if she is having any giveaways:
Website: http://www.patyjager.net
Blog: https://writingintothesunset.net/
FB Page: https://www.facebook.com/PatyJagerAuthor/
Pinterest: https://www.pinterest.com/patyjag/
Twitter: https://twitter.com/patyjag
Goodreads:http://www.goodreads.com/author/show/100 5334.Paty_Jager
Newsletter- Mystery: https://bit.ly/2IhmWcm
Bookbub - https://www.bookbub.com/authors/paty-jager

Thank you for purchasing this Windtree Press publication. For other books of the heart, please visit our website at www.windtreepress.com.

For questions or more information contact us at info@windtreepress.com.

Windtree Press
www.windtreepress.com

9 781957 638799